Crazy-Ass Stories for Crazy-Ass People

ANDY RAUSCH

Burning Bulb
PUBLISHING

Crazy-Ass Stories for Crazy-Ass People
By **Andy Rausch**

Burning Bulb Publishing
P.O. Box 4721
Bridgeport, WV 26330-4721
United States of America
www.BurningBulbPublishing.com

First Edition.

Paperback Edition ISBN: 978-1-948278-13-3

Printed in the United States of America

Dedicated to my best friend Sean Westhoff,
a true crazy-ass people.

I believe the common denominator of the universe is not harmony, but chaos, hostility, and murder.
—Werner Herzog

We're all mad here.
—The Cheshire Cat

TABLE OF CONTENTS

INTRODUCTION

For the record, my partner-in-crime David C. Hayes (of *Rottentail* fame) hates the title of this book. I love that he's not a yes-man and will occasionally fuck my feelings all to hell and tell me when something I do sucks. This is the only way we grow as artists. I'd gladly do the same for him, but I never seem to find fault with his work. (Damn him.) But I'm waiting patiently to pounce, saying, "Aha! This sucks!" Anyway, sometimes I take Dave's advice, sometimes I don't. This time I didn't. Maybe he's right, maybe it's a shit title. I mean, neither Steinbeck nor Hemingway ever had any books with weird-ass bizarro titles like *Crazy-Ass Stories for Crazy-Ass People*, but I believe in truth in advertising, and this book is filled with crazy-ass stories.

But maybe you aren't a crazy-ass people. Hey, I get that. I don't know you all that well yet; we're just getting to know one another. But look, you need to know something right up front... I **am** a crazy-ass people, through and through. So please know that this was in no way meant as an insult. I wear my "crazy-ass people" label proudly, like a badge of honor. (And if you're one of those people right now wishing to correct me and *knowingly* inform me that "people" isn't the correct word and that it should be "person," then you should put this book down now. This probably isn't gonna be a book you'll enjoy, as you clearly have no sense of humor.)

"Humor," you ask? Is this a funny book? Well, I don't know what the hell this book is, honestly. These stories have been popular over the years, but most of them defy any sort of straight categorization. Most have horror elements, some have crime elements, some are funny, some are dark... Hell, there's even a Western tale here; a very non-traditional Western about Wyatt Earp and Doc Holliday battling a serial killer, but it's a Western nonetheless. There are stories in this book for all sorts of people, crazy-assed or no. And as far as its title falling short of those by the aforementioned literary heavyweights, that's okay. I'm cool with that. I wasn't aiming for high art. I wanted these stories to be good, and I think they are, but mostly I just wanted them to be entertaining. And again, I think I succeeded.

But maybe you won't like them. Maybe you'll hate them. Who knows? I mean, I know a guy who hates The Beatles. (I'm looking at you, Michael Steinbacher.) Can you imagine that? How sad an existence must it be to deny the artistry of The Beatles or to be unable to hear and/or recognize it? So if you hate this book, at least I'll be in good company; even The Beatles are hated. But, on the upside, lots of motherfuckers love and adore The Beatles, so there's that to consider. I'm not saying I'm The Beatles (I'm probably more akin to The Monkees or, even worse, the tenth generation copy of a copy that is Oasis), but a guy can imagine, can't he? (It's easy if you try.)

But in all seriousness, if you enjoy these stories, I would suggest that you go back and read my previous short story collection *Death Rattles*, which was published in 2014. I'm pretty proud of that one, but, like a lot of indie books, it failed to find a significant audience and went fairly unnoticed. But it's not too late. As some of the stories I've written depict, sometimes things come back from the dead. So maybe there's still hope for that one yet. Or maybe someone will discover all these stories one day after I'm dead (always a distinct possibility as I just had a heart transplant this past year). I never cared about being rich or famous, I just wanted people to read my writing. So if you like this, tell others about it. Loan them the book, buy them a copy, act out the scenes, whatever. I don't care so long as the stories are being consumed.

I hope you enjoy *Crazy-Ass Stories for Crazy-Ass People*. If you do, feel free to track me down on Facebook or Twitter and tell me about it. Positive reviews on Amazon and Goodreads are appreciated and are extremely helpful to indie authors and publishers. If you hate the book, however, feel free to not send me anything or contact me at all. And you can skip the negative reviews, too. It's cool that you didn't like the book (bully for you), but I don't really need to hear about it. I've got enough neuroses.

But seriously, I hope you dig the book. Laugh, cry, shit your pants, do whatever, just enjoy it.

—Andy Rausch, March 2019

THE DINNER GUESTS

It was just after two in the morning when the idea first came to Troy. To his knowledge, he had never had a craving for something he'd never actually tasted before, but now he did. He was curled up on the leather sectional inhaling plumes of smoke through his bong—the fancy red one he'd gotten on Spring Break that one year, when he had hooked up with that Puerto Rican girl who liked it in the ass—and watching *Plan 9 from Outer Space*. This is when the craving struck. "What would human flesh taste like?" Maybe it was the weed, maybe it was just the relaxed state of mind he was in, but the thought didn't seem the least bit gross to him.

He wondered if human flesh would taste salty. He figured it probably would, basing this on his once or twice licking his own arm as a dumbass kid. He remembered that tasting salty.

Troy supposed these thoughts were coming to him as a result of a recent conversation he'd had with his best friend Chunk. In that discussion, Chunk had talked about all the different kinds of meat that tasted like chicken; frog legs, snake, alligator, bear. "They all taste like chicken." To this Troy had asked, "Then why not just eat chicken?" Chunk didn't have a good response for this, but Troy supposed it was the thrill of eating something exotic.

Well, he thought, human flesh was pretty fucking exotic. Almost no one ate that—at least not in Tulsa where Troy lived. And if they did consume human flesh, no one was really going around bragging about it. After all, no one would understand such a thing, and on top of that, he was pretty sure it was illegal.

So yeah, he thought, what would human flesh taste like? Would it be salty? How would one go about eating it? Would you slice it thinly and eat it on Ritz crackers with little quarters of pepperjack cheese? Or would you put it on Wonder Bread and make a grilled flesh-and-cheese sandwich? All of this begged the question of what condiments might

3

taste best with flesh. He didn't know exactly why, but Troy had a suspicion that deli mustard might be the way to go.

But what if you put strands of human flesh in the trusty old Foreman Grill? That could be good, especially if you seasoned it right. Maybe a little bit of seasoning salt, a few drops of Louisiana hot sauce...

Troy licked his lips, finding he had a real desire for human flesh. It occurred to him that this was strange—not because he would be eating a person, but because he generally didn't like to try new foods. But flesh sounded really good to him.

Troy got up and grabbed his socks. Formerly white, they had turned pink when he'd thrown them in the wash with a red towel. He held the socks up to his nose and sniffed them to make sure they weren't too odorous to wear. After all, he'd been wearing them for a few days now. He figured he could get another day or so out of them, so he pulled them on his feet. He then put on his raggedy old sneakers.

It was time to go hunting so he could satisfy this crazy craving. When he stepped outside his front door, he was surprised to discover that it was still warm at this ungodly hour. Then he realized he hadn't left his house at all the previous day. Instead he had passed the time playing video games, watching TV, and smoking pot. Well, there were worse ways to spend a day, he thought.

So where would he find a person he could eat at this time of night? And if he did find someone, he then had to get them back to his house, so he couldn't really venture too far. He walked a few blocks in the darkness, but encountered no one. Finally he opted to just return home. He was really in the mood to eat someone, but this was turning into a big pain in the ass. It was just too much effort. He would have to wait until the following day to capture someone and drag them home. It was at this moment that he wondered how Jeffrey Dahmer had managed this. Hmmm, he thought. He would have to do a Google search and see what he could find out.

When he got home, he found Chunk inside the house, eating the last of his Chocolate Brownie Fudge ice cream with a plastic fork and sitting there watching *Plan 9*.

"Dammit, Chunk," he said. "What the fuck are you doing?"

Chunk looked at him dully. "I'm eating ice cream." He thought for a moment and then added, "It's pretty good, too."

Annoyed, Troy said, "I know it's good. I'm the one who bought it."

Chunk nodded. "So what's going on?"

Troy looked at him. "It annoys me when you just come into my house without knocking."

"How do you know I didn't knock?" asked Chunk. "Maybe I did. You weren't here."

Fucking Chunk. He was right, but still... fucking Chunk.

Troy plunked himself down in the old Lazy Boy and stared blankly at the TV as a thought came to him—what if he just ate Chunk? That could work. Doing this would accomplish two things simultaneously; he wouldn't have to put up with Chunk's stupid shenanigans anymore, and he'd have a person he could eat right here in his living room, making the whole process a lot easier. It seemed like a pretty logical solution.

But the question was, did he really want to eat Chunk? Chunk didn't bathe properly. Troy wasn't sure he would taste all that good. But hell, he thought, animals don't bathe either and we still eat them. Maybe Chunk would taste okay once he washed the meat under the faucet. And if the meat was gamey, he could just smother it in steak sauce and the problem would be solved.

And it would really cut down on the cost of groceries. Troy didn't eat much—mostly microwaveable burritos and PB&Js, but even that cost money. Troy could now see no real reason why he shouldn't kill Chunk and eat him as leftovers for the next week or so. Sure Chunk was a big dude, but Troy had a deep freeze where he could store the meat. Right now it was filled with old, long-forgotten packages of meat he'd been given years before, which was now covered with a thick layer of ice. But that stuff could be disposed of easily enough.

So now came the million dollar question: how would he do it? He didn't like the word "murder," so he preferred to think of it as "taking care of" Chunk. But how should he go about it? Troy had never killed a person before, so this was a foreign concept to him. He'd never intentionally killed an animal before. One time he accidentally ran over someone's labrador, but that had been a mistake and he'd felt like shit. There was no malice there.

Malice, he thought. Was there malice in his wanting to murder Chunk? He turned this over in his mind for a moment and then decided there was not. After all, it wasn't like he hated the guy or something—he just wanted to eat him. Who could fault a guy for that?

But he needed to figure out a way to do it without making a big mess. And then a method came to him.

He stood up, causing Chunk to look at him.

"Chunk, could you do me a favor and come with me to the kitchen for a moment?"

Chunk didn't hesitate. "Sure thing, boss."

Troy made his way through the dirty-clothes-strewn living room and into the kitchen, switching on the light when he got there. Chunk followed closely behind.

"What do you need me to do?" asked Chunk, trying his best to be helpful.

Troy motioned towards the sink. "I need you to put your head down over the sink." Most people, having any sort of intelligence whatsoever, would ask why Troy needed them to do this at three in the morning. But not Chunk. He just did as he'd been instructed, never once stopping to consider the reasoning behind the request.

"Now what?" asked Chunk, his head leaned down over the sink.

Troy was rifling through the drawers beside the sink, looking for his ball peen hammer. Coming across a steel meat hammer, he considered using it. But no, he wanted the ball peen hammer. That really would be best. So he continued looking.

"What you lookin' for?"

"I'm trying to find my hammer," said Troy, still searching.

"What kind of hammer?"

"The ball peen hammer."

"Oh," said Chunk dully. He thought for a moment and said, "Hammer time," laughing at his own joke.

"Yes," Troy said non-commitally. When he came to the third drawer, he finally located the hammer. "Aha!" he said, pulling it out.

Chunk was grinning like an idiot, still feeling pleased about the unfunny joke he'd made. "What now?"

Troy turned to face him, the hammer down at his side. "Hammer time," he said. He then mustered up all the strength he had and brought the hammer swooping up and then down towards Chunk's rotund head. When the hammer struck the skull, it made a sickening *thunk* sound. Chunk immediately stood upright and started thrashing around.

Shit. The strike had failed to kill Chunk, now flailing around with his hand on his head, blood seeping and spraying out everywhere. Troy raised the hammer back behind him and brought it swooping down hard onto Chunk's head a second time, accidentally striking Chunk's fingers. Chunk staggered back, really wailing now.

Dammit, Troy thought. He hadn't anticipated any of this. The fucker wouldn't die. But then Chunk always had been a pain in the ass.

Troy pulled the hammer back a third time and brought it down hard against Chunk's bloody, battered head. Again there was that grotesque *thunk* sound, and Chunk staggered back against the counter, blood going everywhere.

Now he had him. Chunk wasn't dead yet, but he was no longer here with him. He was conscious, but not by much, and he clearly had no idea where he was or what was happening. Troy struck him in the head a fourth time, finally bringing the big bastard down to the tile floor.

Troy looked at all the blood covering the walls, the sink, the counter, the floor, and the hammer. Fucking Chunk, he thought. He'd made a much bigger mess than he'd expected. "You'd better taste good," he muttered angrily.

Troy felt overwhelmed, unsure where to begin. What should he do first? Cut up Chunk's body and relocate it to the deep freeze or begin cleaning the kitchen? He stood there for a minute considering his options. Then, finally, he dragged Chunk's heavy ass through the house, leaving a thick trail of blood on the green shag carpet, and into the bathroom. It took him a few minutes to do it, but finally Troy managed to get the corpse into the bathtub where he could cut it up later.

He went back to the kitchen. He got out the limited amount of cleaning supplies he owned and squatted down to the floor, wiping up Chunk's blood as best he could. He'd never really been very good at this kind of thing, but he kept at it for a good long time until he was finally convinced that the kitchen could get no cleaner.

Exhausted, he went to the fridge and took out a cold bottle of beer. He twisted it open and downed the thing in three long swigs. Damn, he thought. Killing someone really takes the energy right out of you. He went to the utility room and rummaged through the overhead cabinets until he located the old handsaw. He wasn't really sure why he had a handsaw in the first place, but he'd seen it up there a time or two, pretty sure it was something the house's former residents had left behind. Who knows? Maybe they had used it for the same purpose.

Troy walked back through the living room, following the trail of blood on the carpet, and went to the bathroom.

Several days had passed by before Chunk's brother, Rich, came by to visit. Hearing the knock on the front door, Troy left the frying pan where he had strips of Chunk's flesh frying. He answered the door and found Rich standing there, smoking a cigarette. He said, "Come on in." Rich flipped his cigarette off the porch and followed him inside.

"Have a seat," Troy offered, motioning towards the sectional. "You can watch *Wheel of Fortune* here for a minute while I finish up supper. I don't want it to burn."

Rich nodded. "Sure thing."

Making his way back to the kitchen, Troy turned and asked, "Have you eaten yet? I could make you some, no problem."

Rich smiled. "I haven't eaten, but don't worry about me. I don't wanna invite myself to dinner."

"No, you wouldn't be. I'm asking—would you like me to fix you a plate?"

"Since you put it that way, sure," said Rich, turning back towards *Wheel of Fortune.* "What are you making anyway? It smells good."

"Venison. It'll be ready in about five minutes."

Troy returned to the kitchen, happy to find that Chunk hadn't burned up yet. He pulled some more of the meat out of the fridge and replaced it in the frying pan. He then proceeded to prepare sandwiches with Chunk meat, spicy barbecue sauce, and sliced cheese.

A few minutes passed and finally Troy was finished. He placed sandwiches for each of them on separate paper plates, garnishing them with potato chips. He carried the plates out into the living room, where Rich was attentively watching *Wheel of Fortune.*

Rich looked up as Troy handed him the plate. "Dinner is served, my good man."

Rich smiled gratefully. "I just came by to see how you were doing with it all. With, you know... Chunk's disappearance."

Troy nodded, putting on a good show. "I'm not gonna lie," he said. "It's been really difficult."

"I can imagine. You and Chunk have been best friends for a long time."

"Twenty years if you can believe that."

"I'm sure he'll turn up eventually," Rich said, taking a bite of his sandwich. He chewed for a moment before saying, "This is really good. What kind of barbecue sauce is this?"

"Store brand. I don't get too fancy."

Rich stopped eating for a minute and piled some of the potato chips onto his sandwich. He then went back to eating the thing. He looked up, talking through a mouthful of food and said, "I'm sure Chunk'll turn up. I'm sure he's still around here somewhere."

Troy grinned. "He's probably even closer than you would imagine." Rich nodded in agreement and went about scarfing down his brother's flesh.

SHE HAD A GOOD HEART

I'd had my heart ripped out numerous times throughout my life by a variety of guys who didn't deserve me and didn't appreciate what I had to offer. But this last time I had my heart cut out was different. It wasn't done by some silly boy I'd fallen head over heels for; this time it was done by a surgeon inside an operating room. Somewhere along the way I'd contracted heart disease, and had been told I needed a new heart if I was going to continue living. On February eighth, after a year on the transplant list, I received a new heart.

"You're such a brave girl," my dad told me. That was four days after the surgery. This is my first coherent post-transplant memory. I had been awake for most of the days leading up to that, but was so heavily medicated I no longer remember them. Everyone says that same thing: "you're so brave." But the thing is, I would never have chosen to undertake that procedure if there had been any other way to survive. Because of this, I didn't feel brave. I just feel like a woman who was pushed into doing something she didn't want to do and had lived to tell the tale. But I suppose there was bravery involved. There *had* to be. Simply steeling oneself for such a dangerous and traumatic ordeal requires it. Allowing yourself to be put into a sleep that you may not wake up from is something beyond horrifying. In truth, I still don't know how I did it, other than to simply repeat there was no other way.

My recovery was pretty quick. While it's true that I stayed in the hospital for two months, which most transplant recipients don't, my road to recovery was relatively smooth. I had trouble walking more than a couple feet for the first month or so due to the time I'd spent in bed, but I pushed myself, and the difficulty became less and less. Four months after the surgery I returned to my job as a receptionist at the college. "You've done such a great job recovering," everyone said. But again, very little of that had anything to do with me beyond my will to return to normality. Most people who've had transplants eat better than I do, and they exercise with more frequency, and yet I'm doing better than they are. At my last check-up, my transplant coordinator told me she sees "very, very few" transplant patients who rebound as well as I have. This makes me happy, but I try not to get cocky or take any undeserved credit.

I was almost eight months post-transplant when I was told I could write a letter to the donor's family. This was a big moment and this news was heavier than I had anticipated. Even though there had been several months where the thought or mention of this unknown donor made me cry, I'd wrongly believed I now was past that. But when I was told I could write the letter, it all came flooding back again, and suddenly I was overcome with a plethora of emotions. I couldn't easily identify them. Was it sadness? Was it joy? Was it grief? It was, I think, all of those simultaneously.

So I sat down to write the family, crying as I did. In the letter, I apologized, although I don't know why. The reality is that the donor would have died either way, whether or not I had existed. But that realization changed nothing; I still felt guilty. Once I got past the apology, I told them how exceedingly grateful I was for the gift I'd been given. I made a point to write that I was happy their deceased loved one lived on through me. I know it's corny, but that's what I wrote. I wrote it not only because I thought it sounded good, which I did, but also because I believed it. Those kinds of thoughts make it easier to cope with the guilt, I think. I wrote about how happy I was, and how great I felt, making a point to tell them I would not have felt this way, and probably wouldn't even be alive at this point, had it not been for their loved one. "I want to know more about my donor," I wrote. That was true. Everything had been done confidentially, and I'd been told nothing beyond the fact that the donor had been a young woman.

I thanked the family profusely in my letter, maybe going overboard, but I felt it better to go that way than to appear under-appreciative. I told them I looked forward to getting to know them, and that I hoped we could meet. I signed the letter and sealed it in an envelope. I put a stamp on it and stuck in the mailbox, sending it off to the transplant coordinator. After a week had passed, I started checking my mailbox religiously, hoping to hear from the family, and also knowing I might not. Some transplant recipients don't. I'm not sure why this is, and can only guess. I suppose it's because some families don't want to dwell on their loved one's death any more than they have to. I think that's a shame, because it would probably benefit people to know their loved ones are responsible for saving the lives of others. Maybe it would help them find meaning in otherwise senseless tragedy.

The response letter came back much more quickly than I'd expected. I received it in just over a month. It was a letter from my donor's mother. It read:

Dear Kasey:

I'm glad to hear from you. I'm glad to know my daughter Tricia's heart lives inside you. That fact makes me extremely happy. Believe it or not, I'm crying right now as I write this. My Tricia was only 24, which is a very young age for a woman to die. She was just a year younger than you. I wish you could have known her, although in a way I suppose you do. She got good marks throughout school—primarily As and Bs. She went to college in Maryland, and then became a pharmacist here in Tulsa.

I and Kasey's siblings—she has two older brothers, Dave and Bryan—would love to meet you. Since we all live here in the same city, would you like to come and have dinner with our family on Thanksgiving? We don't get too fancy around here. We just have the normal stuff—turkey and dressing and mashed potatoes... But I'm told it's pretty good. And we have macaroni and cheese. I've heard people say that's a weird thing to have for Thanksgiving dinner, but I don't see what's so weird about it. The kids all like it—it's was Tricia's favorite—and I make it with tons of ooey-gooey cheese.

I hope you can come, but you may already have plans since it's the holiday. Certainly we will understand if that's the case. I'm including my telephone number here. Give me a call and let me know that you received this letter and whether or not you intend to come. Thank you so much for reaching out, Kasey. We are really happy to know you are doing well and that you successfully received our beloved Tricia's heart. You sound like a very sweet girl and we can't wait to meet you.

Warmest regards,
Dorothy Waxman

I read the letter through glistening, tear-filled eyes. I took a deep breath and read it again, finding myself overwhelmed with joy. This first contact had gone much better than I could have anticipated. Thanksgiving was only a couple weeks away, so I called Dorothy Waxman immediately.

"It's Kasey Daniels," I announced.

"Kasey?" the woman asked.

"I received your letter."

There was a pause, and then recognition. *"Oh, Kasey!"* she said happily.

"I'm calling to say I can come for Thanksgiving."

"Great!" said Dorothy. "That would be fantastic!"

"Thank you for inviting me, ma'am."

"Don't call me ma'am. That's for old women. Call me Dorothy, please."

I thought about calling her *"Dorothy please"* as a joke, but instead said, "Okay, Dorothy."

"Will you be bringing anyone along with you?"

"I hadn't thought about it," I said. "I guess I'll be coming alone."

"Fine," said Dorothy. "I just wanted to know so I can make the appropriate amount of food. We'll be eating at two o'clock sharp. Do you have our address?"

"Yes," I said. "It was on the envelope."

"Good. Then we'll see you on Thanksgiving."

"Definitely."

"Okay," she said. "See you soon, Kasey."

"Goodbye," I said, hanging up.

The days passed quickly, and I spent more time than I should have wondering about what I might say when meeting the Waxmans. I hoped it would go well. Dorothy seemed excited enough, so I guessed it would. But I was a worrier by nature, just like Mom had been. It was in my DNA, and there was nothing I could do about it.

When I told my dad about the letter, the call, and the impending meeting, he was overjoyed. He offered to come along, but I felt like this first meeting was something I needed to do alone. After I had realized that I could do anything I set my mind to post-transplant, I sometimes felt a rush of empowerment doing things that scared me. This was one of those things, so the thought of going into this foreign place alone in the face of unusual circumstance thrilled me.

When Thanksgiving finally came, I spent an inordinate amount of time in front of the mirror trying to ensure that my hair and makeup were perfect. After all, I didn't want the Waxmans thinking Tricia had given her heart to an ugly girl. That was silly, I know, but it was an actual thought I had.

I drove over to the Waxman's house. I thought I was ready, but when I came to their street, I panicked and kept driving, right past the house. I drove around the block. I took a deep breath and went back. I sat outside the house in the car for a bit, trying to prepare myself. I looked up at the house, relieved that no one seemed to be watching, and got out. I walked up to the house, trying to act normal, but I felt as nervous as a person could possibly feel.

I knocked. I waited a moment and the door opened. A blonde woman, probably about sixty, looked at me. She lit up, smiling. "Kasey?"

That was when I lost it. I felt another rush of those emotions, all at once, and I burst into tears. Dorothy just smiled knowingly and said, "Bless your heart." She wrapped her arms around me and pulled me close. We hugged for a moment, and then Dorothy released me, stepping back inside the doorway. "The food's ready, dear," she said. I stepped in behind her, wiping my eyes with my sleeve. I saw two guys who were roughly my age standing there, both wearing ugly holiday sweaters.

"This is Bryan, he's my oldest, and this guy over here is Dave," said Dorothy. "He's 25, the same age as you."

I smiled and moved towards them, feeling awkward. They both smiled and gave me obligatory hugs. They were warm, but their hugs were a bit more forced than Dorothy's, which had felt as natural as a mother hugging her child.

Dorothy led us all into the dining room, where the table was set. There was a nice big turkey in the center of the table, along with some cream corn, mashed potatoes, macaroni and cheese, gravy, and wine. "There are two pies for dessert in the kitchen," said Dorothy. "There's a pumpkin pie and there's sweet potato, too, if you like either of those."

"I do," I said. "I like both." I patted my stomach. "I've been eating more lately now that my appetite has come back."

"That's good," said Dorothy. She motioned towards a chair. "Have a seat."

We all sat down. It was a rectangular table, big enough for ten people, but there were only four of us. Dorothy and I sat on one side, and the brothers sat across from us. "Bryan, will you say the prayer?" asked Dorothy. Bryan smiled politely, and delivered a short, stock prayer that sounded like it had been recited verbatim hundreds of times. When he finished, Dorothy raised a bottle of wine and looked at me. "Can you have this? I didn't know."

I felt myself blushing, unsure what to say. "They, uh, they let me have some...in moderation."

Dorothy smiled. "Everything in moderation, right?" She poured me a glass, and then filled her own. She then passed the bottle across the table to Bryan. After the boys filled their glasses, we all started to eat. The food was good, not great, and it reminded me a little of my mom's cooking. I decided to tell Dorothy this, leaving out the part about it being mediocre. "This tastes like my mom's cooking."

Dorothy smiled. "Is she a good cook?"

"She was," I said. "When she was alive." I came to the end of that sentence and found I didn't know what else to say.

"Oh," Dorothy said. "I'm sorry."

"It's okay. She died when I was fifteen. She was in a car accident."

"Just like Tricia," Dorothy said, her voice cracking.

I felt bad. I hadn't known how Tricia had died. I put my hand on her shoulder, and Dorothy looked at me. "It's okay. No fault of yours, dear. It happens to all of us eventually." Dorothy regained her composure. "I hate to ask this, with us still eating..."

"Yes?" I asked.

"I really wanna show you something, and I just can't wait. Would that be okay?"

"Yes, of course."

Dorothy stood. "Come this way."

She led me back through the living room and into a hallway on the left. She took me down the hall to the second of three doors. She grabbed the doorknob and looked at me. "This was Tricia's room."

"Okay," I managed, unsure how to react.

Dorothy opened the door and went in. I followed. The room was still decorated with all the trappings of a high school girl. There were posters and photos of cute male stars, mostly actors and bands who were no longer relevant. They were people who were popular among teen girls back when I myself had been one.

"I restored everything," said Dorothy, turning towards me, spreading her arms to display the room. "I'd kept most of it in place after Tricia went to college, but after she died, I put everything back up the way it had been when she was still in school. This is my shrine to Tricia. I wish you had known her. She was a very sweet girl, like you. She had a good heart."

I looked across the room at a congregation of tennis trophies sitting atop a tall dresser. Dorothy saw me and urged, "Go ahead, take a look." So I walked over and looked at the engravings on them. They were all for first place. "These are amazing," I said, still reading.

"She was a terrific tennis player," Dorothy said.

I turned around to see Dorothy standing in front of me, now holding a huge butcher knife out in front of her. *What was happening?* She had a weird look in her eye. I didn't know what it was, but suddenly I felt scared. I looked to the door, and saw that Bryan and Dave were now standing there staring at me, as well.

"What are you doing?" I asked, panicking.

Dorothy held the knife up between us. "I've collected everything that belonged to Tricia. My collection is complete." She paused. "Well, *almost.*" She moved towards me slowly, her eyes locked with mine.

"What are you saying?" I asked.

Dorothy stared at me, smiling a twisted smile. "I'm gonna need that heart back."

She moved towards me. I tried to push her away, and now saw the boys moving towards me, as well. I stumbled back against the nightstand, and there was nowhere to go. I was trapped.

"Please, no," I begged.

Dorothy's arm slashed out, and I felt the blade rip across my stomach.

"Grab her, boys!" screamed Dorothy.

This was when I felt the blade cut my stomach the second time. And I knew then it was too late. I had been saved by the transplant only to die now because of it. I closed my eyes and started to pray.

CHARLES BUKOWSKI'S COMMAND PERFORMANCE

The Gotham night remained a temperate one, despite the falling rain being pissed from the sky. Having been forced to park his beat up Ford Windstar some two blocks away, Leonard now trudged along, hefting both his knapsack and duffel bag up Eighth Avenue. Still unfamiliar with New York City, he was surprised by the number of pedestrians still making their ways to and fro. He had heard many times that the city never slept, but its inhabitants apparently never went home either.

Finally he came to Twenty-third Street, and he hooked a right. The rain wasn't letting up, and Leonard now feared for the safety of the beloved laptop tucked away in his bag. A short ways in, he now saw the majestic red brick building which housed the Hotel Chelsea. His destination in sight, he started to walk a little more briskly. When he reached the hotel's 222 West Twenty-third entrance, he stepped in, at long last finding relief from the storm.

He shook the water from himself as an animal would, and stood there staring in awe at the spacious-yet-seedy lobby. As he did, he considered the many artists from all walks of life who had inhabited the place at one time or another. The old hotel had seen its fair share of noted talents in its day, from Leonard Cohen to Stanley Kubrick to Andy Warhol. Even Marilyn Monroe had stayed here.

Leonard approached the front desk, manned by a solitary clerk whose name tag identified him as Ray. The twenty-something man with clean-cut, boy-next-door features, said "Hello" in a genuinely friendly tone. "Can I help you?"

Leonard said, "I have a reservation under the name Leonard Trillman."

"Trillman?" Ray asked.

Leonard nodded, and Ray tapped away at his keyboard. "And how will you be paying, Mr. Trillman?"

"With cash."

"And you're staying for two nights?"

"Yes."

Ray tapped at his keyboard some more. His gaze moved up to Leonard. "With tax, that'll be $196.89." Leonard reached into his pocket and pulled out his old tattered wallet. He removed two crisp hundred dollar bills and a ten, handing them to the clerk. Ray then gave him his change and turned away for a moment, finally turning back to produce a room key on a plastic black fob. He handed it over. "Can I get you anything else, Mr. Trillman?"

Leonard said no and turned toward the stairs. When he reached the third floor, he made his way down the corridor in search of his room. Once he'd located it, he unlocked the door and entered. The room was a good-sized one, pulling off the same trick the lobby had of simultaneously being both spacious and seedy. Leonard took off his jacket and sat down on the bed, his soaked Mumford and Sons t-shirt clinging to his body. He opened his duffel bag and retrieved his laptop. The machine, plastered with band stickers, seemed to be in working order much to Leonard's relief. The next item he pulled out from the duffel was a baggie containing weed. He extracted a tightly-rolled joint from the baggie and held it up to his mouth. He fished through the pocket of his jeans, searching for, and finally finding, his Bic lighter. He lit the joint dangling from his lips. The burning paper crackled as Leonard drew on the joint, and he inhaled a big breath of thick pot smoke.

He lay back on his bed and closed his eyes, slipping into the inviting darkness of sleep. When he awoke some thirty-five minutes later, Leonard mentally scolded himself for his *faux pas*. There was work to be done. With only two days in the hotel room, Leonard had to get to it; the Great American novel wasn't going to author itself. He sat upright and went to the bathroom. Once there, he went to filling the large dirtied-porcelain bathtub with steaming hot water. He started to undress. Once he was naked, he took a leak in the toilet and climbed into the half-filled tub. The water was hot, attempting to scald him pink but just hot enough that he could stand it.

Shit, he thought, realizing he'd forgotten something. He climbed out, leaving puddles on the cold tile floor, and made his way to the bedroom. Once there, he went to his bag and retrieved the straight-razor from an outside pouch. He carried it back into the tub, toying with it in his hands. Now sitting in the hot water once again, he turned off the faucet and the cascade ceased to be. Leonard opened the straight razor and stared at it a good long time, eyeballing his shimmering reflection in its blade; maybe it was five minutes, maybe it was twenty. He couldn't say for sure as time was moving at an irregular pace.

Finally, at long last, Leonard opened up the blade, and then his vein. The blackish blood pulsed from the slit like disco lights at a nightclub. He raised his other wrist and followed suit, making sure to slash diagonally rather than horizontally so the wound could be stitched shut when the time came. He stood up, water dripping from his body, and he walked, still soaked, to the bedroom. His wrists were seeping blood at a steady pace, and Leonard went to work outlining a giant, bloody pentagram on the white tile floor with it. Once he had sufficiently painted the floor, Leonard retrieved his laptop and sat it in the center of the drawn shape.

Leonard went back to his knapsack and searched through it, effectively covering it in blood, producing two hot cans of Foster's and a carton of Benson & Hedges. He sat a pack of the cigarettes and the two beer cans inside the marked area. He then reached inside his bag and pulled out five fat black candles—one for each corner of the pentagram. He carefully laid them out around the design and then lit them. He stood back, looking over his work and admiring it. He then went to his duffel bag and pulled out an old, dog-eared book whose dust jacket may or may not have been fashioned from real human skin. He opened the volume to the book-marked page, and carried it to the pentagram. He sat down near the design and began to read from the book. The meaning of the ancient words were lost on him, so he enunciated each word as carefully and clearly as possible. He didn't know what the words meant, but he knew what the outcome would be if all went as planned. Finally he got to the portion of the passage where he was to include the demon's name, and he said "Charles Bukowski," having verified that the author was a servant in Hell through the use of a Ouija board. He went on reading the rest of the gibberish-sounding words.

Once he had finished reading the passage, a cold wind reached out from nowhere, extinguishing all five candles. Leonard watched the pentagram. Now a bright yellowish light started to jut up from the floor in the center of the design, reaching up to the ceiling. He saw the very distinct silhouette of Satan looming over him, and in front of that appeared a second figure, bathed in fire. The thick smell of sulfur was unmistakable. The figure before Satan writhed as if in pain, and then fell to the floor in the center of the bloody pentagram. The fire and light subsided, as did the silhouette of the Dark Lord, and Leonard saw that the man was as naked as he was.

The naked fat man sat up, looking hairy and disheveled. The only thing that looked different about the *Ham and Rye* author from the photographs Leonard had seen was that his eyes now glowed a fiery red. "*Why have you summoned me here?*" the demon Bukowski howled, his voice booming and frightening. Leonard felt as though he might piss himself, intermingling urine with the dripping blood which now covered his legs, but managed to control his bladder for the time being.

"I have summoned you to write for me," said Leonard, trying his damnedest to sound as ferocious as Bukowski. (It didn't work, and Leonard's tiny flaccid penis would do little to make him more intimidating.)

Bukowski's face contorted and he cocked his head, his fiery eye holes fixed on Leonard. "*Write for you?*"

"I've brought you gifts, you'll see," Leonard said, pointing a bloody index finger towards the cigarettes and booze. Bukowski's burning-red stare now turned to the beers, and he was, for the moment, satiated. He reached down and grabbed one of the cans with his long-fingernailed hand, popping it open. He raised the container and guzzled from it, Foster's streaming down his face. Next he tore open the pack of smokes, removing one and lighting it with a flame that emitted from the end of his finger. He went to smoking a cigarette, taking long drags and savoring the moment.

He looked up. "*What,*" asked the demon, "*do you want me to write?*"

"You're going to write the Great American novel." Leonard listened to his weighted words, enjoying the stern sound of his own voice. "And I'm going to take all the credit for it. I will be seen as a great writer, like you."

The demon Bukowski looked at him with those red, hollowed-out eyes, perhaps studying him. His expressions were difficult to discern with his having no eyeballs. "*What exactly would you have me write about, master?*"

Master. Leonard liked that. "Surprise me, Charles," he said. "Write whatever suits you. And make it the very best you can. I command it."

Bukowski sat Indian-style in the center of the pentagram, his long old man testicles drooping to the floor, and he started banging away at the keyboard madly. Leonard was surprised that the author-turned-demon knew how to operate a Dell laptop as he had passed on to Hell way back in 1994, but he figured that was hardly the most astounding aspect of this remarkable occurrence.

And Bukowski wrote, occasionally cackling at his own prose as he did. Leonard did not ask him what he was writing, knowing the words would be his own in a matter of hours. Once the demon Bukowski had finished downing his second can of Foster's, he turned and demanded more. *"More beer!"* he bellowed, his screeching voice sounding inhuman.

Leonard wrapped his wrists with white hotel towels, turning them red in the process, but remaining naked just as the incantation had demanded. Leonard was feeling light-headed now, and he hoped that his demonic slave would complete the manuscript before he passed out from loss of blood. Leonard reached a bloodied hand into the bag and produced another can of Foster's, rolling it into the center of the pentagram. Bukowski clutched at the aluminum can, and tore it open, guzzling its contents and once again spilling it all over his face. He threw the aluminum can at the wall with such force that it shook the room, and for the first time Leonard wondered what might happen were Bukowski able to escape from his pentagram prison. He felt a chill run down his naked, wet spine, and he forced such thoughts from his mind. Much to Leonard's surprise, the demon did not demand another beer, but went on banging away at the keyboard.

Soon, Leonard thought, he would be seen as an accomplished author. He just had to force himself to stay conscious until after the demon Bukowski had completed their novel. Finally, just as Leonard was feeling extremely woozy, the demon spoke in that eery high-pitched voice of his. *"Please read this passage. Let me know what you think, master."*

The light-headed Leonard agreed to read the section, and he inched forward towards the pentagram. Bukowski slid the laptop out from the symbol, and Leonard started to read. The prose he saw there on the laptop was remarkable, one of the finest things he'd ever read and certainly better than anything he could have produced. The words danced on the page. Not wanting to pass out before Bukowski finished his task, he slid the computer back to him.

"It's amazing," said Leonard. "It's one of the best things I've ever read. And just think, I'll get all the credit."

Bukowski looked at him for a beat, his fiery eyes seeming to stare through him. *"Can I tell you a secret, master?"* asked the demon.

Leonard nodded. "Yes?"

"When you slid the beers into the pentagram..."

"Yes?" asked Leonard, biting at his lip.

"And when you slid the laptop into the symbol..."

Leonard didn't understand. "What, Bukowski?"

Bukowski grinned a particularly fiendish smile. *"You broke the plane, freeing me from my prison."*

Leonard now realized the mistake he'd made. His eyes got big, and Bukowski just went on grinning. The demon stood up and dove towards him, snatching him up in his arms and raising him over his head. Leonard was quite light-headed now, and the room was spinning. Or was that him? Bukowski slammed him across the room into the old television set, and Leonard's head went through its screen. He was cut badly, and there was now blood streaming down his face. Despite his light-headedness, Leonard's wounds hurt a great deal. He wiggled out of the television frame, blood in his eyes, his knees being cut by the shards of broken glass which littered the floor. Suddenly Bukowski flung the laptop into the wall beside Leonard, and it shattered.

"Here's your fucking novel, asshole!" raged the demon.

Leonard manged quietly, "My...my...novel..." He stood, swaying as he did, and tried to maneuver towards the room door. He took one step and Bukowski was on him again, clutching at his right arm, the blood seeping quickly now. Bukowski yanked at the arm, and Leonard felt a searing pain unlike anything he'd ever experienced. The demon had torn off the appendage. Leonard stood there, swaying, bloody and confused. The demon Bukowski raised the arm and swung it towards him like a club, knocking him into the wall. Before Leonard could move, Bukowski was on him, beating him over and over and over again with his own arm.

And Leonard, like his appropriated novel, was as dead as disco.

Bukowski turned and sighed. He pulled another can of beer out from Leonard's bag and picked up his smokes. He sat down, naked and trembling, in an aged recliner that had seen better days. The demon popped open the can and took a swig, beer streaming down his chin. He used his finger to light another smoke, and he sat and puffed on the cigarettes and drank the beer his would-be captor had given him. As he did, he wondered where he would get his next drink.

RACHEL IN THE MOONLIGHT

His Rachel had been gone almost two years now, and James still couldn't wrap his head around it. Every morning when he awoke, he turned, expecting to see her lying on the pillow next to him. And every morning was the same; the pillow was empty and the horrible reality would then set in. Rachel was gone, and he would never see her again.

But that wasn't entirely the truth. He saw her *everywhere*. He saw her at the supermarket. He saw her driving by in cars. He saw her walking in the middle of large throngs of people on the sidewalk. But mostly he saw her in his dreams. There she would come to him as if she were still alive, and he would hold her hand and kiss her once more as though there was still a sunny tomorrow.

But there were no more sunny tomorrows in James' life. Not anymore. Now there were only overcast and rainy days, a constant reminder of all he had lost. Not that he had to be reminded. Rachel was all he thought about. In fact, he probably thought about her more today than he had just following her death.

Every day, weather be damned, he went and visited Rachel's grave, flowers in hand. And every day he cleared away the leaves and debris, the flowers from yesterday's visit, and propped up the new bundle of orchids to honor her.

One day he was making his daily walk to the flower shop when a store selling adult movies caught his eye. He walked past it everyday, but he'd never paid it any mind. Despite his mourning, James still had the normal male urges. He didn't own a computer and was interested in obtaining a couple of smut magazines to help satisfy his cravings. He walked inside, the bell over the door ringing as he did. He didn't consider himself a prude, but he was still somewhat shocked by the plethora of dildos and outlandish sexual devices which lined the store. He looked around at them with more than a small bit of curiosity. He eyeballed the devices, amazed by how many there were.

That was when he noticed a sign which read: "CUSTOM SEX DOLLS MADE HERE," with a smaller sign beneath that read "MADE TO HER EXACT SPECIFICATIONS." Somewhere deep down inside this piqued his interest, although he didn't know why.

James made his way up to the man behind the counter, and said awkwardly, "I was wondering about the custom-made sex dolls."

The man's face lit up. "Would you like to see some?"

James nodded.

The man led him through an open doorway in the back of the store. They walked through a hallway adorned with posters of adult movie stars, some of them autographed. James thought the floor felt sticky, but figured that was probably his imagination. The man led him to a big room filled with ultra-realistic sex dolls. These were not the simple inflatable women he had imagined. These dolls were beautiful. There was a doll made to look just like Marilyn Monroe; there was a Scarlett Johansson; a Sarah Palin; and so on. Most of the dolls just looked like normal, beautiful women.

"What are they made of?" James asked.

"Silicone."

"Who makes them?"

The man said, "Kyle, but he's not here today."

"The dolls are made to the exact specifications of real women?"

The man nodded. "We got a very detailed questionnaire you have to fill out when you order one. It asks questions like areola size, pubic hair length, height of the woman, foot size, things like that."

James asked, "Could a guy just give you some photographs of the woman he wanted the doll to resemble?"

"Oh, Kyle will want those, too. But you still gotta fill out the questionnaire."

James stared at one of the dolls, unable to believe how realistic it looked. "The hair looks so real."

"Yeah, they've got real human hair," the man said, grinning. "Up top and down below, too."

"How much does something like this cost?"

"It varies, but the average one costs about $6,000, give or take."

"That's pretty steep," James said.

"But trust me, it's worth it," the man said. "It's the next best thing to having the real woman. If you can't have her, you'll want this."

James took out his wallet and requested a questionnaire.

Fourteen days passed before the big wooden box arrived at his house. James scooted it inside, into his living room. He knew what was in the box, but now felt overwhelmed by a multitude of emotions at the thought of opening it. So he just sat there in his favorite chair for some time, staring at the damned thing.

And he thought about Rachel. He remembered the way she felt in his arms. He remembered the way she smelled. He remembered the taste of her hair in his mouth.

He had to know.

He went to the utility room and got a hammer, bringing it back to open the crate. He went to work on the box, and its lid was off in a matter of minutes. He fished around amongst the packing peanuts, and located the doll. He brought it forward, sitting it in the upright position, packing peanuts falling all around it as he did.

He looked at the doll and found himself amazed by how realistic it looked. It was his Rachel, right here in front of him. She looked just like the real deal; so much so, in fact, that he didn't move for several minutes. He just stared into the doll's glassy blue eyes, and they seemed to stare back.

He considered kissing the doll's lips, but decided against it. No, he would wait until the right time when the doll was ready.

James lifted up the naked doll and found it to be quite heavy. It had to weigh a hundred pounds or so. He carried it up the stairs to the bathroom. Once there, he washed its hair with Rachel's shampoo. He then applied her favorite perfume and lotion to the doll, and the scents immediately brought her back to life in his mind. Wanting to make the experience as realistic as possible, he even put Rachel's lip balm on the doll.

He then took the doll to his bedroom, where he dressed it in Rachel's slinky red lingerie. He tried not to look at the doll's body as he did this, wanting to keep the forthcoming act as special as possible. He put Rachel's ankle bracelet and toe rings on the doll's feet.

Tonight would be a big night. Tonight he would reunite with his Rachel for one last sexual encounter, giving her the proper send-off he had never been able to.

That night, James lit scented candles all around the dark room. He left the curtain cracked just a bit so the light of the moon could fall gently down on Rachel's body. He lay down on the bed beside the doll, gently caressing its hair. He kissed at its temples and nibbled on its left ear. He stuck his tongue in the doll's ear and moved it around. He caressed the doll's neck, finally kissing at the doll's mouth, the familiar taste of Rachel's lip balm in his mouth. He stuck his tongue into the doll's tight mouth, wagging it against its limp tongue, forcing it to come alive and wag back.

For the briefest of moments, James forgot where he was.

He forgot this was a doll.

This was his Rachel, here once more, and they were reunited. Once more they would share their love as they had so many times before.

He moved his hand along her back, kissing his way down her neck towards her big, full breasts. She tasted of lavender lotion. The smell of her perfume filled his nostrils, driving him crazy. He moved the top of the negligee with his nose, his mouth finding her nipples, playing with them, flicking at them. He cupped her breasts together with his hands, kissing between them, moving his tongue all around them. As he did so, he felt himself harden. He was throbbing; pulsing. His desire was consuming him, and he wanted to eat her up.

He moved his hand down between her legs and touched her sticky wetness with his fingers, caressing her clit. He thought he felt her buckle in his arms, and he pulled himself closer to her, his hand moving with ever-increasing speed. He thought he felt her climax on his fingers. Her back arched, and her head went back against the pillow.

James moved closer to her, softly taking his hand away from her wet pussy. He then took his own manhood in hand and stroked it, bringing it to maddening hardness. He made his way on top of her, kissing her lips as he did, and moved his cock around, softly searching for her wet pussy. He found it, rubbed at it gently, and entered her. He moaned as he did, and gently thrust himself deep inside her. He put his right hand behind her back to support her, moving himself in and out of her slowly as he did.

But he knew what she liked. She didn't like this slow stuff. It made her crazy, made her want it faster and harder. She liked it when he pulled her hair. So he gently tugged at it, thrusting his cock harder and harder into her tight, wet pussy. He pulled her tight against him as he did, swearing he could feel her heartbeat against his chest. He pushed himself up on top of her, swiveled his hips slowly, rotating his cock inside her, and then pulled it back to its tip, finally plunging back inside once more.

The moonlight fell against the right half of her face.

She was beautiful. Looking at her blond hair lying across her full, pale breasts, staring at the wonders of her exquisite face, James grew hornier and hornier, overcome with passion and desire. He now fed off what he perceived to be her sexual energy, as well, and he pulled her close, pumping himself in and out of her as hard as he could. He held her legs up over his shoulders, and they swayed hard with each thrust.

He kissed her mouth again, moving his tongue against hers, pushing his cock into her harder and harder as he did. Finally he felt himself climbing, escalating, reaching towards an unreachable high, and he came hard, feeling their juices intermingling as he did. He pulled her up close to him, holding her tightly, and the two of them lay silently in the moonlight in the afterglow of good sex.

SANDWICH BITCH

The day had been a piss-poor one so far, but at long last lunch break had come to the rescue, offering Donny Mead a brief reprieve from his monotonous factory work. The breaks were staggered so only a handful of workers would be away from their positions at any given moment. Because of this, the bright white, overly-sterile break room only contained a couple of occupants at present. Donny approached the old fridge, surveying it to ascertain whether or not the Break Room Bandit had left any messages posted there. Unfortunately, he had not.

The much-ballyhooed Break Room Bandit was some heretofore unknown employee who had repeatedly eaten another worker's bologna sandwiches. This caused the rightful owner of the sandwiches to become angry and post an ignorant, misspelling-laden threat that he (you just know it was "he") would beat the shit out of whomever was eating said sandwiches. This, in turn, caused the perpetrator to go right on eating them, leaving mocking missives on the refrigerator door. One such message read: "It's me, the Break Room Bandit, and I have once again eaten your sandwich. But the thing is, I really, really hate bologna. So, with this in mind, could you please bring either ham-and-cheese loaf or pickle-loaf next time? (I'm really fond of the various loaves.) If you could do that, I would be forever in your debt. Thanks! Yours truly, the Break Room Bandit."

Being mocked infuriated the other guy (Donny still didn't know who the identities of either party), prompting him to write the ever-so-eloquent pronouncement "THIS MY SANDWICH BITCH" on the top of his wrapped sandwich each day. One might think the questionably-literate person scrawling these oh-so-clever declarations might get lucky one day and actually write something semi-intelligent. But no, this did not occur. Each and every day, without fail, the message was the same: "THIS MY SANDWICH BITCH."

As Donny reached into the fridge, stretching his hand beyond the freshly-labeled sandwich, to retrieve his blueberry yogurt, it occurred to him that the person bringing the sandwiches should simply poison them. Of course. It was so simple. Why didn't he just do that? Donny could produce no adequate answer for this question. It would, he believed, be the perfect crime. If the illiterate sandwich scrawler used the right poison, the Break Room Bandit would eat it and then scurry back to his home, dying there as poisoned cockroaches do. This was perfect. How could anyone possibly know the sandwich had originated at the factory? There was no way. Making this scenario even better, if the victim lived with another person, that person would be a suspect long before any coworkers. Since the killer and the victim probably didn't know one another, no one could connect them. Maybe this wasn't quite as clever as stabbing someone with an icicle, which was said to be the end-all be-all perfect murder, but it was still pretty damned good. In fact, this plan was so good that it bothered Donny to think of it going to waste.

Donny sat down with his plastic spoon, digging into the yogurt container, considering possible outcomes of such a poisoning. Then it occurred to him to poison the sandwich himself. He had no way of knowing who might eat it and die. It could really go either way—either the sandwich's owner or this Break Room Bandit fella. Donny found he didn't really care which of them died. This, he thought, would be a grand experiment. He'd always been intrigued by the idea of murdering someone. Here, with the person being completely random and unknown to him, it seemed perfect. *Tomorrow*, he thought. *Tomorrow I will poison someone and see what happens.*

That night when he finally got home, Donny couldn't get to the Internet fast enough. His plan was to investigate different types of poisons and find something suitable for the task. He went to a search engine, stopping. He considered for a moment, trying to decide what he should type. Finally he submitted the words "types of ingested poison lethal." The search produced a variety of websites, and he scanned them carefully. When he came to a listing of the top ten most lethal poisons, he knew he'd struck paydirt. Reading through the list, he passed on a couple of substances, either due to their killing someone too rapidly (when they would still be at work) or their being too difficult to obtain. Then he came to a listing for Strychnine. Donny didn't know much about poisons, but he'd heard of Strychnine. Here he learned it was easy to obtain and that it was a common pesticide that could be purchased anywhere. The thought of the particularly gruesome death it brought about—every muscle in the victim's body simultaneously spasming violently until they died of exhaustion—appealed to him greatly.

After completing his research, Donny scarfed down a bowl of beef-flavored ramen. Then, after he finished, he drove out to Walmart, where he purchased some generic blue after shave, a *Star Wars* t-shirt, a bag of Lemonheads candies, and a $12 bottle of Martin's Gopher Bait, comprised almost entirely of Strychnine. *This could work*, he thought gleefully as he scanned the items through the self-check reader. He paid for the stuff, grabbed the bags, and made his way back out to his Honda Accord, wondering if the taste of Strychnine would be obvious when his mark bit into it.

The next day at work was hell, Donny waiting anxiously for lunch break. He was ready to do this. So when lunch time finally arrived, he made a beeline to the break room. He was the first one in, and he glanced around furtively. There was no sandwich-related correspondence posted on the fridge today. He pulled the door open, looked behind him one last time, and reached in and grabbed the sandwich. He took it to the closest table, holding it close to his body, then lying it down with its proclamation/threat facing down. A couple of gargantuan women meandered into the room, heading directly to a table in the corner. Donny could hear them gossiping about someone being a "dumb sonofabitch." This was good. They were paying him no mind. Donny went to work opening the wrapped sandwich. Once the plastic was peeled back, exposing the food, Donny popped the lid off the yellow mug he'd been carrying. He tilted it over the sandwich, pouring the tiniest bit of gopher bait onto it. The substance puddled up there, resting atop the deli mustard. After looking around to make sure no one would see, he re-wrapped it.

Donny stood up and returned the sandwich, sitting it where he'd found it, its moronic "SANDWICH BITCH" warning on full display. He then reached back further and seized his yogurt. Strawberry today. He returned to his table, listening to the heavyset women carry on about various dumb sonsofbitches, as visions of dead coworkers danced in his head.

The wait for the following day felt like an eternity. When it finally came, all of Donny's coworkers were talking about a dead coworker named Susan. Donny didn't know any Susans, so it didn't seem like any deal to him. No one possessed any details regarding the circumstances of her demise, so he had no way of knowing if she had died by bologna-and-Strychnine sandwich. He figured this was mere coincidence considering the unlikelihood that either party had been female. (Their posted correspondence displayed a type of macho one-upsmanship that was uniquely male.) At lunch, Donny was startled to see a freshly-wrapped and labeled sandwich in the fridge. Now certain that Susan's death was unrelated to the Gopher Bait, Donny went about his workday just as he had a thousand times before.

It wasn't until the following day he heard someone saying the police believed Susan might have been murdered. Poison, they said. But there was nothing beyond that, no details to speak of. Had Donny killed her? There was no way to be certain, but he now found it probable. After all, someone had eaten the sandwich. Who was to say it hadn't been given to Susan, or even stolen by her?

At the end of his shift, Donny saw a flyer taped to the wall. It had a photograph of Susan, announcing her death. Looking at this, Donny recognized Susan as a curvy young woman of about twenty or so that he'd frequently gawked at from afar. She looked a lot like Taylor Swift, at least to him, only a dirtier, meth-using, trailer trash, tattooed version. Because of this, Donny had always thought of her affectionately as "White Trash Taylor Swift." But now she was dead. Donny wondered what name might be appropriate for her now; "Deader-Than-Hell Taylor Swift"? "Worm Food Taylor Swift"? These thoughts made him smile, and then her proper nickname came to him: "Sandwich Bitch." This seemed fitting given the circumstances. While she had (apparently) been neither the person who'd made the offending sandwich, nor the Lunch Room Bandit, their actions, inexplicably, had led to her demise. In considering this, Donny found that he didn't feel one way or another about any of it, but thought he might miss staring at her passably-attractive features.

Several days passed before the local newspaper ran a front-page story explaining that police had concluded Susan had in fact been poisoned. The article made a vague reference to leads the cops were pursuing. Reading this, Donny grinned, feeling proud of what he'd done. This, he congratulated himself, was a perfect murder.

One day in the break room, Donny, eating his yogurt, overheard the two old cows from before, discussing their co-worker's death.

"They're pretty sure it was her boyfriend," said Cow Number One. "They got him in custody."

Cow Number Two nodded, mulling it over. "They lived together?"

"Yeah, but they wasn't married. That was part of it, the reason why Jesus saw fit to take her so young...because of the sin of her living with a man."

"Maybe they weren't having sex."

"No," said Cow Number Two. "They was."

"How do you know?"

"Did you ever look at Susan? She looked...dirty, like the kind of girl that would have sex before marriage. Probably even butt sex."

Listening to this, Donny nodded his head to the melody and cadence of their words. It was literally music to his ears. Not only had he gotten away with murder, but someone else was getting the blame.

Donny found a a level of enjoyment in having killed Sandwich Bitch that was unlike anything he'd experienced previously. This led to the inevitable question: should he do it again? He thought about this long and hard, giving it due consideration, but ultimately decided against it. While it was true that the two idiots trading barbs over the sandwiches were still engaging in this childish behavior, making it possible for him to repeat the act, it was dangerous. It was also selfish, the type of blood-drunken mistake killers made that led to their being captured.

Six weeks passed and Donny's life had gotten back to normal. So much so that he no longer gave any thought to his having poisoned the girl. On this day, however, he was reminded of his actions by the most insignificant of things—a pack of Twinkies.

It was a Saturday afternoon and Donny was visiting the sky-rise where his Grammy June was spending her final days. Donny visited her every few weeks, but he hated going to the apartment building, overflowing with the elderly and disabled, seemingly passing time until their death. On first glance, it looked like any other apartment building. But this one was different. The first indication this was a death house was the shuffle board just inside the entrance, a sure sign of old people, which, in Donny's hundred or so visits, he'd never seen a single person playing. Then there was the television area in the lobby, with a TV that seemed to air unlimited episodes of Judge Judy and Oprah. There was occasionally one or two residents situated there, watching Sean Hannity or the like, but sometimes there would be a single lonely old man sitting there, raptly watching the television, which no one had thought to switch on.

There was an elevator there, with a table beside it. There were religious tracts and stacks of coupons for a nearby pizza delivery joint sitting on it, and occasionally there would be one or two items of food. These random foodstuffs, which ranged from a can of green beans to a box of corn bread mix, were left by residents who had decided they didn't want them. They were up for grabs, free to anyone. Maybe the person who inherited the green beans left behind a food item in its place. Donny wasn't sure how it worked.

But today there was a pack of Twinkies. Donny made a mental note of them, not sure why they were important but nonetheless aware they were. He went up to the third floor and spent time with Grammy June, watching *The People's Court* and discussing life events. (He did not share his murdering Sandwich Bitch with her, which, when left out of conversation, made his life seem awfully dull.) When their visit was over, he left, getting on the elevator once more. When he came to the bottom floor and stepped out, he saw that the Twinkies was gone. He still wasn't sure why he was interested, but found himself thinking about them on his drive home.

Thinking of the Twinkies sitting there, waiting for some stranger to pick them up and carry them back to their apartment, made him reflect on Sandwich Bitch once more. This scenario, he saw, would provide him the opportunity to do it all over again, still going unnoticed. He smiled, feeling proud of himself for being smart enough to recognize this opportunity. Still driving, he saw a Mini-Mart on his right. He flipped on his turn signal, preparing to make a quick stop to buy Twinkies.

POTENTIAL SPACEMEN

Ned Gimler was out on the porch, staring up at the bright, starry night, when he saw the flaming mass come hurtling down to the ground out in his field. "Well, shit," he muttered. After all, this was gonna require some sort of investigation, and he didn't feel like doing much of anything. He just wanted to sit out on the porch and enjoy his cheap wine and chew his tobacco. But no, he couldn't do that, because there was some damned flaming object sitting out there in the middle of that field, and he was gonna have to go and check it out.

More than likely it was just a comet or a falling star, but he figured it might also be one of them flying saucers they liked to talk about in the movies. And if it did turn out to be some sort of spacecraft, that could mean money for him. Big money. And now Ned let his imagination go wild for a moment, imagining lines upon lines of UFO gawkers shelling out their hard-earned dough to see what was out there in his field. Yeah, he could go for that. Money was never a bad thing, so long as it was coming in rather than going out.

Now feeling inspired, Ned stood up and went into the house. An old soap opera was playing to an empty room on his old TV, and some twangy country music was playing over the dusty old radio.

Ned had to find his rifle. He hadn't seen the damn thing in ages, but he sure as shit wasn't gonna go out there rooting around a potential spacecraft without it. He coughed and sputtered a bit, and turned and spit a big hunk of chew on the wall. It dribbled down a bit, a big hunk of it falling to the floor right next to an older hunk of dried chew.

Where the hell is that old rifle? Ned thought.

He went to Peter's old bedroom and made his way through the mountains of clutter to the closet. He pulled it open, just managing to get it open around a pile of long-dirty clothes, and a huge stack of nudie magazines fell out, landing at his feet. *Well, hell,* he thought. He reached down and picked up one of the dusty old magazines, leafing through it, ogling the pretty specimens inside. He figured he hadn't seen these old mags in twenty-some years. He dropped the magazine to the floor with the others, spitting a big hunk of tobacco on top of it.

As he made his way back down the tiny path snaking through the mounds of piled trash, dusty knick-knacks, clothes, and assorted bullshit, he passed by the window. He wasn't thinking about much of anything, but he happened to glance out. There he could see a glowing light emitting from deep in the field. At first he thought the field was ablaze, but then he saw that it was just a glowing light of some sort. Maybe a comet, maybe a spaceman. Who the hell knew?

Despite the realization that there may be aliens out in the field, Ned didn't feel the least bit frightened. Maybe it was the wine, or maybe it was just the fact that he didn't care about much of anything these days, but he felt absolutely no fear whatsoever. But still, he wanted to find his rifle before he went be-boppin' out there. He'd be damned if some alien was gonna catch him unprepared and get the drop on him.

He went to the closet at the end of the hall. There was a huge stack of yellowed, chew-encrusted newspapers there, and he brushed them aside, the pile falling over. He pulled the closet door open. There were more nudie books piled up in there, as well as a stack of dusty paperbacks that had been Jean's back when she was still alive. Ned glanced through the closet, looking past aged creams and ointments and bandages, but saw nothing he could use as a weapon against potential spacemen.

Ned made his way into his bedroom, scanning over the piles of trash and long-forgotten treasures. He didn't sleep in here anymore—not since Jean had passed on. Now he found the dirty stained-up old couch a much more enjoyable place to sleep. So the old rifle could very well have been in here. But it wasn't. Then he remembered his old military stuff in the closet, and began making his way through the piles of clutter so he could get to it. He had to pull out mountains of miscellany, revealing age-old rodent droppings underneath. In fact, there was even the skeleton of a long-dead rodent lying there. But Ned didn't care. Who had time for cleanliness? He spit another wad of chew onto the side of the old dresser and continued digging for the closet.

Once he'd cleared a big enough space to get the closet doors open, he swung them out and looked around at the old clothes inside. He reached up to the top shelf and pulled down an old wooden box that contained his medals. They weren't really so much earned awards as they were the kinds of generalized medals everyone in the military received—glorified participation medals, really—but looking over them momentarily transported him back to another time. He shrugged, and tossed the box onto a pile of dirty clothes. He reached up and grabbed a dusty old box and pulled it down. This one held his old pistol. He looked it over, found that it was still loaded, and tucked it into his waistline, dropping the box to the floor, which was littered with the feces of long-deceased pets.

Now he had a pistol, but he wasn't sure it would be enough if there were indeed spacemen out there. He still needed to locate his rifle before going out there. He made his way back through the house and went through the kitchen to the basement door. He opened it and switched on the light. It came buzzing to life, a dim old thing, swaying from the ceiling, and Ned realized he hadn't been inside this basement in decades. The gods only knew what creepy-crawly creatures were lurking around down there, but maybe his rifle was there, too.

He went down the creaky old stairs, looking around at the dirty old relics from a life that now seemed foreign to him. There were old TVs and chairs and tables and books and anything without value one could imagine.

And then he saw his old rifle, covered in a thick sheen of dust, leaning against a dirty old fridge. He made his way down there, something scurrying past him as he moved, and retrieved the gun.

He made his way back up the stairs to the kitchen, where he regrouped and considered his plan of attack. He made his way into the living room, heading for the door, but realized he'd forgotten something. He then went back into the kitchen, opened the dirty old fridge which smelled of rotten foods long-forgotten, and retrieved the last four cans from a six-pack of beer, pulling one of the empty rings over his belt and letting the cans dangle at his side.

Now he was ready to go into the field.

He passed the old soap opera, past the old radio playing melancholy country tunes, and went out on the porch. He looked out at the dull light emitting from the field, and took another swig of his wine.

He didn't really wanna go out there.

Again, it wasn't fear so much as it was laziness.

Ned knew this was gonna be a pain in the ass.

He made his way down off the porch, stumbling as he did, and approached the edge of the field. He passed the rusty old tractor sitting dead in the yard, hawking a wad of chew on it as he did. He parted the tall stalks and made his way slowly out there, heading towards the light. He started to hum as he moved through the field. This was a bad idea, to be sure, but the alcohol in his blood made it seem like a good one. He continued trudging through the field, the light growing brighter as he approached it.

Finally he parted the stalks and saw that the bright, fallen object was just ahead. He peered through, and could now see what it was. There was no doubt, this was a space craft of some sort. It had some sort of alien insignia and unintelligible writing on its side. It was shaped sort of like a big thimble. It emitted light, and there was a faint mist of smoke rising from the wreckage.

Maybe the aliens inside were dead from the impact, Ned thought.

He could only hope.

After all, he didn't wanna fuck around with no damned spacemen.

Not tonight. Not ever, really.

Now, for the first time, Ned realized he was slightly afraid. After all, this was a space ship. He considered calling the authorities, but then realized he didn't want them coming out and scooping up the thing, taking all his potential money and glory.

No, it was up to him to deal with these goddamn spacemen.

Whatever money there was to be made off this thing was gonna be Ned's and Ned's alone. He now considered just how many bottles of cheap wine and cans of chew that money could buy. Hell, maybe he could even start buying the more expensive wine.

Ned stayed motionless, parting the stalks with the barrel of his rifle. He peered out at the big metallic thing, trying to summon up the courage and strength to investigate it more closely.

But first thing's first, Ned had to piss.

Had to do it right now.

Again, this was a terrible idea, but the wine made it seem like a good one, so he pulled out little Ned and took a piss there, only a few feet away from the spacecraft. As his urine sprinkled and splattered all over the stalks and on himself, Ned heard a hissing noise coming from the spacecraft. He looked over and saw that some sort of hatch was opening on it, a door sliding off to one side. He finished his piss as quickly as he could, shaking the drops off little Ned, and put the thing away.

As the hatch slid to one side, a light poured out. The opening faced upward, at an angle away from Ned, so he couldn't see what monstrosities lurked inside.

Ned could feel himself moving forward, the rifle out in front of him.

He made his way slowly towards the side of the spacecraft. It was small enough, and burrowed far enough into the ground, that once he stood over it, he could see down inside.

And the sight made him sick. He felt his stomach rolling, warm vomit choking him as it rose up his throat. And he puked all over the side of the spacecraft.

He wiped off his mouth and stared down into the hatch at the grotesque monstrosity that was the alien. The sickening-looking creature looked at him and blinked. It started to move a bit, babbling its foreign alien gobbledy-gook as it did. "My name is Steve Smith," said the alien in a tongue foreign to Ned. "I represent the National Aeronautics and Space Administration in the United States on the planet Earth. Can you assist me?"

The gobbledy-gook that the alien spat frightened Ned. He prayed to the gods of the two moons of Candor for strength, raising the two tentacles holding the rifle, and training it on the ghastly space creature.

"Can you help me?" the alien asked, its foreign words sounding scary. Perhaps this was a threat. Since Ned didn't speak alien gobbledy-gook, he had no way of knowing.

He steadied the rifle with his fourth tentacle, squeezing the trigger with his fifth.

Boom!

The rifle went off, its kick knocking Ned back a bit. He stared down at the repulsive-looking creature, just lying there inside that big thimble, staring down at the wound on its torso. Ned raised the rifle to the alien's grotesque head, which had only two eyes (can you believe that?) and squeezed the trigger again.

Boom!

And just like that, the threat was over.

The spaceman was dead.

Ned wasn't sure killing the creature had been the right thing to do, but at least now he would be safe from harm. Thinking of all the money he could potentially make off this thing, Ned turned to leave the field. He looked back at the spacecraft one last time, hawking a ball of warm, gooey chew on its side. And he went back to the house.

KIND OF BLUE

It was a hot night in The Blue Room, and Junior was really going to town on the trumpet, having his way with his audience. Drenched in sweat and enveloped in thick cigarette smoke, he wrapped up his set with a largely-improvised version of "So What." The moment he finished, the audience erupted with cheers and applause, making him remember why he had gone into this profession in the first place. Not every night was like this. Hell, most nights weren't. But tonight was, and Junior wanted to bask in it for as long as he could.

He made his way down off the stage, trumpet in hand, and headed back to the bar. Junior nodded at Jimmy the bartender, and Jimmy fixed his a drink. Junior edged up to the bar, grabbed the shot glass, and downed the thing. When he sat it down, he realized he was being flanked by two of Red's goons.

"Boss wants to see you," said Smoke Daniels, a big mean sonofabitch, putting a meaty paw on Junior's shoulder. Unfazed, Junior looked back at Jimmy, who was watching all this with a look of amusement. "Gimme another drink," he said, and Jimmy did. Junior downed the shot just as he'd downed the previous one, and turned toward Smoke. Seeing no way out, he said, "Let's go for that walk."

The three men made their way through the crowd and out of the bar. The men led Junior to their automobile, and pushed him in the backseat. The other guy drove, and Smoke sat beside Junior.

A few minutes later they were outside The Cuckoo Cock, a rundown old bar that now functioned as Red's base of operations. "Leave the horn in the car," the other goon said. Smoke snatched Junior up, pulling him out of the automobile, and dragged him inside the place.

Once inside, Junior saw Red sitting there majestically, like a king on high. He was surrounded by a few underlings, who were playing

Spades. They all stopped and looked up when Junior and the two goons walked in. Red had a big shit-eating grin plastered across his mug, and he chuckled the way a young boy might after having just killed a cat for fun.

Smoke pushed Junior down into a wooden chair facing Red.

"It's good to see you, Junior," said Red, still grinning. He raised his cigarette to his lips and took a drag.

Junior sneered, but said nothing.

"Do you know why I brought your ass here?"

"Is it 'cause I'm so damned pretty?"

"Well, kind of," said Red. "The thing is, I know all about you and Georgia."

Junior tried to play it cool, but he was certain he looked startled. "What about her?"

Red chuckled again, looking around at his men. "This man thinks I'm a fool." He turned to Smoke. "Tell me, Smoke, am I a damn fool?"

"Nah, Red," said Smoke. "You're not a fool."

Red looked back at Junior, their eyes locking. His smile fell away. "Then why the hell are you trying to talk to me like I'm an idiot?"

"That's how you see it?" asked Junior.

"That's how I see it. Tell me, is there any other way to see it?"

Junior smirked, and Red's eyes got big. He sat back in his chair, and turned towards one of his goons. "Charlie, do me a favor and knock the grin off this motherfucker's face."

Charlie, a big muscular dude in a cheap suit stepped towards Junior. He pulled back and slugged him in the jaw. The blow knocked Junior back in his chair, turning his head in the process. Junior rubbed his jaw and tried to make his blurry eyes refocus.

Charlie asked, "We good, boss?"

"Nah, I don't think we are."

"You want I should give him another one?"

Red nodded, and Charlie stepped forward, slugging Junior again.

As Junior was trying to find his bearings, Red asked, "Why you gotta go around behind my back and screw my lady, Junior? That type of thing is uncalled for. How exactly did you think I was gonna react to this news?"

Junior shook his head, still trying to clear it. He looked up at Charlie, still standing over him menacingly. He looked at Red. "You got it all wrong."

Red looked around the room at his men. He started to chuckle again, and they followed suit. He looked at Junior. "Then explain it to me, my boy. Tell me how I got it all twisted up."

"Me and Georgia, we're just friends. There ain't nothin' there, nothin' at all. We ain't never been like that…"

"I think you're a damned liar," said Red, nonchalantly taking another drag of his cigarette.

"No, no, I swear," said Junior, pleading now. "It's not like that."

"Oh, but it is. You know how I know?"

Junior just stared at him, saying nothing.

Red turned towards one of his goons. "Show him."

One of the guys reached into his pocket and pulled something white out. He tossed it onto the table in front of Junior. It was a handkerchief. Junior opened it and felt sick, knowing at once what he was looking at—*it was a human finger.*

Red grinned. "You recognize that nail polish? Georgia gets her nails done by the Jap broad down the street. Does good work, that broad."

Junior stared at the finger for a long moment before bursting forward out of his chair and reaching out for Red. He came fairly close to grabbing him before one of the goons snatched him from behind and pulled him back down into his chair.

Red looked a little rattled by this. "What do you think you're doing, boy?"

Junior stared at him. "What have you done with Georgia?"

"That's none of your concern," said Red. "But what is your concern is that she told me you and her were planning to take off in the middle of the night and head for New York City. Is that right? Were you planning to set up shop and play house with my woman?" Red caught himself getting overly serious and forced another chuckle. He waved his arm dismissively. "Silly boy, don't you know? You can't turn a hoe into a housewife."

Junior glared at Red, wanting nothing more than to kill the dude, but he said nothing.

Red stood, plucking the cigarette from his lips. He looked to Smoke. "Hold him down."

Red moved forward, cigarette in hand, and pressed it into Junior's forehead. When the cherry from the cigarette touched the sweat on Junior's brow, it hissed a little. Junior wriggled beneath it, letting out a piercing scream.

Red looked past Junior to one of his men. "Go get Tiny. Bring him out here." He looked down at Junior. "You've done it now. I'm assuming you know Tiny."

"Only by reputation," said Junior.

Tiny was a heavyweight fighter who lived in the neighborhood. A real big, tough, mean sonofabitch. Everyone knew he was in Red's pocket. In addition to boxing, Tiny also worked as a collector for Red, roughing up whoever the boss said needed to be roughed up.

Junior's head was throbbing now. Everything was hazy. He was trying to make sense of everything, and Red just kept laughing maniacally, making his head hurt even worse. Where was Georgia? Was she still alive? For that matter, would Junior have any chance of making it out of this place alive?

"Where he at?" came the monosyllabic caveman voice from behind. Junior had never heard Tiny speak before, but he knew at once that it was him.

Red just stood there in front of Junior. He looked down at him. "This here's Junior. He needs to be taught some manners. He needs to be taught not to disrespect me. He needs to learn to keep his goddamn hand out of the cookie jar."

Junior looked up at Red, opened his mouth, prepared to say something smart, but the blow to the back of his head knocked Junior forward, his forehead striking the edge of the table as he went down.

Now Junior was on the floor and everything was *really* hazy. It took Junior a few seconds to realize why—there was blood in his eyes. He turned to look up at Red. The room was moving, his vision blurry.

"Get your ass up," came Tiny's voice from behind.

Junior opened his mouth, his cheek still pressed against the floor. Before Junior could move or formulate any sort of plan of attack, he felt Tiny hoisting him up from the ground. He felt himself arc back just before Tiny thrust him crashing down on top of a table.

"Goddamn, man," said Red. "You gonna kill the boy."

"Is that what you want?" asked Tiny. "You want me to kill his dumb ass?"

Red chuckled that sickening chuckle again. "Nah, I just want you to play with him a bit."

Junior was lying on the floor, his head and ribs hurting like hell. He was staring at the floor, unable to move. Then he felt Tiny's hands on him again, lifting him up. Junior mustered up a bit of strength and swung his elbow back hard, surprised when it actually struck Tiny in the face. Junior, still being held at chest height, felt Tiny stagger back a bit. Then Tiny growled an awful gutteral growl and he raised Junior up over his head, hurling him down onto the floor again.

Junior landed hard, crumpling like paper-machete. Junior looked down, seeing his blood all over the floor before him. Still face down, he pulled his arms back and adjusted himself on the palms of his hands, trying to push himself to his feet. He raised himself a little bit, but fell limply to the floor.

Junior couldn't see him, but he could hear Red. "Why'd you do it, boy? Surely a talented young man like yourself could find another woman without having to go sneaking around trying to steal my woman..."

Junior was going to try to stand again. He pressed his palms down against the ground, stretching his fingers out. Just as he did, Red came forward and stomped down hard against his hand. He did it again, and again, and again, finally squishing Junior's broken fingers around beneath his heel.

Through his own screams Junior could hear Red taunting him. "I guess you won't be able to play the trumpet anymore, huh, boy?" Red laughed heartily, as did his goons. Junior felt tears welling up in his eyes, and soon saw them falling to the floor before him. He spread out his broken fingers and tried to push himself up again.

"You got heart, boy," said Red, sounding genuinely impressed. "Don't he got heart, Smoke?"

"Yeah, boss," said Smoke. "He gots a lot of heart."

Junior lay there on the floor for a long beat, trying to push himself back up to his feet. As he did, he heard Red say, "What do you think I should do with a young buck who got heart? Should I let him live?"

There was a moment of silence before Charlie spoke up. "I don't think that's a good idea, boss. What if he comes back someday?"

"Ain't nobody give a good goddamn what you think," growled Red angrily. "I'm the boss here, not you." There was another moment of silence before Red said, "Say it. Say I'm the boss." And Junior, still looking down at the blood-covered floor, heard Charlie sheepishly repeat, "You're the boss, Red."

"You're goddamn right, I'm the boss!" After another long moment of awkward silence, Red said, "Get that boy back up on his feet."

Junior felt hands reach around beneath his arms, lifting him up. Junior found himself on his feet again. He was wobbly, and he started to fall, but the goon held him up until he regained his composure enough to stand without toppling.

Red got up in his face, the smell of collared greens strong on his breath. "What if I let you live, boyr? What you gonna do? What if I let you live, but I told you I never wanted to see you in Kansas City again, so long as you live? What would you do?"

Junior just stood there, swaying, but said nothing.

"You'll do nothing, that's what you'll do," said Red. "I'm gonna let you live out the rest of your pathetic miserable life with nothing. You're gonna be a testament of what I'll do if anyone crosses me. I messed up your hand so you can't play that horn no more, and I took away your woman... The love of your life, huh, Junior? Do you know what her last words were?"

Junior looked up at Red, trying to convey an expression of hatred.

"She said, 'Tell Junior I love him.' That's what she said." Red stepped back to get a good look at Junior's anguish. He laughed, looking up at Smoke. "Take this trash out to the street and leave him there."

Smoke grabbed Junior, practically dragging him out of the place. As he did, Junior heard Red from behind him. "Don't ever come back, Junior," he said. "Not ever. God as my witness, if I see your face again, you're a dead man."

Smoke dragged him through the door, tossing him down to the hard pavement, where Junior lay crumpled like a discarded piece of trash. "Don't ever come back," Smoke advised one last time before going back inside.

Junior lay there for a moment, broken and pathetic. He thought of Georgia and he considered the fact that he'd never see her again. He could see her face now. "Christ," he muttered, reaching for the neck of a broken beer bottle lying beside him. He pushed himself up, slowly finding his way to his feet. He stood there for a moment, swaying as if he were standing in a stiff wind. He turned back towards the entrance of the bar.

He gripped the broken bottle as tightly as he could and walked back into The Cuckoo Cock.

STEVE MCQUEEN AND THE THANKSGIVING ELVIS DECANTER

Turk Kellerman wasn't the most attractive guy. He wasn't even the most attractive guy in his own house. That honor went to his roommate Kyle, who wasn't really very attractive himself. But, to his credit, Turk was arguably the second best-looking guy in the house, even if there were just the two of them.

Turk had a bit of a body odor problem. But maybe body odor problem wasn't accurate. A better way to describe it might be a lack of caring problem. Turk didn't really give a shit about much of anything and found washing his ass to be too difficult a chore, so he simply lived life dirty, only showering a couple of times a month. Even then, he rarely used soap.

Turk was unemployed. He'd briefly had a job at Scooter Burger, but had ended up leaving over an argument with Todd, the assistant manager. Todd had asserted that Charles Bronson was a better actor than Steve McQueen. It wasn't really the disagreement that sealed the deal with Turk's leaving so much as it was his punching Todd in the throat. So Turk lost his job, but he was okay with it. He'd be damned if he was gonna stand by and listen to someone bad-mouth Steve McQueen, the coolest cat ever to walk the earth. (In Turk's mind, this included Jesus Christ, because if Jesus was in fact a real person, there was no way he was pulling the kind of hot tail Steve McQueen had. And there was no chance he was as cool as McQueen. After all, in Turk's mind, there was no way anyone could be as cool as Steve McQueen while wearing sandals. Sandals? Get out. Steve McQueen would have never worn sandals, because sandals were dumb.)

So now Turk spent his days sitting in front of the living room TV playing video games, shirtless and smelly, an ever-growing collection of empty Mountain Dew bottles piling up around him.

After a few months of this, things had gotten so bad that Turk no longer got up to take a piss. If he felt the urge, he would just whip out his dick and urinate into one of the empty bottles. As a result, there were a good half dozen piss-filled Mountain Dew bottles lying around the room.

One day Turk was in the middle of a first-person shooter game, talking smack to some 15-year-old Vietnamese kid through a headset, when Kyle came home. When Turk saw his roommate signaling for him to take off his headset, he did so begrudgingly.

"What's up, man?" he asked, his eyes glued to the TV screen.

"I got you something," said Kyle. "Against my better judgment, I found you something at the flea market."

Now he was speaking Turk's language. He looked at Kyle. "You got something for me?"

"I did."

"What's it for?"

"Thanksgiving, I guess."

Turk stared at him in disbelief. "Who gives gifts for Thanksgiving?"

"I do, I guess," Kyle said sheepishly.

"But Thanksgiving's still over a month away."

"No, dude, it's this week."

"Shit," said Turk. "Time's really flown by. I guess I haven't been paying much attention lately. I've been busy here playing my game."

"Yeah, I guess you have."

"So what'd you get?" asked Turk, reaching his hand down into his sweatpants to scratch his balls. He pulled his hand back out to smell his fingers. As he did, Kyle reached into his duffel bag and pulled out a bottle. He handed it to Turk. Turk looked at it and saw that it was an Elvis decanter.

"Oh, shit," said Turk. "These are cool. My dad's friend Chuck used to have one of these in his trailer house. I always thought that was cool, because you know, the King was a cool dude. Not as cool as Steve McQueen mind you, but pretty damned cool."

"What is it you like so much about Steve McQueen?" asked Kyle. "He was cool, sure, but was he really all that great? I mean, I can only name a few movies he made." Kyle thought for a minute, looking away. "Let's see... *The Getaway*...that one with Faye Dunaway where he does that heist... Then there was the one where he was in prison with that guy from *The Graduate*..."

"You're not really a movie guy, and I get that," said Turk, trying to be condescending. "But Steve McQueen was the greatest actor of all time. Not just the greatest actor, mind you, but also the coolest dude ever to walk on two legs."

"What was so cool about him?"

Turk stared at him, wanting to slap him. "What kind of question is that? There are so many reasons why he was cool. Far too many to list. If I need to explain that to you, then you're worthless. There's no point in even talking to you."

"I don't get it," said Kyle.

Turk stared at him again. "Steve was a good-looking guy, could bed any chick he wanted to. If I could be him, in his prime, for a single day, I would sleep with all the girls. And not just the ugly ones, the ones we usually get, but the really fine, really sexy ones with asses you can actually hold in your hand and don't take two hands just to kind of get around."

"Steve McQueen was bisexual," said Kyle.

"Fuck you," said Turk indignantly. He didn't like when people said bad things about Steve McQueen.

"No, really, I read it in a book."

"I know about that book," said Turk. "I don't believe it though. I don't believe he was bisexual or whatever, but who cares? Good for him if he was. I mean, he was Steve McQueen. He could have anybody he wanted, male or female. So what? It ain't gay when it's like that."

"Like what?"

"Where you can literally have anyone you wanted."

"If it's guys, how is that not gay?"

"I dunno," said Turk. "But it ain't. It ain't gay when it's Steve McQueen. Look, if you're gonna do something, then you do it all the way. So if you were gonna be gay, not that he was, but if you did, then you'd wanna do it like Steve McQueen."

"What does that even mean?"

"It means if you're Steve McQueen you fuck *everybody;* man, woman...whatever."

"You were gonna say child."

"No," said Turk flatly. "I was not. Steve McQueen mighta screwed both men and women, I dunno, but I assure you he didn't fuck kids."

"How do you know?"

And Turk lost it. *"Because he was Steve McQueen, goddammit!"*

Kyle hook his head. "You're ridiculous."

"No, Steve had the world in his hands. He was the epitome of cool. He drove race cars and screwed models and actresses. He was rich. That guy could do anything he wanted, and probably did. If I had my choice and I could be anybody who ever lived, I'd be Steve McQueen."

"Why not just make your own life better and be yourself?"

"That's stupid," said Turk. "I'd rather be the worst of Steve McQueen than the best of me any day."

"Why's that?"

"It ain't that I'm bad or anything, but it's that Steve McQueen was a fuckin' superman. He was the single greatest guy who ever existed. Seriously, think about it and you'll see that I'm right."

"You're silly," said Kyle. He stood up. "Do we got anymore Hot Pockets in the fridge? I'm hungry."

"I think so," said Turk. He was examining the Elvis decanter now. "This is pretty cool, man."

Kyle said, "I'm glad you like it."

"There anything in it?"

"I don't think so." He thought about this for a moment and then added, "Please don't piss in it."

Turk looked up angrily. "Why would I do that?"

Kyle stood there, looking down at the piss-filled Mountain Dew bottles strewn around the room. "I don't know, Turk. Why the fuck would you?"

Turk opened the decanter. He was fiddling with it when tufts of smoke started billowing out from its mouth. "Whoa!" he said. "What's this shit?" He looked at Kyle, who was standing there staring.

Kyle said, "I don't know. I didn't know that smoke was in there."

They both watched the plumes billowing from the decanter, still in Turk's hand. A moment later the smoke congregated in the center of the room between Turk and the television. It started to grow darker, all seeming to settle in the same area. Slowly it materialized into a figure without legs, floating there. As it formed before their eyes, it became apparent that it was a person, a man, an Indian dude, wearing some sort of ancient garb, all blue, and a matching silk hat.

The legless Indian man stared at Turk. "What do you want, master?"

Turk said, "Who are you?"

"I am Kimba."

"Why are you here?"

"I am a genie. I live in the bottle, master, and you rubbed it, summoning me."

"You're a genie?" asked Turk.

"I am," said Kimba.

"And you live inside an Elvis decanter?" asked Kyle.

The genie looked over at him, annoyed. "I do. So what?" Then he looked back at Turk. "So what would you like, master?"

"What do you mean?" asked Turk.

"You get one wish," said Kimba. "Your wish is my command. Anything, master."

Turk's face lit up. "I get to make a wish?"

"Yes, master. One wish."

"And you'll grant it?"

"Yes, master."

"Anything?"

The genie nodded. "Anything."

Turk turned his head a bit, his eyes looking up at the ceiling, and then he immediately looked back at Kimba. "I know what I want."

"So quickly?" asked Kimba, starting to grin. "You don't wanna take more time?"

"I don't need to. I've been wishing for the same thing for years."

Kimba stared at him, his eyes twinkling. "Name it and it's yours, master."

"I wanna be Steve McQueen," said Turk. "Do you know Steve McQueen? The actor. I wanna be Steve McQueen, the famous actor, and not some other dude with the same name. That would suck."

"The guy from *The Great Escape*?" asked Kimba.

"Yeah, him," said Turk.

"Why do you desire that?" Kimba asked.

"Because Steve McQueen was the coolest man who ever lived, and I wanna be just like him."

Kimba nodded. "Then stand up and I shall grant you this wish."

Turk lit up, looking as happy as ever. He stood up, wobbling a bit from the lack of standing he'd done recently. He looked at Kimba, and Kimba looked back.

"Alakazam, zamba zoom, bee baa bee baa, zippity zoo, now you are Steve McQueen!"

There was a flash of light before Turk and he transformed into a darkly decayed corpse, wavering there for a moment. Kimba stared at him, laughing a loud belly-laugh. Kyle watched Turk standing there, swaying, and then he fell to the floor in a pile of death.

Kyle's mouth hung open. He looked at Kimba. "What the fuck?"

"Steve McQueen is dead," said Kimba, smirking. "But he wanted to be the alive version of Steve McQueen!"

Kimba shrugged. "He didn't say that though, did he?"

Kyle nodded. "No, I guess not."

Kimba looked at him. "How about you? Would you like to make a wish?"

Kyle looked around the room and sighed. "Could you just get rid of Turk's body?" He thought for a moment before adding, "And all these bottles of piss?"

The genie nodded. "Sure thing."

"Then I'll just be in the other room."

"What are you doing?" asked Kimba.

"I'm gonna start working on an ad for tomorrow's paper. It looks like I need a new roommate."

"One thing, kid."

"Yeah?"

"Can I give you some advice?"

"Go for it."

"Find somebody clean this time," said Kimba. "And less stupid."

Kyle grinned, knowing the genie was right.

THE MAN WHO HATED PICKLES

The lunch crowd was just starting to die out around the time Marty entered the dingy old diner. No doubt the dive had seen better days, probably before Sputnik caused millions of Russkies to raise a toast to the skies. The joint smelled of greasy burgers and body odor, and the Box Tops were warbling "The Letter" out of small distorted speakers strategically placed around the establishment. Marty had taken two steps inside the door before a twenty-something brunette baby doll in an apron walked out to greet him.

Baby Doll ushered him to a red vinyl booth that seemed to be held together by silver duct tape. Marty slid into the booth and picked up a menu.

"Can I get you a glass of water?" asked Baby Doll. Marty didn't look up from his menu, but said yes, he would take some water. He scanned the typo-laden menu, which looked as though it had been printed around the time Ronnie Raygun took his bullet, when a small blonde girl clutching a stuffed Teddy bear approached his table.

Marty looked up at her, blinking. "Mister?" she inquired, utterly unfazed by his adultness.

Marty nodded, signaling that she had his attention.

"Do you got a quarter?"

He grinned uneasily, looking around to see where the child's mother was. He spotted her, standing up at the front counter paying her bill. "Suppose I do," he said. "What are you gonna do with it?"

The little girl's eyes lit up. "I'm gonna put it in the gumball machine and get me a gumball. Hopefully it's a red one."

"You like the red ones, huh?" he asked, producing a shiny quarter. The little girl nodded. "Uh-huh."

"The red ones are the best," he said, winking as he held out the quarter.

The little girl snatched the shiny coin. Already turned and halfway to the gumball machine she said, "Thanks, mister!" Marty looked back down at the menu, trying to make the important decision of just what to have for lunch. It was a difficult decision. Should he have the open-faced roast beef sandwich? Or maybe a mushroom swiss burger? Or a double-decker cheeseburger? And then, even after he'd made his selection, there would still be sides to consider; mashed potatoes with brown gravy or a helping of French fries?

He was still weighing his options when Baby Doll reemerged with a green, plastic cup of ice water. She sat it down on the table beside the napkin-rolled silverware. Still peering down at his menu, Marty asked, "What's good here?"

He looked up at Baby Doll, her big brown eyes twinkling, a ready-made howdy-do service smile plastered on her features. "Everything's good here," she chirped, her voice annoyingly happy the way only morning people who actually liked Mondays could manage.

"What do you suggest?" he asked, trying again. "What do you eat here?"

She flashed a perfect brilliant-white weather girl smile and said, "I eat here every day. Mr. Thompson lets us eat on a discount. It's not much, but at least it's something. Every little bit helps, you know?"

Marty showed her a fake smile. "But what do you eat?"

"Oh, I only eat salads," she said. "With little chunks of chicken, French dressing, and extra croutons."

Marty shook his head. "No, no, that won't do for me."

Baby Doll's face twisted in confusion. "Why's that?"

"I hate vegetables."

"My little brother hates vegetables, too," said Baby Doll, as if she was trying to comfort him about something he should be embarrassed about.

"I *really* hate vegetables," said Marty. "I hate them more than anything."

Baby Doll bit her lip. "Anything, in the whole world?"

"Pretty much," he said. "But pickles are the worst."

Baby Doll smiled as if she might laugh. "I didn't think anybody hated pickles." She said it in a judgmental way that made it sound ridiculous, as if he was the only son of a bitch on God's green earth that hated the briny bastards.

"Yep," he said. "I hate 'em."

"Why's that?" inquired Baby Doll, her order pad and pen held steady at her chest.

"Who can say? I'll tell you what—I'll just have the double-decker cheeseburger. Is that pretty greasy?"

Baby Doll looked unsure of what her answer should be. "I guess... Well, not *too* greasy. Do you, uh, do you *like* greasy cheeseburgers?"

Marty laid the menu back down on the table, still looking at the girl's soft China doll features. "Shit yeah," he said. "Who doesn't love a good greasy cheeseburger? Otherwise, what's the point?"

Relieved, Baby Doll shifted her weight from one foot to the other. "Good," she said. "Mr. Thompson makes the greasiest burgers you've ever seen. The grease just drips off of 'em. They're real messy. Some people love that, but then others..."

Marty nodded. "They don't care so much for that."

"Right," she said, repositioning her pen to write. "What kind of side would you like?"

"I'll go with the French fries."

Baby Doll smiled. "I'll bet you eat 'em with gobs of ketchup."

Marty grinned. "Guilty as charged. I drown 'em in it."

"I thought so," she said, nodding happily. "I'll get your order in and it'll be out in a jiffy."

He stopped her. "One more thing."

She looked back. "Yeah?"

"No lettuce, tomatoes, onion, and above everything else, absolutely no pickles."

She nodded in a perky way that made him wonder what she would be like as a sexual partner. "Got ya, boss. No pickles."

"*At all*," he said. "Seriously, no pickles."

She smiled big, flirting just a bit. "Or what, mister?"

He grinned back. "Let's just say I'll be really displeased."

"Well, we don't want that," she said, still flirting. "After all, I want my tip."

And Baby Doll turned and walked back to the counter, making a point of swishing her ass as she did. Marty watched her as she walked away, nodding his head to some crusty old banjo-laden country song about broken hearts and cowboy boots.

About eight minutes passed before Baby Doll appeared at his table again. While waiting, Marty had tolerated the grating music playing, occasionally glancing up at a muted soap opera on the old black-and-white TV hanging at the front of the room. Baby Doll sat the plastic plate, piled with French fries, down on the table. It smelled good and Marty was ready to dig in.

Seeing that he had drained his water cup, Baby Doll asked, "Would you like me to get you a refill?" Already anticipating the answer, she picked up the cup before he could speak, and she turned and walked away.

Marty inhaled the pungent fried potato smell and reached for the ketchup bottle. He unscrewed its lid, dumping a ridiculous amount of the stuff onto his fries. He then lifted the hamburger bun to apply ketchup there, as well. When he did, he was horrified to see three slices of neon green cucumber affronteries to humankind sitting there atop his cheesy burger patty. He forced himself to avert his gaze, fighting back the feeling that he might vomit. He slid the plate away from him.

"Goddammit," he said, his stomach still turning from the unexpected pickle sighting.

A moment later Baby Doll returned with the condensation-coated cup, now fully refilled. He looked up at her, their eyes locking, and she knew instantly that something was wrong.

"There a problem?" she asked.

He nodded, looking down at his defaced burger. "I'm afraid so," he answered grimly. He looked up at her. "It's all fucked up."

Baby Doll cocked her head like a puppy hearing a high-pitched sound, wrinkling her brow as she did. "What do you mean?"

Marty raised his hand and pointed at the plate. Her eyes tracked from the tip of his finger to the burger sitting a few inches away.

"Go on," he said. "Take a look at it. Look under the bun."

Confused by what was he happening, Baby Doll reached out and pulled back the bun, revealing the nasty little bastards in all their abominable glory. But she still didn't understand. She looked at him questioningly.

"Pickles," he said. "They're all over the damned thing."

She started to laugh, unable to control herself. "That's it? That's the big drama?"

Marty glared at her. "I told you—I really hate pickles."

And he stood up.

It was just after two when Sgt. Malone pulled his cruiser into the diner's parking lot. He switched off the red lights and climbed out of the car, walking over to where the other officers were congregated. They turned to him.

"What 's the story here?" asked Malone.

"Nine people dead inside," responded the cop. Malone had never seen him before and figured him a newbie.

"How'd they do it?"

The cop made a face. "Shot up the place, blood all over the walls, everywhere. It's a goddamn slaughter party. It's like the fuckin' *Wild Bunch* in there."

Malone nodded, letting it sink in. "Robbery?"

"It doesn't appear to be," said the young cop. "There appear to be other motives."

Malone nodded again. "Surveillance cameras?"

"No, sir," the young cop said. "But there was another thing—a really strange thing—that I gotta show you."

"Take me to it," said Malone, already on the move towards the diner's entrance. He read a sign in the window as he did. "Their sign says they got the best burgers in town. You figure that's true?"

"Beats me," said the young cop, leading the way.

"I kinda doubt it," said Malone. "Everybody always says that. Then you get the burger and it's just a regular old burger."

"Right," said the cop, not paying attention. He led the older officer into the blood-drenched crime scene. He walked towards one of the bodies—a young Amish man with a dingy *Duck Dynasty* beard lying there on the tile—and squatted down over him. "I want you to see this," said the cop.

Malone knelt down beside him, looking at the bloody corpse. That's when he noticed that the corpse had something covering its eyes. "He's got something in his eye sockets," he observed.

The younger cop nodded. "All of 'em do."

Malone reached down and plucked the tiny object from the dead man's eye. "Well, hell. It's a goddamn pickle," he said. "What do you make out of that?"

"I have no fucking idea, sir," the cop said, trying to parse it all out. "Maybe someone just really hated pickles." The two cops remained there squatting, laughing at the improbability of the scenario.

IT'S NOT ENOUGH

The following story is a modern-day re-envisioning of "The Dog and the Sparrow" by the Brothers Grimm.

Kiki was an Australian Shepherd with a beautiful, shiny black coat. Everyone who saw her commented on her beauty. But her fur was the only aspect of Kiki's life that was beautiful, for she had a very cruel owner who beat her and often forgot to feed her. (This was usually when he was drunk, which was a great deal of the time.) Because of this, the outline of Kiki's ribs soon became visible through her fur.

Each day Kiki diligently chewed at the rope that bound her. Finally, after many days, she managed to chew through the thick cord and free herself. She quickly dug a hole under the wooden privacy fence which surrounded the yard, hoping her master would't discover her digging. After several hours, the hole was big enough that she was able to squeeze through it and escape.

She walked along the street for some time. She stopped when she came to a dead bird in the street, and briefly considered eating it. Only moments later, a sparrow landed on the pavement before her and asked, "What's the matter? You look sad."

"I haven't eaten in days," Kiki replied. "I'm weak and my stomach hurts."

"Well then, let's correct this at once," said the sparrow.

"How?"

"Follow me and I'll feed you."

So the hungry dog followed the sparrow through the alleyways of the city. Finally they came to a dumpster behind a butcher shop. "Let me get you some meat," said the sparrow, and off he flew, into the dumpster. He then returned a moment later with a large piece of steak. He dropped it at Kiki's feet, and the ravenous canine quickly consumed it.

"I'm still hungry," said Kiki, licking her lips.

"No problem," said the sparrow. "I'll get you another piece."

The sparrow returned to the dumpster and retrieved a second piece of meat, this one larger than the first. The hungry dog quickly scarfed down the meat, barely taking time to chew.

The sparrow asked, "Are you satisfied now?"

To this Kiki replied, "I could use some bread to wash down the meat."

"Then follow me and I will get you bread."

The dog followed the sparrow through a labyrinth of alleys until at last they came to a dumpster behind a bakery.

"Wait here," said the sparrow, and off he flew into the dumpster. A moment later he returned, dropping a loaf of bread at Kiki's feet. The hungry dog devoured the bread, and was now quite satisfied.

"Thank you very much," she said.

The two continued on as traveling partners, eventually going so far they exited the city. They followed the road several miles before Kiki finally stopped and said, "I'm very full from having eaten so much. I think I'll take a nap."

Kiki lay down in the road.

"I'm not sure this is a good idea," warned the sparrow.

"Nonsense. I'll just sleep for a short time and then we'll proceed."

Within seconds the dog was fast asleep.

Soon an old Ford pickup truck came roaring down the road on the opposite side of where the dog was lying. The sparrow was alarmed at first, but relaxed once he realized Kiki should be safe. The man driving the pickup truck, however, did not share this sentiment. When he reached the sleeping dog, he went out of his way to swerve into the opposite lane and run it over. The truck bounced when its tires ran over the dog, and the driver laughed. Kiki died without waking from her slumber.

"You son of a bitch!" cried the sparrow. "I'll have my revenge!"

The driver heard the bird's proclamation, but only spit a glob of chewing tobacco out his window in response.

Seeing the truck was hauling a load of furniture in its bed, the sparrow had an idea. The truck was missing its tailgate, and the furnishings were held in place by a single rope. "I'll have my revenge!" cried the sparrow. But the man didn't hear him this time, as he'd turned up the volume of his stereo, which now blared Led Zeppelin. So the sparrow went to work pecking at the rope, until finally it snapped.

Immediately items of furniture began falling from the truck and breaking to pieces all over the road. But the man was oblivious to this, as he was listening to Robert Plant screaming "Whole Lotta Love."

When the man finally noticed he'd lost half his load, he stopped the truck and hopped out to see if any of the fallen furniture could be salvaged. He quickly assessed it could not. While he was arriving at this conclusion, the sparrow started to peck at the old pickup's front driver's side tire, flattening it immediately.

When the man saw this, he screamed, "You filthy little bastard!"

He reached down to the road and picked up a broken chair leg, and came up swinging at the bird. The sparrow quickly moved, and the man accidentally broke the back window of his truck, causing him to become even angrier. The sparrow then flew around the vehicle, and the man gave chase, still swinging the chair leg like a madman. Finally the sparrow landed on the windshield, and the man brought down the piece of wood hard. But the sparrow moved, and the chair leg smashed through the windshield.

"Goddamn bird!" screamed the man.

"It's not enough," said the sparrow. "I'll have my revenge!"

And the bird flew away down the road, leaving the man to walk back to the city alone. Several hours passed, and finally the man reached his old ramshackle house. When he arrived, his wife was there waiting for him.

"Where's the truck?" she asked.

"It's a long story."

"Thank goodness you're here."

"Why is that?"

"Because a bird flew into the house," she said. "Soon it was followed by hundreds of other birds, and they're pecking on the walls and shitting everywhere!"

This angered the man. He grabbed a hammer from the shed and went running into the house like a crazy person, swinging at every bird he saw. But he struck none. Instead, he hit his own furniture, breaking it to kindling. The wife saw what the man was doing, and tried to stop him from swinging the hammer, but to no avail.

Finally the man grew tired and gave up.

"Look what you've done," said the wife. "You've broken every piece of furniture we own!"

"Still not enough!" said the sparrow, fluttering around the man's head. "Still not enough!"

But the man got lucky as the sparrow grew cocky, and he reached out and snatched the bird. Now holding it in his arms, he instructed his wife to retrieve his hunting rifle. The woman disappeared into the next room, finally returning with the gun.

"What do I do now?" she asked frantically.

"Shoot this goddamned bird!"

The man had expected the woman to know enough to shoot the bird from a side angle, but she did not. Knowing nothing about guns, she fired at the bird dead on, but only grazed it. She did, however, manage to shoot her husband in the chest, killing him instantly.

"No!" she screamed, falling to her dead husband's side.

"I told you," said the sparrow, "I'd get my revenge."

And off he flew through the open door, singing as he did.

GRANNY WILKINS' LAST SUPPER

Theodora Wilkins had more than thirty grandchildren and great-grandchildren, and she loved them all very much. In fact, Theodora was so associated with her family that even the other seniors called her "Granny Wilkins."

She was eighty-seven and had just found out she was dying. The doctors had given her two-to-three months to live. Old people died every day, and Granny Wilkins figured she'd had a good run, but the cause of her imminent death annoyed her to no end; despite having never smoked a single cigarette in her entire life, she now had stage IV lung cancer. She felt it was unfair, sure, but what could she do? So instead of focusing on the negatives, she chose to remain happy and look at life's silver linings.

Her children and grandchildren were naturally upset by the news, but again, she was eighty-seven and had already outlived her late husband Earl by nearly fifteen years, so no one was really all that surprised.

Granny Wilkins didn't have much money to leave behind after funeral expenses, so she decided to spend it all on a single lavish meal for her entire family. It would be her last supper, so to speak. She would use her money to fly in family from all over the country. She wanted all of her family to be there for this one last hurrah. It was decided that the dinner would be held in the park on a nice, warm Saturday afternoon in May. Much of the meal would be catered from that nice young man, Mario, who owned the little Italian restaurant next to Granny Wilkins' church. The rest of the meal would be provided by Granny Wilkins herself. After all, sick or no, she couldn't possibly have a dinner without her famous fried chicken, butter potatoes, and Waldorf Astoria red cake.

The meal was scheduled only two weeks away, so there would be little chance of Granny Wilkins dropping dead before the big day. She quickly got everything into place (all by herself, which was something she prided herself in) and had everything ready for the occasion.

On the day of the big dinner, there was a slight wind, which threatened to blow everything around a bit. More than one hundred and forty family members showed up. Granny Wilkins' brother, Ned, was the only notable no-show, and she didn't give a damn about the old so and so anyway.

As everyone found their seats and got situated at the rows upon rows of picnic tables, Granny Wilkins milled about, checking on the meats and pies and refreshments. She wanted everything to be just perfect for this meal. She had left no stone unturned, and had purchased the very finest meats and cheeses and foods for the side dishes. Despite her age and illness, she had prepared a great deal of the food herself and had personally overseen much of the food preparation at Mario's.

Finally everyone was ushered through the lines to get their helpings of food. This whole rigmarole was overseen by Granny Wilkins herself.

"Don't be shy," she told them. "Get a huge plateful. I don't care if you're on a diet or you're a vegetarian or gluten-free, eat up today, on this one day, for me. Please. No need for any of this fine food to go to waste."

Once everyone had their plates of food, they nestled themselves back into their positions at the picnic tables. Granny Wilkins led the meal with a prayer, which focused very little on her sickness. She figured why talk about it more than she had to? Everyone knew why they were there. No need to make this event a depressing one.

"Dig in!" said Granny Wilkins, happily. She, like her Earl, came from the old school of thought where the person throwing the dinner ate last. Besides, she was so enraptured watching everyone eating the food and having a good time that she didn't care much about herself. Everyone seemed to be having a grand old time.

"These peas are marvelous," Betty Jean said. "What did you put in them?"

"Cumin," said Granny Wilkins. "Cumin's the secret, dear."

Donald said, "This chicken is ever bit as delicious as I remember it being. I don't think I've had your chicken, Granny, in...what? Twenty years?"

"At least that."

"It's been far too long."

Granny Wilkins just smiled. "Well, I'm glad you enjoy it."

"Is there a secret with the chicken's breading?" asked Annette.

"Oh, yes," said Granny Wilkins. "I use fluffy, milky egg yokes in the breading."

"It's magnificent," someone said.

Granny Wilkins winked. "I've never had any complaints, and I've been making it for nearly seventy years."

"Everyone loves Granny Wilkins' fried chicken," said Albert.

"Everyone except the chickens themselves," said Tommy.

There were a few complimentary laughs, and Albert said, "I'm sure the chickens gladly bow down and give their lives freely to be a part of such an exquisite meal!"

"Grandma," said Tony.

"Yes?"

"Are you afraid?"

Granny wrinkled her brow. "Afraid?"

"Of death?"

"Tony!" said Martin from down the table. "We don't talk about such things!"

"I'm sorry," Tony said sheepishly.

"No, it's no problem," Granny Wilkins said, still smiling. "No, deary, I'm not afraid. I have faith in God and I believe in an afterlife where I will ultimately spend it with everyone I love."

"That's a nice thought," said Tony, nodding.

"It's more than a thought," Granny Wilkins said. "It's how I make it through my life, from one day to the next. I believe I'll see Earl there, and I want that more than anything else in the world. He was my entire life. I loved him so much."

"That would be great, Mom," said Tammy.

"Oh, wouldn't it?" said Granny Wilkins. "Nothing means more to me than spending time with my family. I know a lot of people—a lot of people who are maybe smarter than me—place value in things like their jobs and sports and entertainment, but what I love most is my family."

Granny looked around the tables and saw that people were tearing up. This wasn't her intention. "No, no," she said. "This is a good thing. This is a positive thing. It's the circle of life. An old woman like myself lies down and makes way for a newborn baby somewhere. It's the way of the world. It's God's way. Besides, we'll all be together one day in Heaven. No tears."

"I'm going to miss you so much, Grandma," said Tony.

"It's okay, dear," Granny Wilkins said. "I promise you everything's gonna be okay."

"Mom, you've meant so much to all of us," said Barbara. "We won't ever forget you and everything you've done for us."

"I know, deary," said Granny Wilkins. "You've all meant the world to me."

Everyone finished their meals and then Granny Wilkins served up her famous Waldorf Astoria red velvet cake, which was as well-loved as her fried chicken.

"This is delicious," said Martin. "I don't know how you do it. No one else makes red cake the way you do. It's so moist."

"I use lots and lots of butter," she said. "That's the secret."

"Better watch out," said Betty Jean.

"Why's that?" Granny Wilkins asked.

"Because that stuff'll kill ya," Betty Jean said.

Everyone laughed, including Granny Wilkins. It was a poorly-timed joke, just the kind the Wilkins clan had always been known for. Earl, especially, had had a dark sense of humor, and that had carried over to the rest of the members of the family.

"I've had a good life," Granny Wilkins said. "I have nothing to be sad about, and there's nothing you should be sad about either. I'm an old woman, and I've been alone for a number of years. I'm ready to go on to Heaven, where I'll be able to spend eternity with my friends and family."

"Cheers!" said Martin.

Everyone raised their cups of soda and clinked them together.

Granny Wilkins looked over at the children's table and saw two of the kids—it looked like Billy and Sarah—lying with their faces down in their plates.

And so it began.

At first no one noticed.

Granny was watching and she saw Chip lean back and close his eyes, but no one else saw it. Then Mikey decided to stand and toast Granny Wilkins. He stood up and raised his cup of Royal Cola over his head and said, "I would like to propose a toast to our wonderful host, Granny Wilkins. She has—" And then a strange look came over his face. He struggled to finish his sentence. "She...she...she..." And then he fell over face first, his head hitting the table hard.

By this time others were getting into the act, as well, and falling over and dying.

"What's happening?" asked David.

"Now we can all be together in Heaven!" Granny Wilkins said, happily.

Now things were fully underway, she finally started in on her own meal. The peas were good, she thought, but a little dry. As everyone fell dead around her, Granny Wilkins ate her food slowly and thoughtfully.

She was happy. Her day had gone perfectly.

THE SWEETEST ASS IN THE OZARKS

Staring at the shelf filled with snack items, Roach managed to stand out as a dirtbag, even here, smack dab in the middle of *Deliverance* hillbilly country. His body hadn't been washed in weeks, and his clothes—the standard-issue uniform for a midwest meth head—were just as dirty. He wore a filthy black beanie, despite it being mid-July when the temperature was ninety almost every day. He reeked of body odor, and his remaining teeth—all eight of them—were the color of piss, complimenting his breath, which smelled like something akin to that.

As he stood there mulling over which type of cupcakes to steal, he noticed a ridiculously-attractive young woman entering the convenience store. She was obviously a spoiled little rich girl, probably about 20, wearing tiny designer shorts painted on her ass that highlighted its perfection. Her face looked like that of a porcelain doll—something so flawlessly crafted that one feared it might break if you touched it. Looking at her there, oblivious to his very existence, Roach instantly assessed her as being a stuck-up bitch.

He finally settled on a pack of Ding Dongs, carefully sliding them down the front of his boxers, exposed above his sagging jeans. He turned towards the counter, waited in line for a moment, scratching his nuts, and then purchased a pack of grape cigar wraps. When he turned around, he found the girl now standing right behind him, waiting to buy a single bottle of water. He grinned, exposing his missing teeth.

"I'll bet you got the sweetest ass in the Ozarks," he said, making a point of looking her up and down. As he'd said the line, he'd felt proud of it, genuinely believing she might appreciate it and find it flattering.

She didn't.

She made a face of revulsion. Roach grinned and strode past her, exiting the store. When he got outside, he pulled out the Ding Dongs from beside his own and climbed into his dirty, rust-covered 1990-

something Honda Civic. He sat behind the wheel, munching on the stolen cupcakes—the first meal he'd had in days—and watched the door of the store. The chick with the nice ass walked out, making her way to a little red Corvette, still unaware of his presence. Roach was surprised to see that she was alone.

She got into her car, sat there for a moment, and then pulled out of the lot and onto the street leading back to the interstate ramp. Roach followed at a distance, careful not to draw her attention. He stared ahead through the dirty bug-guts-covered windshield, making sure to leave considerable distance between their vehicles. Having done this very thing on many an occasion, he was somewhat of a pro at this.

He reached down to the floorboard, littered with a couple years' worth of trash, and felt around for the pack of smokes he'd accidentally dropped earlier in the day. After feeling around amongst a moldy half-eaten Egg McMuffin, dozens of damp cigarette butts, and a few empty beer cans, he finally located the Pall Malls. He picked up the pack, fished out a cigarette, and put it to his lips, lighting it.

He stared at the Corvette, imagining the sexy little girl inside it. He remembered every single curve of her body. Her beautiful face. Her plump breasts. He started to fantasize about the many things he would do to her if he caught her alone. He planned to make sweet love to her if given the chance. Of course society had other less savory words for the act, like rape or sexual assault, but to Roach this was lovemaking, and he had made his share of love in his day. Now driving in the opposite direction he'd originally been traveling, this little side mission would add time to his trip to visit his old cellmate Russell. But Russell would understand. Russell knew the importance of a good piece of ass, and if he could get an eyeful of this chick, he'd have fully understood Roach's motivations.

Getting bored and needing stimuli to entertain his short attention span, Roach turned on the radio. He scanned through the stations. After discovering that the local radio stations were all Christian, Country, or even worse—Christian Country—he switched the damn thing off.

Roach had followed her for about fifteen miles when he saw the Corvette's right turn signal begin to blink. He slowed a little, careful to maintain an adequate distance. She turned off onto a small blacktop road heading off into the boonies. When Roach came to the road, he turned as well, continuing to follow her. Maybe he wouldn't lose as much time as he'd thought. If he could catch her out in the middle of BFE, he could hold her down and make sweet love to her. Then he could turn back around and head for St. Louis.

A few minutes later he saw the Corvette stop on the side of the road. He looked around, making sure there were no witnesses anywhere around. There weren't. In fact, he hadn't passed a single vehicle since they'd started down this road. Roach slowed down, idling toward her vehicle. He watched the Corvette, but the girl didn't emerge. He edged slowly towards her car, their distance shrinking rapidly. Finally, he was right behind her. He pulled over and stopped. He left the motor running, thinking this wouldn't take long. He climbed out and closed the door. He stood there for a moment, scanning the area once more to make sure they were alone. He moved slowly towards the driver's side door, creeping around the car like a cautious cop during a traffic stop.

When he came to the window, he was happy to discover it was already down. The chick looked up at him, smiling. This caught him off-guard, momentarily confusing him. Had she known he'd been following her? Had she decided she wanted to have sex with him out here in the middle of nowhere? Maybe. Anything was possible, and Roach considered himself to be a pretty good-looking dude.

He smiled, flashing that winning smile again. "Is everything okay?"

"Yeah," she said, chewing gum. "What makes you ask?"

"I thought maybe your car broke down."

"And what? You thought you would be a Good Samaritan, help me out?"

He grinned, now believing she was warm for his form. "Yeah, something like that."

She grinned a mischievous grin, really laying it on now. "Can I show you something?" she asked in a tone that was upbeat and sexy.

"What you got?"

"Something hot," she teased.

"Sure," he said. "I'd love to see anything you got that you wanna show me."

"Come over here, real close to the window."

He could feel his erection starting to writhe around in his boxers. He grinned, leaning in towards her. It was then that she raised her arm, holding out a large pistol, training it at his face.

"What the fuck?" he asked, startled and unsure how to react. He stiffened, stepping back.

"You move and I'll shoot your dick."

"Okay, I won't move."

"So, I guess this wasn't what you thought I had?" she asked.

He shook his head. "No."

"What were you gonna do out here? Were you gonna rape me? Were you gonna hurt me?"

"No," he insisted. "I swear, you got it all wrong. I was just tryin' to help."

"Be a Good Samaritan."

He nodded. "Exactly."

She extended her arm towards him, pointing the pistol for emphasis. "Open my door, fucker," she said. He nervously opened the door, and she climbed out, never once taking her eyes or the gun's aim away from his face. She stood before him now.

"Get in the car," she said. "You and me, we're going for a ride."

His mind was reeling. "Why would I want to do that?"

"Because I said so."

"But—"

That was the moment she squeezed the trigger and shot him in his right arm. The impact knocked him back and he yelped with pain. He reached up with his left hand, grabbing the bloody wound. "God help me!" he screamed, looking up at the sky, searching for divine intervention.

"He won't help you now," she said. "That's rich though. A minute ago you were planning to rape me, you rapist piece of shit. Now you're asking God for help."

Roach said nothing. He just stood there, holding his blood-covered arm, crying and heaving in a way no adult man should. She motioned with the pistol. "Get in the fucking car."

He stared at her, hesitant, still in shock.

"You want me to shoot your ass again?"

"No," he managed, sort of stuttering the words.

"Then get in the goddamn car."

He turned for the passenger's side, but she stopped him. "No, you're gonna drive. That way I can keep my eye on you."

Roach didn't say a word. He opened the driver's door and climbed in behind the wheel. As the woman walked around the back of the vehicle, he had the idea he should start the car and take off. The only problem was she had taken the damn keys. She climbed into the passenger's seat, the pistol still aimed at his head.

She handed him the keys. "Start her up and then turn around and head back to the interstate."

He did as he was told.

"You ever drive a Corvette before?" she asked.

"Can't say I have."

"I kind of figured. Most scumbag crank fiends don't have high-end sports cars. Most of them got trashy old beaters like you got... at least 'til they sell them for meth."

He started to feign offense at the suggestion he was a meth addict, but thought the better of it. So he kept his mouth shut and drove. Neither of them said a word except for the occasions on which she gave him directions. She was turned towards him in her seat, still looking hot as ever. Even now Roach thought about the love-making he would probably never get to do with her.

About thirty minutes later, they exited the interstate, heading into Springfield. She directed him to her house. It was a tiny little blue house, something quaint and middle class you might expect a grandma to live in. It didn't look like someplace a little rich bitch like her would live. He wondered if she had pissed off Mommy and Daddy and they had cut her off. Roach looked around, hoping some random neighbor or two might see them, but there were none in sight. She ordered him to get out of the car. He did, and she followed him up the driveway and to the front door. She handed him the keys and he unlocked the door. He entered the house first, and she and the gun followed close behind.

She grinned. "Do you mind if I show you something?"

Recognizing the familiar question, he steeled himself for whatever might be coming.

"That didn't work out so good for you last time, did it?" she asked.

Roach said nothing. She opened a door inside the kitchen, revealing wooden stairs that led down into a darkened basement. She instructed him to walk down them. He took two steps on the rickety wooden stairs before she flipped a light switch, lighting up the place. It had the smell of every basement ever, bringing back memories of the summers he'd stayed with his cousins, Mel and Jenny, who'd had a basement that had been converted into a nice little family room. As he walked down the steps, Roach saw that this basement was very different. There was no nice little family room here.

He looked down at what was there in disbelief.

"You like that?" she asked, sounding pleased with herself.

Roach stared at the heavy chains bolted to the brick wall. There was dried blood splattered on the cement floor and on the walls. This was a goddamn torture room! What kind of girl was this?

When they reached the bottom of the stairs, he started to turn back towards her. She pointed the gun at the chains. "Go over there and put the cuffs on, you piece of shit."

He begrudgingly did what she told him to do. He put his back to the brick wall, reaching up and fastening the metal clasp around his left wrist. It locked into place with a metallic snap. With his left arm tethered there, he couldn't fasten his right wrist. Before he could say anything, she muttered, "I know, I know..."

She walked towards him, striking him hard across the face with the hard pistol, cracking and bloodying his nose. She grabbed his right arm and held it up to the hanging cuff, fastening it around his wrist. Now he was completely at her mercy, and that fact was not lost upon him.

Blood poured from his nose, running into his mouth, down onto his chin, and dripping onto his yellowed once-white Sublime shirt. The blood was thick and salty, and he knew eventually he would gag on it. "What now?" he asked weakly.

She sat the pistol on the floor.

What was this?

She started to unbuckle his belt. Roach was unsure what this meant, unsure if this was a good thing or a bad thing. Maybe this was just some kind of kinky shit she was into. Maybe all of this was part of some detailed sex game. Maybe they would still make love. She yanked his jeans and his boxers down around his ankles, exposing his flaccid penis, poking out through a dense foliage of curly hair. She chuckled, staring at his dangling manhood. "That all you got, sport?"

She turned and walked across the room to a solitary green Army foot locker sitting against the wall. She leaned down and opened it. The lid now sat open, but its contents were obscured from Roach's view. She crouched over the box for a moment before standing again. When she turned towards him, Roach saw that she was now holding a large hunting knife, the kind hunters used to skin their prey.

"No," he said. "Please don't. I'll... I'll be good."

She moved towards him, her face now completely slack, as if this was simply some mundane chore she had to do; a task that brought her no pleasure. As she approached, Roach stared at the blade, which caught a glint of light from the overhead lamp. She came to him, close enough that he could smell the gum she was chewing.

He closed his eyes, frightened, hoping it would all go away. Soon he felt the flat side of the blade caressing his testicles. She moved it slowly along them, loosely hanging skin dragging behind. When she brought the blade upwards, still torturously slow, it rubbed across the head of his penis. This contact, unwelcome as it was, nevertheless brought his dick to life. It started to stir. She rubbed the blade against it slowly.

"What do you think? Should I cut your dick off?"

"No," he said, starting to sob again.

"What were you gonna do with it?"

He said nothing.

"Where you gonna rape me with it?"

He remained silent.

She turned and walked back to the foot locker. She knelt down again, hovering there for a moment. When she finally stood, she held her arm behind her back, concealing whatever she now held. She walked towards him, and he wondered what sort of weapon she now possessed.

When she was up in his face again, she brought out her arm, revealing a giant black dildo.

Roach was instantly terrified, his mind imagining a plethora of possible scenarios, none of which were good. *"No,"* he pleaded. *"Please, no."*

"Were you gonna rape me, motherfucker?" she asked, staring past the plastic dick and into his eyes. "Is that what you wanted?" Her voice grew angrier and more venomous with every word she spat.

"What was it you said to me?" she asked.

"What?" He had no idea what she meant.

"Back at the store. What was it you said?"

"I don't know."

"I do." She smiled, pushing the dildo into his face.

He turned his head, wimpering.

She repeated the words: "I'll bet you got the sweetest ass in the Ozarks."

And Roach started to scream.

It was almost dark when she pulled the Corvette into the gravel driveway of the abandoned farmhouse. She drove to the end of the gravel, then pulling off into the yard. She drove slowly through the weeds and high grass, around the farmhouse to the old stone well.

As she idled the car towards it, she considered its history, wondering how old it was. Probably a hundred years or so, at least. She stopped the car and pushed the button to pop the trunk. She got out and walked to the back of the vehicle, seeing Roach's dead, naked body in the trunk, half covered by an old My Little Pony blanket. At least this guy was skinny, she thought. He would certainly be lighter than the gross old truck driver she'd picked up the previous month. Getting him into the well had been a real chore. Moving this meth-smoking dickhead wouldn't be a walk in the park, but it should be at least a little easier.

She grabbed the green backpack she kept in the trunk. She unzipped it and pulled out a pair of latex gloves, sliding them onto her hands. She then reached into the trunk and grabbed Roach under his arms. She didn't like doing this. The rancid scent of his arm pits would be on her person, even with the gloves. She shrugged to no one and then hefted the body out of the trunk, letting it fall hard to the ground, head first, Roach's neck snapping upon impact. She looked over at the well, only a few feet away.

I just have to do it and get it over with, she thought. Once she was finished, Roach would be with all the others in the bottom of the well, and she could go home and have dinner with her cat Bedelia and watch *Grey's Anatomy* before bed.

THE MAN WHO WOULDN'T DIE

Today was to be Frank "The Hammer" Peretti's execution, and he couldn't wait for his last meal. For the past seven years Frank had been a prisoner at Millwood Maximum Security Prison, and he had spent much of that time dreaming about eating barbecue ribs. Frank was tired of prison life, and ready to get the execution over with, especially if it meant he could have barbecue ribs and potato salad.

The meal was wheeled into his cell at five after four. He was scheduled to be executed at six. The ribs were okay, if a little bland, and the potato salad tasted like the cook had used too much mustard. Despite these shortcomings, Frank devoured the meal in a matter of minutes. He wanted to eat slowly and savor its flavor, but found himself unable to do so.

Frank Peretti wasn't the worst man at Millwood, and he was one of the least offending prisoners on death row. He had worked for the Mafia for a number of years collecting debts, but had made a single mistake which had landed him in prison. He'd brutally beaten a man, accidentally killing him. It could have happened to anyone. The thing was, Frank used a ball-peen hammer and hit the man until there was nothing left of his head to strike.

But Frank didn't complain about his lot in life. He never had. He simply accepted his fate and waited for his impending execution. He'd submitted a number of appeals, but had finally given up on awaiting reprieve from what he saw as a flawed system. If he was to die, he was to die, and that was that.

At a quarter till six, Millwood's warden, Sherman Wilkins, came to Frank's cell. Frank was whistling.

"What is that you're whistling?" Wilkins asked. "Jimmy Crack Corn?"

Frank nodded.

"I just wanted to tell you I enjoyed working with you," Wilkins said.

"Thank you. I wish I could say the feeling was mutal, warden."

A faint smile touched Wilkins' lips. "Let me tell you, there ain't many of the prisoners I can say that about—especially here on death row."

"I appreciate that."

"You always obeyed instructions and did what you were supposed to do, and you never complained or caught an attitude with any of the guards. You've been a model prisoner."

Frank nodded.

"You scared, Frank?" asked Wilkins.

"Not really."

"How come?"

"I don't know," Frank said. "I guess I'm just tired of prison life. You hear about old people who are ready to die... I suppose that's where I'm at. I'm just ready to go."

Wilkins said. "I don't think I could be so calm in the face of death."

"I guess I just don't care enough to get all worked up about it."

A few minutes later the guards came to Frank's cell to escort him to the electric chair. They walked down that long corridor, and a priest read Frank his last rites. Once he was finished, Frank politely thanked him. As they walked, one of the guards literally announced, "Dead man walking." This made Frank chuckle. He'd always thought that was just a fiction of TV and bad movies.

The guards strapped Frank into the big wooden chair.

"It's gonna be tight," one of them said. "I'm sorry for that."

"Don't worry about it."

Once the guards had him strapped into the chair, they put a black satin mask over his face. Just before the mask fell, he looked up in the observation window and saw a few people sitting there. He didn't recognize any of them, and figured they were probably friends and family of the victim. To their credit, none of them glared at him or gave him dirty looks. In fact, several of them were weeping into Kleenexes.

The mask now covered his face and there was only darkness. They then clamped the metal bowl down over his head.

"You ready, Frank?" asked Warden Wilkins.

Frank grinned. "Ready as I'll ever be, I suppose."

The clock struck six and one of the guards started counting down from ten. Once he reached one, he pulled the lever and electricity surged through Frank's body, causing him to buckle in the chair.

The pain was immense—worse than anything Frank could have imagined. Frank prayed inside his head for a quick and merciful death, but the electricity just kept coming, coursing through his body, feeling like fire inside him.

And it kept coming.

His bowels and his bladder let go, but he did not die.

Finally the electric current stopped coming, and Frank could feel them checking his pulse. There was a pause and then the doctor said, "He's still alive." There was another long pause and then Warden Wilkins said, "Give him some more juice." And once again the electric current came, causing Frank to jump around in the chair.

But he did not die.

After they checked his pulse, they lifted the mask to find him staring back at them.

"Well, I'll be damned," said Wilkins. "What do you make of that?"

The doctor shook his head. "I've never seen this before."

Wilkins turned to a guard. "Can we turn it up higher and leave it on longer?"

"No. If we do that, we'll wipe out all the energy in the Eastern seaboard."

"Damn," said Wilkins.

"What's that smell?" Frank asked weakly. "It smells like cooked meat."

Wilkins and the doctor looked at each other.

"It's you," said the doctor.

Frank looked up and saw that half of the observation gallery was empty, and that the other half was either vomiting or looking sickly blue.

Frank was too limp and worn out to walk, so he was carried back to his cell. That night, as he lay there silently in his bunk, Wilkins came to see him.

"I'm awfully sorry about what happened out there, Frank."

"It's not your fault. Don't worry about it."

Wilkins stood there, hanging on the bars for a long moment, saying nothing.

"So what happens now?" asked Frank.

"I think we're gonna have to try again."

"In the electric chair?"

"No, something different. I'm awaiting the word."

"Damn," said Frank. "Well, will I at least get another last meal?"

Wilkins smiled. "I think that can be arranged. After the bullshit that happened today, I'd say it's the least we can do."

"I want fried chicken and mashed potatoes with gravy—the white kind."

"Duly noted," said Wilkins.

The following day Frank received word that he was to be hanged, and that the event would be occurring the following Saturday at six p.m.

The days passed quickly, Frank's body still sore but mending. He now felt less enthused than he had before about his impending execution. After all, the electric chair had caused him an immense amount of pain, and Frank now knew what to expect.

A makeshift gallows was built, as there hadn't been a hanging at Millwood in some sixty years, and everything was prepared for the big event.

Finally Saturday came, despite Frank's futile attempts to will it away.

At just after four they brought him his fried chicken. This time Frank was wise enough to eat it slowly so he could truly experience its flavor. He found the chicken to be much better than the ribs had been, although it was nowhere as good as what his mother used to make back in Brooklyn.

Once again Warden Wilkins made an appearance in the doorway of his cell. Frank continued to eat as they spoke.

"How's your food?" asked Wilkins.

"Not bad," Frank said. "Although I sort of hate what it represents."

"Yeah, I can see that. So you're not as gung-ho to...er...*go* as you were before?"

"No, sir, boss. That electric chair took a lot out of me."

Wilkins made a pained expression. "I have no doubt about that. Again Frank, we're all awfully sorry about what happened in there. None of us knows why it happened. After you got out of there, we tested the equipment and it was working just fine. Apparently it was just a fluke."

Frank laughed. "A painful fluke."

"Well," said Wilkins, "we should have better luck today."

"I don't know whether that's a good thing or a bad thing."

A few moments later, the guards came to escort Frank to the gallows. If the previous walk to the electric chair had seemed like a mile, then this now felt like twenty. Frank swore it was the longest walk of his life.

But he still wasn't scared. He was more apprehensive than anything.

The guards took him to the gymnasium and led him up to the top of the gallows. Once there, the priest read him his rites again. Frank thanked him for his time, just as he had before. They then put a black hood over his face and wrapped the noose tightly around his neck.

"Francis Peretti," read Wilkins. "You have been sentenced to death by hanging, and are to be hanged by the neck until you are dead."

Frank then heard him say. "You ready, Frank?"

"Sure," Frank said. "Let's give it a try."

One of the guards counted down from ten once again, and the lever was flipped at one, dropping Frank through the gallows. The rope at Frank's throat immediately became tight, so tight he couldn't breathe. The darkness inside the hood gave him the heebie-jeebies.

And he dangled there.

Alive.

Literally kicking and (attempting) to scream.

Finally Wilkins said, "Climb on up there, Joe, and see if you can weight him down some more."

Frank felt the guard climbing up his legs and dangling there, but it was to no avail.

Frank did not die.

Finally, after more than a half an hour of Frank's hanging there, Wilkins said, "Goddammit, cut him down."

Frank was then let down from the noose. He gasped for air, finding it, and gulped it in in large breaths. Again Frank felt weak, so he was carried back to his cell.

About an hour later, Frank was lying there limply on his bunk, considering all that had taken place. Warden Wilkins came to him again.

"I don't know what to say," Wilkins said.

"I'm not sure there is anything to say."

"It doesn't make sense. No one here has ever heard of this happening before."

"Me neither," said Frank.

"How bad does it hurt?"

"Real bad."

"I'm sorry."

"So now what?"

"We try again."

"How?"

"I'm not sure," said Wilkins. "I'm sure the method has to be something more drastic this time. Something impossible to walk away from."

"Great," said Frank. "Sounds fucking painful."

"How could it be worse than what you've already endured?"

"I have faith that it could." Frank grinned at this.

"Together, we'll figure this thing out, Frank."

"I suppose so."

"Try and get some rest," Wilkins said.

"Rest up for my death?"

Wilkins smiled uneasily. "Something like that."

And he left.

Two days later, Frank was led out of the prison to a nondescript white van. He was then escorted by Warden Wilkins and two guards. They all climbed into the van, and pulled away from the prison.

"What now?" asked Frank.

"We try again."

"How come there was no build-up this time? No warning?"

"The powers that be want this one off the books," Wilkins said. "They're becoming increasingly embarrassed by this whole fiasco. So this won't be a publicized thing. It won't be official. They've already marked you down as dead. Now it's our job to make sure you really are dead."

"How will it happen?"

"I hate to even say this out loud," Wilkins said. "It's going to be quite terrible."

"How so?"

"We're going to incinerate you."

Frank felt a chill run down his spine.

"Incinerate me?"

"We really have no choice. This has to be the last time."

Frank was really uncomfortable now. He was no longer excited about the prospect of dying. He was now afraid. Really afraid. Afraid of the pain, afraid of living.

"Why don't you turn on the radio?" Wilkins said to one of the guards. "I think poor old Frank here could use some music to calm his nerves."

They listened to music—oldies rock like "Johnny B. Goode"—but it did little to calm Frank's nerves. After all, he was about to be incinerated.

Once they got to the big white building, they led Frank out of the van. They went inside the building.

"So this where the magic happens?" Frank said dryly.

No one said a word.

Frank was then made to strip down to the nude, the cement floor cold on his feet. The room was cold and he felt his cock shrinking towards his balls. *I guess I won't have to worry about being cold for long*, he thought.

He was then made to lie down on a long metal tray. Frank wondered how many bodies had been incinerated on this very tray.

"Any last words, Frank?" asked Wilkins.

"Let's just get this over with."

And Frank was pushed slowly into the fire, the door shutting behind him.

And he burned. The smell of his own flesh burning overwhelmed him, and he screamed out in agony as the fire consumed him. He screamed and screamed and screamed.

But he did not die.

Frank was left screaming inside that incinerator for the better part of an hour. His flesh baked and charred, his hair burned away, but he lived.

Finally they opened the door to the incinerator and pulled the tray out.

Between the smell of Frank's burned flesh and his now-gruesome appearance, the two guards started to vomit. Only Wilkins and the incinerator-operator maintained their composure.

Frank tried to cry, but could not. His tear ducts had melted.

There was smoke coming off his body.

"How bad is it?" asked Wilkins.

"It hurts so bad," Frank said weakly, trying to cry. "Worse than anything."

The guards would find it difficult to load Frank back up in the van, as every time they touched a place on his charred flesh, it would come off in their hands. But nonetheless, Frank was loaded into the van and returned to Millwood.

Once there, he was taken to the infirmary so he could be treated for his burns. The doctors there said these were the worst burns they had ever seen. "He shouldn't be alive," Frank overheard them saying.

And yet he was.

He was alive.

The following day Frank was taken by wheelchair to a dimly-lit room in the basement. Only Warden Wilkins and the two guards from the incinerator mishap were in attendance.

One of the guards, Ted, was now wielding a giant, extravagant sword with dragons inlaid on its blade.

"What is that for?" Frank asked.

"I really hate to have to do this," Wilkins said. "But we're gonna have to cut your head off."

Frank's eyes grew big. *"Cut my head off?"*

"There doesn't seem to be any other way."

Frank looked at the sword. "You're gonna cut my head off with a Medieval-looking sword? That doesn't seem very official."

Wilkins looked pained. "Well, it's not, but no one knew where else to get a sword. Ted here already had one."

"I like to go to Renaissance Fairs ," said Ted.

"So I guess this is it," said Frank. "You're gonna cut my head off."

"I guess so," said Wilkins.

They laid Frank out on an old wooden bench, his charred black neck exposed.

"Ted here's gonna do the honors," explained Wilkins.

"Since it's my sword and all," said Ted.

Wilkins looked at Frank. "Any last words?"

Frank was irritated. "Just fucking get it over with."

Wilkins looked at Ted and nodded.

Ted turned sideways, putting the sword down beside him, so he could swing it with enough momentum to chop Frank's head off.

"Ted," Frank said.

"Yeah, Frank?"

"Try not to miss."

Ted said he wouldn't. He then counted to three, whipping the giant sword up over his head, and bringing it down flush against Frank's neck. Frank's bald, blackened head fell off onto the cement floor, bouncing as it did.

"Ouch!" yelled Frank's head. "That fucking hurt!"

All three of the prison employees gasped simultaneously.

How could this be possible?

Frank's headless body sat upright and started moving around animatedly, its arms waving wildly.

"Well," Frank's head said, "this fucking sucks."

So Frank was then taken to the prison cemetery, where he was laid in a coffin, his head down next to his body. A fresh hole was dug in anticipation of this.

"So I don't get to die?" asked Frank.

"I don't know how to kill you," Wilkins said. "But this is becoming a huge embarrassment. We have to get rid of you, and there doesn't seem to be any other way."

The coffin lid was then put on, forever encasing Frank in darkness. The lid was then nailed down to the box. The coffin was lowered down into the grave, and dirt was thrown onto it. As the gravediggers covered the hole, they could hear Frank whistling "Jimmy Crack Corn" from beneath the soil.

THE GYPSY'S CURSE

Crank loved a lot of things in life, but there really was nothing he enjoyed more than hurting people. That, to him, was the epitome of happiness. So here he was, out on this old single-level houseboat, breaking this old gypsy's fingers, and loving every minute of it.

"How you like that, you old fuck?" Crank asked as he snapped the old man's right index finger, twisting it in ways fingers weren't supposed to be twisted. The old man didn't say anything, but only screamed out. But what the fuck was he gonna say that had any relevance? "Ow"? "That hurts"?

Crank and the other members of the Disciples motorcycle club had been out on these "fishing trips" more times over the years than he could possibly account for. There was no way he could have remembered them all.

The Disciples were an outlaw MC that had been established way back in the early seventies, back when the Vietnam War was still a thing. The MC had set up shop in Miami, Florida. In those early days, under the leadership of Horse Cock Davis, their primary focus had been on the choppers. Today, some fifty years later, their focus had shifted. Obviously the bikes were still a major aspect of the club, but today the Disciples' main objective was making money selling drugs and running hookers. The Miami cops pretty much let them do as they pleased, as the MC kept all the right palms greased and dicks sucked. The Disciples were making money hand over fist, and life was good.

Despite this prosperity, examples still had to be made and heads needed to be cracked. For several decades, the MC had disposed of such problems in a small unnamed cove they'd discovered about twenty miles downshore. If some asshole crossed the Disciples or tried to screw them over, he would inevitably find himself chained to bricks and dumped in the cove, problem fucking solved.

So here they were today, Crank and three other members of the club, Slash, Hannibal, and Russo, taking care of yet another problem.

The problem they were handling today was an old silver-haired gypsy bastard named Looney. The Romani man had sealed his fate when he'd come at the Disciples' leader, Schizo, wielding a knife after Schizo had beaten the man's daughter. The attack resulted in a huge gash across Schizo's cheek.

So here there were now, out on the houseboat, taking Looney to meet his demise. When they'd first gotten onto the boat, Looney had sat there at gunpoint, putting a curse on the bikers. "You will die," said the old man, a twinkle in his eyes. "All of you will die soon. *All of you!* I will have my revenge, I assure you." None of them believed in bullshit curses, so they laughed at him, mocking his name. "You really are looney, old man!" But the old man just smiled at them, promising his curse would take their lives. This promise did nothing to prevent them from doing him harm. In fact, it made things worse.

It was the utterance of the curse that had caused Crank to start snapping the old man's fingers like twigs. Crank hadn't felt like coming on this trip in the first place, and he hadn't felt like hurting the man, even though he loved doing these things. He'd stayed up all night and drank way too much, and today his temples throbbed like a motherfucker. But still, the old bastard needed to be hurt.

"Christ," muttered Crank, standing over him.

"What is it?" asked Russo.

"My head," said Crank. "It hurts like a bastard."

Russo looked at him. "Why don't you just have a seat and let me take care of him?"

Crank shrugged. Russo was right. There was no reason to make more work for himself. "Fine," he said, shrugging. "Go ahead and do it."

The old man watched all this, his eyes big, but he said nothing. Crank sat down in the seat across from Looney. Russo moved forward a few steps, opening a small hatch and retrieving a snub-nosed .38. Gun in hand, he stood up, looking at the old man. He walked over to him, casually raising the pistol and firing a round through Looney's eye.

"*Goddammit!*" said Hannibal. "You got brains all over the fucking seat! Who's gonna clean that shit up?"

Russo just looked at him, sliding the .38 into his waistline. "I dunno," he said.

"I know who's gonna do it," said Hannibal. "You're gonna do that shit. I get tired of it. I told you last time you did that to take them outside and fire towards the water so their blood and brains go there and not on the boat. I hate cleaning brains off vinyl seats, man. They smear all over and it makes a mess. And some of it's on the carpet, man. That's gonna be a bitch to clean."

"Whatever," said Russo. "You think I ain't never cleaned brains before?"

"You never clean anything," Crank interjected. "You're a lazy dick."

Russo muttered and went off looking for cleaning supplies.

A few minutes later the old houseboat was sitting in the middle of the secluded cove. Crank and Hannibal went to work chaining the old man to a large cement brick they'd brought along. They then hefted the brick-tethered gypsy overboard, watching him sink. Crank rubbed his hands as if cleaning them and said, "Goodbye jerk."

"Fuck that guy," said Russo, now back with a rag in his hand.

Crank turned, and Slash handed him a bottle of beer. Crank then went and climbed behind the steering wheel, trying to start the boat's engine, but it wouldn't turn over. "Shit," he said. He looked at the others. "Do any you fuckers know anything about fixing a boat engine?"

"Shit no," said Slash. "All I know about technology is when the TV remote stops working, I bang it on my leg. If that don't work, then I pop it open and spin the batteries."

"I don't think that's gonna work here," Crank said.

"I'll just call the MC and have somebody come get us," said Hannibal. He reached into his pocket and produced an old-school flip-phone. He opened it and punched in the number, then holding the phone to his ear. "Damn," he said. "Ain't no service out here."

"What now?" asked Crank.

"Don't worry, brother," said Russo. "I'll swim to shore and find a phone and call for help. We'll be stuck here for a bit, but eventually we'll get home. You guys cool with that?"

"Where you gonna find a phone?" asked Slash. "You think they're growing on trees up there?"

"I got no idea," said Russo. "But do you see any other alternatives?"

Slash shook his head and the other guys agreed. "See you guys in a bit," said Russo, diving overboard in his t-shirt, jeans, and boots. They all watched him swimming towards the shore, which was probably sixty yards away. Crank noted that Russo was a pretty good swimmer and wondered where he'd learned to swim like that. As they all watched

Russo swim, they suddenly saw him bob underwater. A second later he reemerged, flailing and screaming. *"Help me!"* he yelled. His head then bobbed underwater a second time, then popping back up. Then a second head emerged from the water behind him. It was a dark head, its features difficult to discern. The bikers all squinted and saw that it was a decayed human's face, very little remaining beyond the skull. The figure was holding Russo tightly as the biker fought to get free. Finally the decayed human pulled Russo close and bit into his neck. Dark blackish blood instantly appeared around its mouth. Russo was screaming like crazy now, and the decayed human continued biting and chewing his neck. A moment later Russo stopped screaming and went limp. The decayed human continued gnawing at his neck.

"What the fuck?" said Crank excitedly.

"What is that...that...*thing*?" asked Slash.

"You guys ever watch zombie movies?" asked Hannibal.

"Zombies don't exist, you dumb fucker," said Slash. "Don't even say that."

Hannibal looked at him, dead serious. "You sure about that?"

Before Slash could answer, they heard a loud gunshot from behind. Hannibal and Slash turned to see that Crank had fired his .45 into the side of the decayed man's skull, opening up a big hole there. But the dead man was still chewing on Russo. "I shot that fucker right in his head," said Crank. *"He's got a fucking hole in his head!* And he wasn't affected in the least. He didn't even stop for a moment. He just kept right on chewin'!!"

"I told you it was a zombie," said Hannibal. "But you guys never listen."

Crank noticed something in the water in his peripheral vision. He turned and saw another skeletal head, only the slightest amount of bluish decayed flesh and hair still attached, emerging from the depths of the ocean. "Guys, look," he said, pointing. "There's another one!" As Slash and Hannibal turned, they saw other skeletal heads popping up from beneath the water. The houseboat was surrounded by water zombies, only their heads visible.

"Holy fuck!" said Slash. "Now what do we do?"

"I didn't even know zombies existed," said Hannibal.

Crank nodded. "They didn't cover water zombies in science class."

The three bikers stood there for a moment, each of them terrified and trembling, on the verge of pissing themselves.

Crank started firing his pistol at the water zombies. His shots were accurate, making more holes in the zombie heads but achieving nothing. The zombies were just kind of floating there, still for the moment. They weren't really looking anywhere in particular since they no longer had eyes, only gaping black holes.

"I feel like they're starin' at me," said Crank. "But the fuckers ain't got no eyes."

"Where do you think they come from?" asked Hannibal.

"Probably hell," said Crank.

"No," said Slash. "They're all the people the MC has killed and sunk out here."

"There sure are a bunch of 'em," said Crank.

Slash went inside the houseboat, the other two bikers just standing there watching the water zombies and trying to figure out their plan of attack.

"Where's he goin'?" asked Hannibal.

Before Crank could answer, a water zombie emerged from behind Hannibal, reaching out and grabbing the biker. Hannibal was turned away from the zombie, flailing and trying to wriggle free from its grasp. He elbowed the bluish zombie in ribs visible beneath torn flaps of skin. The zombie's rib bones crushed inward, but the zombie didn't ease up its clutch on Hannibal. Hannibal was screaming and wriggling. Crank was moving towards them, not even knowing what he would do when he reached them. Before he could even get close, he heard the loud blast of Slash's shotgun to his left. Crank was staring at Hannibal when he heard the shot. Slash missed, hitting Hannibal in the chest. Hannibal's chest opened up in a bloody mess as his body flopped backwards, disappearing overboard with the zombie still hanging from his back. Crank heard the splash. He moved forward to look over the side, seeing Hannibal in the water, only twitching now, the zombie pulling his ear off in its teeth.

"Dammit to hell," muttered Crank. He turned to Hannibal. "You got this out here? I'm gonna go in and try to start the engine again."

"I got it," Hannibal said confidently.

Crank went inside and sat down behind the steering wheel. He reached to his right and turned the key, grinding it. As he did, he heard the 350 engine suddenly whir to life. He was about to shift the thing and take off, but then he heard Hannibal screaming behind him. He hopped to his feet, reaching for his .45. When he emerged onto the back deck he saw Hannibal on the ground, screaming and trying to fight off two water zombies. One of them had chewed off Hannibal's nose, leaving a grotesque mess in its place, and the other was ripping out his entrails with its hands.

Crank positioned himself where he could get a clear shot at Hannibal. "I'm sorry, old friend," he said as he shot a round into Hannibal's forehead. Hannibal's head thumped back, and the two zombies continued eating his remains. Crank reached down, grabbing the fallen shotgun and dropping his pistol. He moved towards the feeding zombies, approaching them from behind. When he was close to them, he swung the butt of the shotgun hard into the nose-chomping zombie's head, knocking it completely off. It flew back, crashing into the side of the boat, its jaws continuing to grind Hannibal's flesh. The body, now headless, fell over, but continued moving.

The other zombie was standing there, leaned forward, eating Hannibal's intestines. He was holding them up to his face, the rest of them hanging down. Crank stepped forward, as if he was Ted Williams swinging into a fastball. He swung the shotgun upwards into the zombie's head, causing it to detach and sending it flying out into the ocean.

Crank ran back to the driver's seat and shifted the thing into drive. The houseboat started moving forward. He swung the boat around to leave the cove, motoring over several zombie heads, which he heard crunch as they were obliterated by the engine's propellers.

Crank laughed as he left the cove, happy to have escaped.

"Fuck yeah!" he said, raising his fist into the air triumphantly, completely unaware of the water zombie shambling up behind him.

THE DAY FAT TERRY BROUGHT DEAD HITLER TO IOWA

Today was the single greatest day in all of Fat Terry's thirty-four years of life. Today was the culmination of everything he'd hoped and dreamed about these past four years. After hundreds of hours of planning and organizing (over Hot Pockets and D&D in his mom's basement), the day had finally come. Today was the first annual Aryan White Dudes Unite conference, here in his home town of Tibbetsville, Iowa. Today was sure to be a banner day, one of those three or four days you look back upon fondly when you're in your eighties and near the end of your string. In fact, Terry couldn't envision a day he might someday be more proud of. He doubted he would ever have children, since no one would fuck him (he still had his v-card), and he hadn't done much else in his life. Today even ranked ahead of the time Fat Terry had placed thirty-fourth (out of thirty-six) in the national Dig-Dug championship. Fat Terry wanted every aspect of the conference to be perfect, but his therapist had advised him to relax and enjoy his accomplishment ("even though it's really stupid," he'd said).

Standing here now, looking over the crowd, Fat Terry was starting to feel anxious. He had felt confident the event would bring in several hundred white Aryan brothers from across the nation, but there were only eight dudes present in the VFW event room. (Fat Terry had spent fifty bucks to secure the large room, but had figured it would be worth it. Now he realized he could have just held the conference in the back room at Toby's Chinese and Mexican Good Eatins Buffet for free.) But maybe there would be more people coming, he thought. After all, it was only forty-five minutes after the conference had been scheduled to begin.

Terry had pulled out all the stops for this thing, making every effort to ensure this would be a top-notch affair. He'd scheduled a speaker, Kenny Marshall, the guy who worked over at the farm store, to talk about how the holocaust was completely made up. Kenny hadn't gone to college and didn't have a Ph.D (he'd actually dropped out in the sixth grade) and he wasn't an expert, per se, but he'd once had a conversation online (in a Naruto chat room) with someone revealing himself to be a government employee working for a top secret organization located a hundred miles beneath the ground. In that conversation, the guy, going by the moniker ILOVETITTIES42, told him three secrets that would change Kenny's life forever: that Bigfoot existed (he'd been shaved and was now passing as a human somewhere in Poughkeepsie), aliens existed ("there's lots of 'em," he'd said. "Barack Obama was one of 'em!"), and that the holocaust "was total bullshit, made up by a Jewish guy who wrote for some big newspaper somewhere and couldn't think of nothin' else to write about". But that wasn't the biggest thing Fat Terry had scheduled for the event. Not even close. His secret weapon was a guy named Nathaniel Honeysuckle.

Nathaniel Honeysuckle was a retired Walmart auto mechanic and former felon (convicted of having sex with an eleven-year-old girl, but hey, Nathaniel had only been thirty-four at the time himself) who had found his true calling in life ten years ago, at the age of forty-one. After reading a few books at the library, watching a few YouTube videos, and having had a conversation with God (his friends had said it was the mushrooms, but Nathaniel knew better), he'd embarked upon a new path, essentially becoming a real-life Dr. Frankenstein. As silly as it sounded, Nathaniel had come up with a method to reanimate the dead. His method, secret as it was, involved brake fluid, mayonnaise, and jumper cables. At least that was what he'd told Fat Terry, saying he could reveal no more.

But today all those years of research would pay off, and Nathaniel would be unveiling the resurrected body of the Fuhrer himself, Adolf Hitler.

"Are you sure it's really Adolf Hitler?" Fat Terry had asked.

"Of course it's Adolf Hitler," Nathaniel had snapped. "Who else would it be?"

"I dunno, maybe somebody else."

"No, he's definitely Hitler."

"How do you know?"

"I seen his cock. It's a real big one."

"What does that mean?" asked Fat Terry.

"Duh," responded Nathaniel. "Everyone knows Adolf Hitler had a big cock. The guy was hung like a fuckin' T-Rex."

"How do you know?"

"I read it online somewhere."

"Oh, okay," Fat Terry had said, realizing it must be true.

"I still can't believe I located Hitler's body. This is a big thing."

"Fuck yeah, it is. This is huge."

"Like Hitler's cock," Nathaniel had said.

"You sure like to talk about that cock."

"Well, it's a good one. Even bigger than mine."

"How big is yours?"

"None of your business," Nathaniel said, then adding, "But it's big. Way bigger than two-and-a-half inches, that's for sure."

"Where did you get Hitler's body?"

"I bought it from a guy over in Hartley, works at the hospital."

"He works at the hospital?"

"Yeah."

"Does he work in the morgue?"

"Yeah, how did you know?"

"Are you sure he didn't just steal a body at the hospital and tell you it was Hitler?"

"Hell no," said Nathaniel.

"How do you know?"

"Because he told me it was Hitler. He said his grandpa had uncovered the body while he was working as a juggler on tour in Germany back in the fifties."

"Okay, yeah, then I guess it's Hitler," Fat Terry had concluded.

"You bet your ass it's Hitler."

Fat Terry said he'd purchased the corpse a couple years ago, having paid $500 and given a love seat, a Jack Russell terrier named Cosmo, his Darth Vader action figure carrying case, a stack of *Betty and Veronica* comics, and his broken down Toyota Celica for it. "Hitler was expensive, but it was a once in a lifetime opportunity," Nathaniel had said. "Hitlers don't grow on trees, you know."

When Fat Terry had first mentioned his idea about the conference to Nathaniel, whom he'd met in a Fox News forum, Nathaniel had come up with the plan to unveil Dead Hitler for the first time. "They'll love it," Fat Terry said. Nathaniel agreed, saying, "Then we can discuss how we'll use Dead Hitler to start a new Third Reich in America. We'll call it the Fourth Reich." After further consideration, Nathaniel decided "Nathaniel Honeysuckle's Fourth Reich" had a better ring to it.

Finally, after having waited for more than an hour, Fat Terry concluded that no one else was coming. So the first annual Aryan White Dudes Unite conference would consist of just eight people, plus Fat Terry, Kenny, and Nathaniel. But that was okay, he figured. Soon, after everyone else learned about the reanimation of Dead Hitler, things would change and neo-Nazis from around the globe would join their ranks. Baby steps, Fat Terry told himself. These things took time.

Fat Terry started the event by standing up in front of the meager crowd and introducing himself. "I'm Terry Hullinger," he said. "My friends call me Fat Terry." (He didn't really have any friends, but thought it sounded cooler to say he did. Fat Terry was just something the guy who used to come over on Saturday nights to bang his mom called him as he passed through Terry's room naked to get to his mom's adjoining bedroom.) "I'm glad to see you guys here," Fat Terry said. "We got long johns and nacho chips and fiesta dip back there on the table if anybody wants some. We've also got three different flavors of Shasta available if anybody's thirsty. Unfortunately it's hot because my cousin Skeeter couldn't locate his cooler this morning. But it's still good warm. The secret is you gotta hold it in your mouth for a minute and sorta get used to it before swallowing. It goes down easier that way."

"*Get on with it!*" screamed a bearded guy wearing a HILLARY FOR PRISON 2016 shirt. Fat Terry took this in stride, keeping his composure. "Today we're gonna have a good day. First we're gonna listen to a real cool guy named Kenny Marshall talk about the holocaust and how the Jews made the whole thing up. Then we're gonna have a thirty minute break where everyone can just mingle and talk about our Aryan white brotherhood and listen to music. I brought Air Supply and Journey CDs, so we can listen to those. I got some Styx, too. Then, after that, is the big thing I promised you. Today Nathaniel Honeysuckle is gonna unveil the reanimated corpse of Adolf Hitler. So it's a good thing there's only eight of you guys, really, because you'll be the first ones who get to see this thing that's gonna change the course of history, not just here in the US of A, but everywhere, because once we take over this place, we're gonna take over the world, and then maybe even the other planets."

After Fat Terry had introduced him, Kenny Marshall, a heavyset guy who was bald but had a ponytail and Spongebob face tattoo, addressed the group, explaining how he'd learned that the holocaust was a lie. Everyone cheered and yelled out things like "fuck yeah!" as he spoke. One particularly high point of Kenny's speech was when he explained how the six million supposedly dead Jews had really just faked their deaths and moved to Mexico, giving everyone just one more reason to hate the Mexicans. "This is why we need a wall on the border," someone said, causing everyone to cheer.

When Kenny was finished speaking, they took a break and mingled, listening to music. Several people yelled out music requests, ranging from Night Ranger to Def Leppard. One guy suggested Foreigner, eliciting anger. A big guy wearing Oakleys screamed out *"I fuckin' hate foreigners,"* and then the other seven guys attacked the poor bastard who'd made the request. At first Fat Terry thought this was a bad thing, but then he realized it just showed how fired up and dedicated to the cause these guys were.

Then Fat Terry stood up in front of the seven attendees who remained. "This is the reason you all came," he said. "Today we're gonna do something that's gonna change everything. This is gonna be a day that's gonna go down in history. I invited the reporter from the newspaper over in Culver to come and see, but he said he was busy covering a girl's high school volleyball game and couldn't come. But eventually everyone's gonna know what happened here today. This, my friends, is a special day. But don't listen to me, listen to Nathaniel Honeysuckle, a guy who's on the cutting edge of science stuff. He's gonna explain it all." Fat Terry then introduced Nathaniel, who was still wearing his McDonalds shirt as he'd come directly from a morning shift.

"Hey guys," he said, giving them the "live long and prosper" parted fingers gesture. "Who wants to see Dead Hitler today, alive and well, ready to take over the world?" The seven guys cheered. "Who's ready to take back our country?" They cheered again. "Give me a minute and I'll go get Dead Hitler and bring him on in. This is big. You guys are the first people in the world to see reanimated Dead Hitler other than my friends and my brother. This is a special event." Nathaniel left the room for nearly ten minutes, causing the crowd to wonder if he was coming back. But finally he did, leading in another man, whose head was obscured by a My Little Pony sheet.

Nathaniel led the sheet-headed man up to the front of the room. "Here he is, guys," he said. "Are you ready?" Everyone cheered, saying they were. "Wait no longer," he said. *"Here he is, Dead Hitler!"* Nathaniel pulled off the sheet, revealing a guy who looked suspiciously black.

"What the fuck?" screamed the biker guy. "Hitler wasn't no damn coon!"

Others started raising their voices.

"Hold it down," urged Nathaniel. "You'll scare him. He's never been around a crowd before."

Everyone continued screaming, and Dead Hitler's eyes looked around the room, bulging, big and panicked. He was starting to shake, just a little at first.

"This is bullshit!" someone screamed. *"I drove 200 miles to be here so I could see Hitler. That ain't Hitler! That's a black dude!"*

Nathaniel tried to calm the crowd. "I know he looks like a black guy, but he ain't. I'll tell you what the guy I bought him from told me. He just looks black because he's been dead for a long time. Dead people look like that after a while."

"Horse shit!" screamed a guy wearing a JESUS IS LOVE t-shirt. *"He's got half a fuckin' Afro! He's black, he ain't dead!"*

"He's dead and he's Hitler," Nathaniel maintained. "Calm down everybody." He looked over at Dead Hitler, looking nervous. "You guys are scaring him."

"Fuck Dead Hitler!" screamed a guy wearing a Chewbacca shirt.

Suddenly Dead Hitler started flailing around crazily, waving his arms, striking Nathaniel in the side of the head. Nathaniel crumpled to the floor like discarded trash.

"Jesus Christ!" yelled one guy.

Someone else yelled, *"Get the sonofabitch and beat the shit outta him! He's black anyway!"*

The seven men swarmed on Dead Hitler, and Dead Hitler started striking them, displaying superhuman strength.

"Why the fuck is he so strong?" someone asked.

"Only Nathaniel knows, and he's unconscious," said Fat Terry.

The men continued to attack Dead Hitler, and he continued striking at them. He reached out and grabbed the guy in the Chewbacca shirt, picking him up. The others backed up a bit as he did. Suddenly Dead Hitler tore the guy's body in half at the stomach and there were entrails and viscera everywhere.

"Good fuck!" screamed someone. The crowd was becoming panicked now. Everyone rushed to the back of the room. Someone tried to open the room's only door and said, *"It's locked! The fuckin' thing's locked!"*

"It ain't locked," said Fat Terry. "I had my cousin Skeeter block the door from the outside so nobody could interrupt." Meanwhile, Dead Hitler was ripping the head off a dude dressed in camo. Everyone was screaming and panicking, and Dead Hitler was moving forward, flipping over tables and tossing people around.

"Call your cousin and tell him to unlock the door!" someone yelled.

"I can't!" explained Fat Terry. "He ain't got no phone!"

"What are we gonna do?" someone asked.

"I got an idea," said a dude who looked like the resulting baby if Willem Dafoe and the old guy version of Mickey Rourke fucked. The guy pulled out a Bowie knife from a sheath on his belt. "Watch this," he said. Willem Dafoe Mickey Rourke Fuck Baby moved towards Dead Hitler, lunging at him, burying the blade deep in Dead Hitler's eye. Dead Hitler gave a long pained moan, knife still sticking out of his face, and reached out and grabbed the guy. He held him up over his head, hurling him hard into the brick wall, killing him instantly.

The remaining men in the room were clustered around the door, pushing against it. Dead Hitler stalked towards them, moving with purpose now. He lifted another table over his head, slamming it down on the guy with the HILLARY FOR PRISON 2016 shirt, crushing him. Dead Hitler then raised the table again, hurling it into the crowd, striking a number of the Aryan White Dudes. Dead Hitler grabbed one guy by the arm, tearing it off. He then took the arm and used it like a club, beating another man to death.

This carnage continued until Fat Terry was the only one left alive. He cowered in the corner. "Please let me go, Dead Hitler," he pleaded. "Please, man, let me go." Dead Hitler stood there for a moment, the two of them watching each other. "I'll suck your dick if you let me go," said Fat Terry. Dead Hitler came closer, cocking his arm back. He punched hard, burying his fist in Fat Terry's face, causing blood and brains to explode from it, and Fat Terry was no more.

THE TRUTH ABOUT JOSH

I had been friends with Josh for a long, long time.

The thing about Josh is that, well, he's crazy. He doesn't recognize his insanity, and he takes no medications whatsoever. And when craziness goes untreated, it only gets worse over time.

But Josh wasn't always crazy, at least not in ways that show; not like now. No, when we were kids I thought he was one of the sweetest people I'd ever met. That's what pulled me in. Well, that and the fact that he was my only friend. So instead of it just being me out there getting my ass kicked by the bullies, it was the two of us. I always thought that was nice.

Josh didn't start changing for the worse until he we were in high school. At about 16, I watched him slowly start to pull away from the world and become reclusive. He was always paranoid—he thought everyone was out to get him. No one was out to get him, but he refused to listen to reason. He started playing with his father's guns.

The first time I saw Josh exhibit true craziness was one night when he telephoned in the dead of night.

"What is it?" I asked.

"I'm in a bad place," Josh said.

"What do you mean?"

"I got a gun."

"Please don't hurt yourself."

"No," Josh said. "Not me."

"Then what?"

"I'm gonna kill some people tonight."

So I rushed across town and caught him pulling out of the driveway. I got in the car and talked the gun away from him. I didn't know much about guns, so I then took it to my father and he took the bullets out for me.

Josh didn't kill anybody that night, which seems like a miracle in retrospect. But I know—I mean, *know*—I'm gonna get that call one of these days that Josh has slipped over the edge and killed a few people. It's inevitable.

You need more proof of Josh's craziness? One night Josh texted me that his mother had just died. I was on good terms with his parents and knew them fairly well, so I was on the phone within seconds.

"What happened?" I asked.

Josh was giggling.

I didn't understand. "What is it?"

"The bitch is dead," he said.

"Josh!"

"No, I mean it. She's dead. I'm celebrating."

I could never get over how cold it was to hear someone so giddy about the loss of their own mother. That was another pretty big tell-tale sign for me that things had gotten a bit cuckoo in Josh Land.

No, you don't want to make Josh angry.

The thing is, it's real easy to do.

Most of the time you don't even know you've done it.

One time I got a package in the mail from Josh. We hadn't spoken in a few days and I had no idea what it was. When I opened it, I found a dead bird and photographs of me with my eyes x-ed out. Josh had written some sort of voodoo mess on the back of the photos, along with the words, "YOU ARE DEAD."

That was fun times. But that, my friends, was life with Josh.

Another time he got mad at me over some perceived slight and called the cops and told them where I kept my weed stash. It wasn't much—not enough to lead to any long-term legal problems—but it did get me thrown in jail for a night.

I know, I know, you're wondering why I didn't end our friendship years ago. Well, the reason for that is pretty simple—I was scared. I was frightened that Josh might become angry and hurt me and/or members of my family.

So I stayed around, but it wasn't easy.

My mother and I had had serious conversations about the inevitability that Josh might hurt someone some day, and also that he was in desperate need of psychiatric help. But none of that ever came, and Josh just grew crazier and crazier.

So when he called me on that Friday evening, I had no idea what to expect, but with Josh, you always expected something out of the ordinary.

I had just gotten off work and was about to take a nap. But that wasn't to be. No sooner than my head hit the pillow, Josh was on the phone.

"I need you to come over right now." Urgency in his voice.

"What's wrong?"

"I just need you to come now."

"Why?"

"I've got something I need to talk about."

"And it has to be now?"

"It needs to be right now, Andy."

Dammit, I thought. I was really looking forward to that nap.

I said, "Okay, I'll be there in fifteen minutes."

Josh being Josh, he just hung up, saying nothing.

Fifteen minutes later, I was at his house. I knocked at the door. He opened it, looking both ways, obviously paranoid.

"What's the matter?" I asked.

"Just come in."

I entered the house, which smelled of a thousand stale cigarettes, and Josh led me to his bedroom.

"Sit down," he said.

So I did.

"What's wrong?" I asked again.

Josh was on the verge of something; I couldn't tell if it was tears or a nervous breakdown, or maybe both.

"I've got something to tell you."

"Okay, sure."

"This isn't going to be easy."

Josh started wringing his hands, also wringing all the drama out of the situation he possibly could.

"Go ahead," I said.

"You may not like me anymore after I tell you this."

I said, "I'm sure I'll like you, Josh. You're my best friend."

Truth be told, I was horrified he was going to tell me he'd finally snapped and murdered someone.

"I just...," he said.

"What?"

"I don't know how to say it."

"Just say it."

"You're not going to believe me."

I assured him that I would.

"I'm..."

"Yes?"

"I'm..."

I was growing tired of this routine. I was ready for him to say whatever the hell he had to say and get it over with.

Or so I thought.

"I'm a werewolf," he said.

Okay, this was clearly nothing I had imagined I'd be hearing today (or any other day for that matter).

"What?" I asked, trying not to sound judgmental, but probably sounding judgmental.

"Yeah."

"Yeah, what?"

"I'm a werewolf."

I didn't even know what to say to that bullshit.

"You're a werewolf?"

"Yessir, a bonafide werewolf."

"Since when?"

"What do you mean?"

"When did you become a werewolf?"

"I don't know."

"Well, how do you know you're a werewolf?"

"Because I change," Josh said.

"You change?"

"When the moon is full, I change. Into a werewolf."

"Okay..."

"I can tell from your tone you don't believe me."

"Of course I do," I lied.

"You do?"

"Of course. So how did you become a werewolf?"

"I don't know. I guess I got bitten by one."

"You don't remember?"

"No, I have must have been in a trance-like state."

"Huh," I said, trying to decide how to handle all this.

"Are you sure you believe me?"

"Yeah, I believe you."

"I'm just afraid."

"Afraid of what?" I asked.

"Afraid of hurting other people."

"When you're a werewolf."

"Right."

"Like who?" I asked. "Who do you think you might hurt?"

"Well, what if you and I were hanging out and the moon was full?"

"And you turned into a werewolf?"

"Yeah, I'd probably kill you."

"I see."

"I wouldn't want to," he said. "But I wouldn't be able to control it."

"Sure."

"Tonight's a full moon, Andy. I need you to leave before it gets dark."

"Or I could be killed."

"You probably will be."

"Look," I said calmly, trying not to provoke him. "I believe you. At least I believe you believe you're a werewolf."

"But you don't believe I really am one?"

"Well...no, not really."

"Why?"

"Because there's no such things as werewolves."

"Then how do you explain it?"

"Explain what?" I asked.

"Why I wake up naked and bloody with dream-like memories of killing people and animals."

"I don't know."

Actually I did know—he was nuts.

"I'm gonna prove to you you're not a werewolf," I said.

"How?"

"Tonight's a full moon?"

"It is."

"Then I'm gonna stay here with you."

"What?"

"You heard me."

"Then what?"

"One of two things will happen: either you'll transform into a werewolf and kill me, or you won't transform and then we'll go have some beers at the bar and try to figure all this out. Then maybe we'll go and get some dinner."

"This isn't a good idea," he said.

"I'll be fine. I'm a big boy, Josh."

"I'm serious."

"So am I."

And that was that. I stayed.

We sat closed in the bedroom, him on the computer chair, me on the recliner, and we talked to pass the time. It was growing dark outside, and Josh spoke a lot about being a werewolf. He acted genuinely afraid he was going to transform and murder me, and I suppose I appreciated that. Of course I knew he wasn't a werewolf, but something about his sincerity touched me.

"So what happens if I turn into a werewolf and kill you?" he asked.

"Then I guess that'll be that."

"It's probably gonna happen. I hope you know that."

"I'm not all that worried."

"Why is that?"

"Because I don't believe you're a werewolf."

"That's not a very nice thing to say."

"I'm sorry."

"Sorry why? Because you don't believe I'm a werewolf?"

"Yeah," I said. "I guess so."

"It's okay. I'm sure it's difficult to believe."

I just nodded.

"I didn't believe it at first myself," he said.

"How long has this been happening?"

"What do you mean?"

"When was the first time you woke up naked and covered in blood?"

"About six months ago."

"Where did you wake up?"

"In an alley behind a liquor store."

"And you were covered in blood?"

"Yeah, covered in blood."

"How did you get home?"

"I took a cab."

"You took a cab, naked and covered in blood?"

I didn't believe a word of this horseshit, but I could see that Josh genuinely believed what he was saying. But then he was a goddamn loon.

I asked, "When you wake up, is there blood in your mouth?"

"There's blood everywhere."

"So you're sure you're eating some kind of animal?"

"Yeah, definitely."

I thought for a moment before asking, "Where else have you woke up?"

Josh thought for a moment. "Once under a bridge, and another time at the library."

"At the library?" I asked.

"Yeah."

"Okay then, at the library. And you're sure the blood isn't your own?"

"No, it's never my own. They'd have to have a silver bullet to hurt me."

I nodded. "Sure, I can see that."

And the rest of the night went on like this as we waited.

It was about ten o'clock when I started to make the transformation. I looked at Josh, his eyes huge, and he was not transforming. Just me.

"You," he said. "You're a...werewolf!"

I didn't say anything. I just cried out in pain.

The transformation is always very painful.

My legs grew wider, tearing my pants. My torso grew wider, ripping my clothing. My spine now protruded from my back. The hair started to emerge from my pores—that's always the worst, most painful part of the process. Then came the fangs. And the claws.

I looked at Josh while I was still able to see him through my own human eyes.

He was blurry because my eyes were turning.

As I looked at him, Josh pissed himself. He was trembling. He was, as I had figured, not a werewolf at all. He was just a man. A very frightened man.

And for a moment I feared what would inevitably come next, but then I remembered that Josh's death would be for the good of all mankind. This way he couldn't hurt anyone. Besides, I was hungry.

SANTA'S LITTLE HELPER

This was Carl's third house of the night, and he still had two more he wanted to hit before morning. As he'd gotten older, he'd become a much better robber, but the downside was that he'd come to loathe his work with a fiery passion. Maybe it was the two falls he'd already taken for B&E, or maybe it was because he felt like the Last of the Mohicans now that all his old road dogs were behind bars. But mostly Carl believed it was just a part of his getting older. Even as he'd become wiser and had learned to take less chances, he still had to take some. Chances came part and parcel with this line of work. And topping it off, Carl's body was showing signs of fatigue. He became tired much more quickly these days, and the treasures he carried out of the houses were getting getting heavier and heavier.

Carl hadn't wanted to go out robbing tonight, but he had no choice. He'd been dating Porcupine Tina for a couple weeks now, but she refused to put out. She said she'd only screw him if he agreed to take her to this new highfalutin' expensive-ass restaurant in Manhattan. She'd read about it in the *Times*, and had told him it was all the rage. "Movie stars go there," she said. "There was a picture of Nicole Kidman eating there!" She thought going there might somehow give her class, but Carl doubted it, just as he doubted that all the women in the place combined had seen as many dicks as Tina had. When Carl was growing up, his dad had a saying about girls like her—if she had as many dicks sticking out of her as she'd had stuck in her she'd be a porcupine. Hence the name Porcupine Tina.

Carl was in the dark house, shining his flashlight down on a laptop. It was an older model, probably five or six years old. That wasn't old for most things—Carl had underwear that were older by a mile—but it was literally a lifetime for a laptop. "Fuck it," he muttered, sticking the laptop in his bag. He turned around and was shocked to find himself face to face with a little boy.

"Who are you?" asked the boy, squinting into the light. "Are you Santa Claus?"

Seeing his way out, Carl jumped on this. "Yeah, I am," he said. "I'm Santa Claus."

The boy tilted his head. He looked unsure, like he was trying to work out a mathematical equation in his head. "Are you sure?"

"What? You don't think I know who I am?"

"Why are you here?"

Carl paused. "Well, I'm here, you know, doing Santa stuff."

"But Christmas is eighteen days away," said the boy.

"Eighteen days, huh?"

"Yeah, I count 'em off every day. I got a Santa Claus face calendar with cotton balls on his beard over each day. I remove a piece of cotton every morning until Christmas, and right now there are eighteen cotton balls left."

Carl nodded. "That's a good system."

"But my Daddy told me you didn't exist," said the boy.

"He did?"

"He sure did. But I knew he was wrong. *I knew it!*"

"Why do you think he did that?"

The boy scrunched up his face, looking perplexed. "I don't know."

"Well, I know," said Carl.

"You do?"

"He did it because he was naughty."

The boy's eyes got big. *"Daddy's naughty?"*

"He lied about me not being real. You know what that is? Naughty with a capital N."

"Maybe he just didn't know," offered the boy.

"No, he knew. He just did that to be naughty. He was lying to you, trying to hurt your feelings. So that's why I'm here. Normally I only come to houses and leave presents on Christmas. But this is something different. This is a special occasion. Your Daddy's been naughty, so I had to come to teach him a lesson."

"Good," said the boy. "Daddy needs to be good and stop lying. It was shitty that he did that." The little boy looked at him. "Can I say that? 'Shitty,' I mean?"

"Don't worry about it," said Carl. "It'll be our secret."

The boy's eyes dropped to the bag in Carl's hand. Next his eyes moved to the spot where the laptop had been. Then he looked at Carl.

"You lookin' for the laptop?" asked Carl.

"Yeah. Where is it?"

"I gotta take it for a while, to teach Daddy a lesson."

The kid's face brightened. "But the laptop's Mommy's."

"Oh," said Carl. "Well, she let him lie, so she's in trouble, too. I'm gonna take some of their stuff for a few weeks. Then I'll bring it back on Christmas after they've learned their lesson."

"That's a good idea."

"What's your name, kid?"

This confused the boy. *"Don't you know?"*

Carl knew he'd said the wrong thing. "I'm not gonna lie to you, kid, it's hard to keep everybody's names straight. Sometimes I forget."

The boy nodded. "I forget stuff, too. I got an aunt that's got a big mustache like a cowboy. Sometimes I forget her name. My sister Tammy and me call her Chewbacca, so then when I see her I wanna call her Chewbacca, but I know that's not the right name."

"What is her name?" asked Carl.

"I still don't know."

"Fuck it," said Carl. "Call that bitch Chewbacca."

The boy started to laugh and then caught himself. He looked at Carl. "You said a bad word."

"Actually I said two. So, what was your name?"

"Billy," said the boy.

"Oh, now I remember," said Carl. "Well, I gotta get back to work. I've got other houses I gotta go to tonight."

Carl turned to take a second look at the TV he'd passed in the dark living room. It was a decent set, probably middle-of-the-pack in terms of price and quality, but he wasn't sure he could get it out of the house without making a lot of noise.

"If you really wanna teach my Daddy a lesson, you should take his baseball card collection," said Billy.

This caught Carl's attention, and he turned back to Billy, shining the flashlight on him. "Your Daddy collects baseball cards?"

"Oh yeah. It's his favorite thing in the world. He's always bragging about how much they're worth. He says the Hank Aaron card he bought this summer cost about the same as a ski boat."

Carl's eyes got big. "Really?"

"Yeah," said Billy. "And he's got a whole bunch of Mickey Mantle cards, too. Mickey's his favorite player, even though he retired before Daddy was even born."

"He's got a bunch of Mickey Mantle cards?"

"He's probably got about twenty, all expensive and locked in a glass case in the study. Well, most of 'em anyway."

Carl felt his heart drop. "They're locked away?"

"Yeah," said Billy. "But I know where the key is."

"Lead the way, kid."

As they walked through the house, Billy turned and asked, "Do you need another bag? I can get a trash bag. There's a whole bunch of cards. Daddy says there's probably enough to pay my way through college."

Carl said, "Sure, I'll take a trash bag."

Billy went into the kitchen and switched on the light. He grabbed a trash bag from beneath the sink, and then turned and led Carl to the study. There was a big glass case full of cards along the wall. Carl could have broken the glass easy, but it would have made a helluva racket. Billy walked across the room and grabbed the key out of a desk drawer. He unlocked the case, and the two of them cleaned it out, putting all the cards in the trash bag.

When they were done, Billy asked, "Do you think that's enough to teach Daddy a lesson? Or do you need more stuff?"

"I should probably go, kid."

Billy nodded. "Are you sure?"

Carl almost laughed. "I think we're good."

He started towards the door when he heard Billy ask, "What about the safe?" Carl stopped and turned around. "What safe?"

"Daddy's got a safe in the study."

"What's in it?" asked Carl.

"Stacks of money and some papers." He looked at Carl for a moment, still thinking, and then said, "Oh, I forgot! And Daddy's favorite thing."

"What is it?"

"Daddy's got a baseball card he spent $60,000 on. It's a Mickey Mantle rookie card. Daddy says it's mint." Billy stopped for a minute, his face twisting into a confused expression. "If it's mint, does that mean I can eat it?"

"No," said Carl. "It's a different kind of mint." He paused for a beat before saying, "Let's go to the safe. I really need to get going."

Billy led him back to the study. They walked past the empty card case and Billy approached a framed painting of Babe Ruth, pointing towards the outfield. "It's behind there," said Billy.

Carl approached the painting, sitting down his bags. He pulled back the picture, finding that it was on hinges. When he did, he saw the face of a gray safe staring out at him. He looked at Billy. "Do you know the combination?"

"Yeah, it's my birthday."

"When's that?"

Billy studied him. "Don't you know?"

Carl sighed. "I forget stuff. Cut me some slack, kid."

"My birthday is May 4, 2010."

Carl turned back to the safe, twisting the nob to five, then four, and then ten. He turned the handle, and he heard the bolt unlock. He opened the safe and saw two fat stacks of hundreds, which would be more than enough to take Porcupine Tina to that rich la-di-da burger joint. He pulled out the cash and tossed the stacks into the bag. Peering into the safe, he moved a stack of documents and found the Mickey Mantle card lying there inside a hard plastic sleeve. He pulled it out and stared at it for a moment, admiring it. "She's a beaut," he said, sticking it in his back pocket.

He picked up the bags and looked at Billy. "I gotta go, kid. Santa's got shit to do."

Carl walked out of the study and through the dark living room, moving towards the door. When he reached it, he realized Billy was standing behind him. Carl turned and looked at the kid, slightly illuminated by the light from the kitchen. Carl turned back towards the door, pulling it open. He opened the storm door and stepped out into the cold night.

"Goodbye, Santa." And for a moment Carl felt bad about all this. He stopped and turned towards Billy. "I got something for you, kid." He reached into the bag and pulled three hundred dollar bills out, handing them to Billy. "Go get yourself some candy," he said. Billy's eyes were as big as silver dollars. "But whatever you do, don't tell your Mommy and Daddy about this. No matter what happens, this is our secret and the money is yours. Deal?"

Billy looked at him, smiling big, a gleam in his eye. "You bet, Santa!"

Carl turned and walked towards the stolen Chevy pickup parked at the curb.

Billy watched him climb into the truck, hoping he'd look back so they could wave at one another, but he didn't. But Billy didn't care, because he knew he'd definitely be on the nice list now. He'd helped Santa, which was a thing none of the other kids at school had done, and this made him special. Billy smiled, closing the door. He looked down at the bills in his hand.

"Thank you, Santa," he whispered.

And he went to bed, dreaming sweet, innocent dreams about he and his new friend Santa Claus.

EARLY RETIREMENT

Mr. Mapplethorpe had been a high school history teacher for nearly forty years. It was his whole life. He felt blessed. He was one of the only people he knew who got to do exactly what he wanted in life. He loved history, loved everything about it, and he loved teaching impressionable young minds.

It was a Friday afternoon in late May when Mr. Mapplethorpe got called in for a meeting with the new principal, Eddie Deacon. Eddie was a young guy, still learning the ropes. He had been one of Mr. Mapplethorpe's students a few years back, and they had always had a mutual respect for one another. So when Mr. Mapplethorpe got called into Eddie Deacon's office, he figured the young principal needed his advice on some matter.

He knocked at Eddie's door, and the principal, seated at his desk, asked him to come in and close the door behind him. "Have a seat," Eddie said. Mr. Mapplethorpe did, a wide smile on his face.

"You probably know why I've asked you in," Eddie said.

"Not really, no, but I figured it might have something to do with the History Club."

Eddie gave him a pained look.

"The History Club started out a little bit shaky," Mr. Mapplethorpe said, "but it's really doing well now. We have almost twenty members."

Eddie folded his hands on his desk in front of him.

"As you probably know, the district is undergoing severe budget cuts," Eddie said.

Mr. Mapplethorpe nodded. "Is there anything I can do to help?"

Eddie looked at him pitifully. "As a matter of fact there is, Tom."

"Just name it."

"We're going to be making some cuts. And one of those cuts is going to be in the History Department."

"Oh," said Mr. Mapplethorpe, frowning. "You need to get rid of Ben Neal." Eddie said nothing, letting him talk. "He's a good guy, and a heck of a basketball coach. I'm sure he'll land on his feet somewhere. And you know, I think it may be for the best. Ben Neal is a great guy, but I don't think he engages the students. And his grasp of history barely reaches back to the 1960s."

Eddie looked uneasy. "Actually, we're keeping Ben."

"Oh," Mr. Mapplethorpe said, still not sure what was happening.

"We're getting rid of you."

Mr. Mapplethorpe was stunned. "You're getting rid of *me*?"

"I sure hate to do it this way, Tom, but Ben means too much to the school. He is, after all, the coach of the basketball team, and they had a winning season this year. And you know how important basketball is to this community."

"But I've been here for thirty-eight years."

"I'm sorry."

"But..."

And again Eddie said, "I'm sorry, Tom."

"What about the union? Won't they have something to say about this?"

"They've already okayed the decision," Eddie said. "There's nothing to do now but draw up the paperwork."

Mr. Mapplethorpe looked down, tears welling up in his eyes. "But what will I do now? This is...this is all I have."

Eddie smiled. "This doesn't have to be a bad thing, Tom. Think of it as an early retirement. You can go fishing whenever you want. You can go visit your daughter...what was her name? Lily?"

"She's dead."

"What?"

"She died three years ago," Mr. Mapplethorpe said. "A drunk driver swerved into her lane and hit her head-on. Killed her son and her husband, too. And she was pregnant."

Eddie looked uncomfortable, as if he didn't know how to end the conversation. "I'm sorry, Tom."

Mr. Mapplethorpe looked up, tears streaming down his cheeks. "When will all this happen?"

"What?"

"When am I being terminated?"

"You can still come to work for the remainder of the year," Eddie said. "That should give you time to say goodbye to everyone and get your affairs in order. I figured it was best to tell you on a Friday so you could have a few days to regain your, uh, composure."

And that was it. It was that easy for Eddie Deacon and the school board to terminate him after nearly four decades of service.

Mr. Mapplethorpe stood up and stumbled towards the door.

Eddie came around the desk and shook his hand.

"It's all gonna work out for the best," Eddie said.

Mr. Mapplethorpe said something, although he didn't know what it was, and headed for the sanctuary of his classroom.

Mr. Mapplethorpe spent the better part of the weekend fishing. The hope was that it would remind him how much he enjoyed the act, and then he wouldn't have to feel so bad about his impending retirement.

And, to his surprise, it worked. He started to see his retirement as a good thing rather than a bad one. He had given most of his life to teaching. Now it would be his time to live life. He didn't know what he would do, but he saw the possibilities as being endless, stretched out ahead of him as far as the eye could see.

Eddie Deacon was right; things were going to work out for the best. They always did.

Mr. Mapplethorpe had always wanted to take up golf, and his pal Jim Norris had offered to teach him sometime. Well, here was his chance to take Jim up on the offer. And that was just the beginning. There was no end to the things he could do in retirement.

Yes, life was good. This really was for the best.

Monday morning was a normal one for Mr. Mapplethorpe. He had become so accustomed to this idea of retirement that he didn't even think about it. He just went through his normal routine. He fed Oscar, his cat, and he took Arnold, his schnauzer, out for a brief walk. He then went back into the kitchen and packed his lunchbox. He prepared two bologna and cheese sandwiches, removing the crust from each. He then bagged them up and placed them neatly into his lunchbox. He then bagged up a handful of cheesy crackers and put them inside the lunchbox. He filled a thermos with black coffee and put it in next to his sandwiches. He then packed his Colt .45 handgun, shut the lunchbox, and went to work

When he got to the school, he found that his favorite parking spot was open, which was a rarity. When he got out of the car, he was approached by Mr. Scott, the Civics teacher. As they walked towards the school, they talked about the weather and a student they both had who'd made their school year a living hell.

"You're in a chipper mood today," remarked Mr. Scott.

Mr. Mapplethorpe smiled. "I'm not sure why, but I am in a great mood today."

Mr. Scott held the door open for Mr. Mapplethorpe, who thanked him.

He then produced the handgun and shot the Civics teacher in the face.

Monday or no, today was going to be a glorious day. Mr. Mapplethorpe could feel it in his bones.

It was an ordinary day at school, just like the ones he'd experienced for almost four decades now, and Mr. Mapplethorpe found comfort in that familiarity. On his way to his classroom, he stopped by the restroom. Old age was apparently getting to him, and his bladder wasn't what it used to be. It seemed like he was always pissing these days. As he urinated, he could hear the slapping sounds of a student masturbating in one of the stalls. Mr. Mapplethorpe smiled.

Boys will be boys, he thought.

He walked over to the sink and washed his hands. He then took a paper towel out of the dispenser and dried them off. He turned, fired his .45 through the door of the stall, and walked out of the bathroom.

He looked at his watch. It was still a little bit early.

He went to his classroom and put his briefcase and lunchbox in the closet. Having a few minutes to kill, he decided to sharpen some pencils. As he was feeding a pencil into the electric sharpener, he heard a knock at the door behind him. He turned and saw Mrs. Beauregard, the Home Ec teacher, standing there, a great big smile on her face. He liked Mrs. Beauregard, particularly her shapely legs, and he smiled back at her.

"What can I do for you?" he asked.

Her smiled widened. "I was wondering if I could borrow your TV for a bit."

"No problem," Mr. Mapplethorpe said. "Your class watching a movie?"

"We're going to be watching an excellent documentary on parenting in China."

Mr. Mapplethorpe smiled. "That sounds fun."

"I thought so."

"Why don't I get that for you?"

"You're such a gentleman," she said.

He smiled and went to the cart holding the television and DVD player. He unplugged its cord from the wall, wrapped it up in the cart, and turned towards her, pushing the cart to her room. They walked slowly down the hallway to the Home Ec room. It was only two doors down, so it didn't take long to get there. Once he had the cart in her classroom, he turned to her, reaching into his pocket.

"Thank you very much," she said happily.

"Always a pleasure," he answered, shooting her in the throat. She flopped back against her desk, flailing like a shot animal, but Mr. Mapplethorpe didn't notice. He put the gun back into his pocket and left her there to die.

He walked down the hallway, heading back to his classroom. There was a student leaning over the water fountain. Mr. Mapplethorpe couldn't remember his name, but he knew he'd taught him. The kid was looking down the hall towards Mrs. Beauregard's room.

"Did you hear something?" he asked.

"No, I don't think so," Mr. Mapplethorpe said, shooting him in the back.

Mr. Mapplethorpe continued to make his way back to his classroom, but decided to stop by the teacher's lounge to get a Coke from the pop machine. The English teacher, Mr. Grassman, was in there, standing over the table, reading an article in *The New York Times*.

"How are you today, Mr. Mapplethorpe?"

"Just fine. And you?"

"I'm fine," he said, giving him a sad look. "I heard about the school letting you go."

Mr. Mapplethorpe put his change in the pop machine. "You did, did you?"

"Yeah, I think it's bullshit. Pure bullshit. A man teaches as long as you have, he deserves to leave on his own accord."

Mr. Mapplethorpe leaned down to retrieve the Coke can from the machine's mouth, and came up with the .45. He fired once, shooting Mr. Grassman through his newspaper at point blank range. Mr. Mapplethorpe popped open the can of pop, raised it to his mouth, and took a drink, finding it refreshing.

When he walked back into the corridor, sunlight was peering in through the windows at the end of the hall. With the weather being so beautiful, how could Mr. Mapplethorpe not be happy? This was going to be a wonderful day. He could feel it.

He took another swig of Coke, lowered the can to his left side, the .45 held at his right side, and walked back to his classroom.

Yes, he thought. Early retirement would suit him just fine.

SNOW WHITE AND THE SEVEN BASTARDS

As they sat drinking in Joe's Tavern, Prince Charming couldn't stop thinking about Snow White's past. It had been weighing on him lately. Sure, she was beautiful, but she was also white trash. She was beneath him. They were from different stations in life, and their differences were becoming ever more apparent. Despite her claims that she'd never slept around, Prince Charming was having a difficult time taking her at her word. She had drank her fair share of tequila tonight, and the inebriated men in the bar were talking to her like they'd been intimate. The worst offender was a sloshed cowboy in a camouflaged cap who kept making remarks about her tits.

Being the gentleman he was, Prince Charming defended her honor, but it became more and more difficult to do so as horny slobs continued swarming out of the woodwork to make lascivious remarks. *She was his wife, goddammit!* Why didn't these men respect that? Even if they had screwed her, why would they be so cruel as to rub it in his face? And Snow White herself was no help, as she was drunk and flirting back.

Prince Charming took a swig of his Jager and excused himself to the restroom. Inside, the urinals were nasty and overflowing, so he was forced to piss in a stall. As he stood there relieving himself, he glanced down and saw a sentence scrawled on the wall. It read: "Call Snow White for a good time." But the word "time" had been scratched out and replaced with the word "fuck." Her cell phone number was written beneath. It was an outdated number, but it was one he knew.

"Goddammit," he muttered. The scrawling was down low to the ground, just at the height of a dwarf. Prince Charming's mind began to race. She'd insisted that she'd never slept with any of the loathsome little sons of bitches, but the graffiti told a different tale. Prince Charming could feel his face turning flush with embarrassment. He stalked back to his table to find another redneck leaning over his wife.

When Prince Charming reached them, the man staggered away without acknowledging him.

"Another friend?" asked Prince Charming.

"Just a guy I used to know," said Snow White, taking a drag from her cigarette. This was another sore spot with Prince Charming—he didn't smoke and he absolutely loathed the stench of her Pall Malls.

"It seems like you know a lot of guys here."

She looked at him. Despite her being drunk, she understood the insinuation. "Is there somethin' you wanna say? If there is, don't fuck around. Just say it."

So he did. "Are you sure you told me the truth when you said you'd only been with five guys before me?"

Snow White was visibly pissed. "I've never lied to you."

"I don't know about that," he said.

Anger flashed in her eyes, and she stubbed out her cigarette. "Why is that?"

"You're awfully chummy with quite a few guys here."

"And?" she asked.

"Well, let me ask you this: just how was it that you convinced the Woodsman to release you into the woods instead of killing you?"

"What does that mean?"

He stared at her, unrelenting. "Did you fuck him?"

"No, he was atrocious."

At this Prince Charming turned and looked at the other men at the bar. "And these guys aren't?"

"Everyone's got a past, Charming," she said. "Even you."

Prince Charming took another drink. "You're full of shit."

"What are you saying?"

"I'm saying that you're a liar."

This infuriated her. "How can you say that to me? Where do you get your balls?"

He looked at her. "Those dwarves you lived with—are you sure you didn't fuck them?"

She threw her hands up, implying there was no talking to him. "Are we really having this conversation again?"

"Have we ever had it?"

She glared at him, fire in her eyes. "And what does *that* mean?"

"It means we never really had the conversation, because you put an end to it. God forbid you should have to talk about something you don't wanna talk about." Prince Charming took a drink. "You're a spoiled bitch."

Snow White lit another Pall Mall with shaking hands. "Where is this coming from? Why tonight?"

"You're so chummy with all the guys here. Are you really gonna tell me you never screwed any of them?"

She looked at him, saying nothing.

"That's what I thought," he said.

"What do you want from me?" she asked, fidgeting nervously.

"I want you to be straight. I think you screwed those dwarves."

"You would think that," she said, taking another drag.

"There's a message written in the bathroom. Care to guess who it's about?"

She looked up. "What kind of message?"

"It says to call you for a good fuck. And it has your number on it! And it was written about two feet from the ground—right at dwarf-level."

She blew out smoke. "So what?"

"I want a divorce," he said, pulling the ring off his finger. He dropped it into his drink. He started to stand, and she reached out to stop him. "Please don't," she begged. "My lawyer will be in touch, Snow White."

He turned and walked out, leaving her sitting there with her tequila and a half-smoked Pall Mall. George Strait was singing on the jukebox, and even though he was her favorite, Snow White didn't notice. She raised her cigarette, tears welling up in her eyes.

Prince Charming was the only thing she'd ever really wanted.

He was the only man she'd ever loved.

She sat there crying, her tears serving as man-repellent, and no one came to her aid. There were no more comments about her tits or anything else.

She reached into her purse and caressed the chrome pistol with her fingers, making sure the gun was there.

Someone was going to pay.

She stood up, George Strait sounding muted in her ears, her balance just a little off. She drank the last of her tequila and turned for the door. She had tears streaming down her face like tiny snakes slithering their way towards her neck.

She walked out, surprised to find her Camaro still parked outside. Prince Charming must have walked home. She thought this as if home was where he was headed. And for the briefest of moments, Snow White considered shooting him in his preppy fucking smug face. But she knew what she had to do, and she knew who had to pay.

She unlocked the car door, climbing inside. She turned the key, Lorrie Morgan coming to life from the speakers. She peeled out of the gravel parking lot, kicking up a cloud of dust behind. Her hands still trembling, she lit another cigarette. She stomped the gas, and the car lurched forward, speeding towards vengeance.

Minutes later she was there, parked in front of the dwarves' trailer. She turned off the ignition and stared at the house, contemplating what she had to do. She reached into her bag and grabbed the .45, pulling it out. She climbed out of the Camaro and marched up the driveway towards the trailer. She made her way up the stairs, flicking her half-spent cigarette into the yard. She raised her right hand, the one clutching the gun, and banged on the door. She could hear Megadeath blaring inside.

No one came, so she knocked again, harder this time.

Finally the wooden door opened and Doc peered out through the tattered screen.

"*Let me in, goddammit,*" she screamed.

Doc opened the door and let her in, her pistol raised.

Doc raised his arms to show he didn't want trouble. She swiveled the pistol to her left, seeing Dopey snorting a line of crank from an aluminum TV tray.

"What's the problem?" Doc asked.

She turned the pistol back towards Doc and squeezed the trigger, shooting him in the face. Dopey looked up, startled. He started to run towards the back of the trailer, but Snow White caught him with a shot to the back of his head. The bedroom door on Snow White's right opened and Grumpy peered out. *"What the fuck is going on?"*

Snow White shot through the particle-board door, catching Grumpy center mass, and he fell from sight. She turned and kicked the door open, seeing Sneezy there naked and crouching on all fours, waiting for Grumpy's return. She shot Sneezy, painting the blinds behind him with blood and brains.

Snow White turned back towards the living room, where she saw Bashful standing there with a naked dwarf woman clutched in front of him, his Glock aimed at her temple. "Shoot and she dies," Bashful said.

"Who wrote my number in the bathroom stall?" Snow White asked, trembling with anger.

"It was Doc," Bashful said. "I told him not to write that shit, but you know how that motherfucker is..."

Snow White squeezed the trigger, firing off a round through the female dwarf's chest and hitting Bashful behind her. They both fell dead in a heap of flesh and bones. Snow White moved past them in search of the two remaining dwarves. She peered down the hall, and Sleepy peeked out through the doorway at the far end. Snow White fired two rounds, splintering the wall and catching him in the throat. She made her way down the hall, past the row of stockpiled Pepsi two liters. She stumbled, momentarily losing her footing, and she fell towards the floor.

She heard the gun cock behind her. She turned and saw Happy standing there, his nine-millimeter Glock trained on her. She went for her gun, which she'd dropped in the fall, and Happy fired a round through her left shoulder.

"*Unnnngggggg!*" she cried.

"Turn around and look at me," said Happy.

She turned to her right, twisting a bit, and looked him in his eyes. He had his pistol trained on her, but Snow White came up with the .45 and shot a bullet through his forehead. The diminutive gunman toppled back into the kitchen.

Snow White raised herself from the ground, her shoulder hurting like hell. She could hear the police sirens in the distance, getting closer by the second. She raised the .45 to her temple and squeezed the trigger.

And Snow White was no more.

IT'LL MAKE YOU FEEL BETTER

Paul Novitz had been mourning his twin brother Reggie's suicide for the past six months. Paul had always had a difficult time handling death, but he was finding this one particularly hard to deal with. In the months since Reggie had taken an entire bottle of his antidepressants with a bottle of whiskey, Paul had been wracked with guilt. Reggie had committed suicide because his wife Brenda had left him. That had been instantly apparent to everyone who knew Reggie, and it was something he'd confirmed in his suicide note. Reggie had always loved Brenda, no matter what she did or how she treated him. So she'd left him, and he'd killed himself. But the thing was, it had largely been Paul's fault.

Beginning in early fall the year before, Paul and Brenda had begun having an affair behind Reggie's back. Brenda would frequently comment about how easy Paul was to talk to, comparing him to Reggie, whom she said didn't know how to communicate with her. Paul didn't believe he was really all that easy to talk to, knowing he had simply been playing a role, saying and doing the things needed to get into his sister-in-law's pants. And it had worked splendidly.

So Brenda would open up about Reggie's inadequacies in the bedroom, as well as his inability to meet her emotional needs. And as she spoke about these things ad nauseum, Paul found himself doing the unthinkable—falling in love with his brother's wife. While Paul knew he was developing these unwanted feelings towards Brenda, he was completely oblivious to the fact that the advice he was giving her was subconsciously intended to sabotage she and Reggie's marriage.

Paul should have known better. He knew that Brenda was Reggie's entire world. She meant everything to him, but Paul hadn't cared. He'd just known that she was beautiful and intelligent, and he came to see her as a conquest both sexually and maritally. Sure, everyone in the family would disown them if they were together, but who cared? Paul was in love, or at the very least deeply in lust. Brenda had many fine attributes that Paul admired, not the least of them being her small shapely ass. So Paul did what he felt any man would have done, and he ultimately convinced his sister-in-law to leave his brother, hoping that she would then want to be with him.

But that was where trouble came into paradise. Brenda did not want to be with him. After she left Reggie, Paul made a play for her but was quickly shot down. "I don't think of you that way," she said. "What the hell, Paul? You're my brother-in-law, for God's sake!" But that fact hadn't stopped her from letting him put his dick inside every orifice of her body. It hadn't stopped her from going down on him during a matinee screening of *Toy Story*. And it hadn't stopped her from being talked into a three-way with Paul and his secretary, Desiree. But in the end, none of that mattered. Paul being her brother-in-law may not have stopped her from doing the horizontal mambo with him, but it definitely shut down any chance he might have had at being her significant other. Only weeks after leaving Reggie, Brenda had started dating a Pakistani surgeon from Cleveland.

Paul had never wanted his brother to die. It's true that they had talked very little as adults, but it wasn't because Paul hated him per se. It was more that they had nothing in common and were virtual strangers. It also had a bit to do with the fact that their parents had openly favored Reggie, showering praise on him for every little thing he'd ever done. That had left a bad taste in Paul's mouth. This may also have been the reason he'd slept with his brother's wife and then tried to steal her away, but he was no expert on these things. Who could say for sure?

He'd brought up his guilty feelings to his shrink, Dr. Berdinski. Of course he'd only told him half the story—that he may have given his sister-in-law advice that may or may not have influenced her decision to leave Reggie—conveniently leaving out all the times he'd had sex with her. He also made the decision not to mention his attempt to steal Brenda for himself. So based on the limited amount of information Dr. Berdinksi had, he'd advised Paul to sit down and write a journal entry about his feelings. "It will be cathartic," he'd said. "You can even write a letter to your brother telling him what you did. That will help you get it off your chest. It'll make you feel better." Paul thought about the shrink's advice, but had never considered actually doing it.

One day Paul was at the car dealership where he worked, fucking around on the computer. It was raining out and had been a slow day, so he'd spent almost an hour perusing Internet porn. Once he was finished with that, Paul checked his e-mail inbox. There were a couple of messages from the auto company, but nothing very interesting. As Paul was maneuvering through them, he accidentally came across an old e-mail from his brother Reggie. It had been from last November, when Paul had been banging his brother's wife on a daily basis, and Reggie had e-mailed him to ask what dish he was bringing to their parents' house for Thanksgiving dinner.

Paul sat there staring at the e-mail for a few minutes, feeling extremely guilty. He had the same urge to e-mail his dead brother that he'd had when other people he'd known had died. It was a silly knee-jerk thing, and Paul obviously knew his brother could no longer send or receive e-mails. But what if he sat and composed an e-mail to Reggie, confessing what he'd done? Obviously Reggie would never see it, but it might be cathartic, as Dr. Berdinski had suggested. Maybe it would make him feel better.

What the hell? Paul thought. *What could it hurt?*

So he clicked "reply" and began to write his dead twin brother a letter. In it, he apologized for Reggie's death and informed his brother that he thought about him each and every day. He also came clean and told him, in detail—because why not?—about his many sexual adventures with Brenda. He told him about the time he had anal sex with her in the parking lot of the Super Saver, as he'd simultaneously eaten a can of Sour Cream and Onion Pringles. He even told him about the time he'd had sex with her in her and Reggie's marital bed, wiping his love juice on his brother's pillow. But most importantly Paul told his brother about how he'd convinced Brenda that she deserved better than what she'd been getting from her husband. He told Reggie how he'd painted a beautiful picture of the way her life could be without Reggie in it, and he told him how he'd hoped she'd end up being his wife. "At the end of the day, I don't know if I really wanted her," wrote Paul, "or if I just wanted to take her away from you simply because I thought I could. I probably would have dumped her, just because I could." When Paul finished composing the e-mail, he felt as though a tremendous burden had been lifted off his back. He stared at the screen for a long hard minute before finally hitting the "send" button, sending the e-mail off into the ether.

Or so he thought. But then later that evening, he checked his e-mail and discovered something he had not expected—a response! There, in his inbox, was a message sent from Reggie Novitz! Of course he knew it couldn't really be Reggie. After all, Reggie was stone cold dead. So what was this?

Paul clicked on the e-mail, opening it. He read its contents. It was a letter, supposedly from Reggie. It read:

You have no idea how much it saddens me to read about what you've done to me. You destroyed my life, dear brother. Literally. Brenda meant the world to me. I would have done anything for her. And you took that away from me. And why? Was it all merely sport for you? I guess I shouldn't be surprised. You were always a mean little bastard. Always, even as a child. That's why Mom and Dad never liked you. You've spent your entire grown life moping around and complaining about that, but you've never taken the time to analyze your own actions to see if you might have played a role in that.

You were right, Paul. You were always right. Mom and Dad didn't love you. None of us did, really. We were all afraid of you, what you might be capable of. We kept you at a safe distance, and it now appears we were right to have done so. Look at what you've done, brother. You killed me. No, you didn't shoot me with a gun or pop all those pills in my mouth, but you did the next closest thing. And you slept with my wife—just to hurt me. I stayed away from you, kept you at a distance so you wouldn't hurt me, and apparently that drove you to try even harder to hurt me. It drove you to kill me.

I'm not sure what you want me to say here, Paul. That I forgive you? Is that what you're looking for? Because I don't. I can't. I never will. The truth is that I hate you, brother. I hated you before you even pulled this shit, but now I hate you with a passion and intensity unlike anything I ever experienced as a living, breathing person. I absolutely hate you, Paul.

You will pay for what you've done, brother. Oh, yes, you will most certainly pay.

Your (dead) brother, Reggie.

Paul read the missive, and then read it again, not sure what to make of it. There was no way it could possibly be his brother. After all, Reggie was dead. Paul had been at the funeral and had seen his lifeless body lying there. He had seen his brother being lowered into the ground. Sure, he hadn't stuck around to watch the gravediggers toss dirt on top of him, but he knew Reggie was gone. Yet he couldn't escape the knowing feeling that this message was actually Reggie. Somehow, some way, deep down, he was sure this was him.

Paul sat there at his computer, considering this for a moment. Being the compulsive person he was, he immediately went about typing a response. He didn't even know what he was going to type, he just typed, the words coming to him as he did.

How can this possibly be you, Reggie? If it's really you, prove it to me. Tell me something only you and I would know.

After Paul had typed those three sentences, he hit "send," and the e-mail went out. He sat there for an hour or so, just watching his inbox. If it was really Reggie, he figured his brother wouldn't have much else to do in hell but check his e-mail. Paul caught himself, realizing the improbability of such a thing. Improbable? It was less than that. It was downright impossible! Paul finally gave up waiting for his brother to write back. Just as he was about to log off, he received a notice informing him that he had an e-mail. He went to check it and saw that its sender was Reggie Novitz. He knew it was impossible, but that didn't change what he was seeing.

He hesitated for a moment, scared to open the thing. At that moment he absolutely knew it was his dead twin brother. He couldn't have said how if he'd been pressed on the subject, but he knew. He clicked the file, opening the e-mail.

Remember that time when we were kids and I caught you looking out the window, jerking off to our little sister swimming in the backyard?

This was the entirety of the message. Paul's first reaction was to be angry. He had tried to explain to Reggie that he hadn't been jerking off to Janice and that he'd actually been looking at her friend Candace in her little red swimsuit. Sure, Candace was still young at the time, and sure, it was still creepy, but at least it wasn't little sister-level creepy.

But then Paul's anger started to fall away as he realized the implications of the message. Unless Reggie had told someone about the incident, there was no one else who could have known about it. But Paul decided this wasn't conclusive evidence because, again, Reggie could have told someone else. Paul highly doubted it, but he needed to cling to that possibility. He needed to hold onto that belief if only to save his own sanity. So Paul sat down and started composing a response.

> *I'm still not convinced you're really Reggie. Tell me something else that only you and I would know.*

Again Paul hit "send," firing the e-mail out into the stratosphere. There was no long wait this time. The response came back in less than two minutes. It read:

> *Remember that time when we were little and you tried to get me to touch my penis against yours? You said you wanted to touch my balls, but I didn't let you. You do remember that, don't you, dear brother?*

Paul felt the blood rush to his face. His first reaction was one of embarrassment, even if it was only he and Reggie who knew about it. His second reaction was fear when he realized that this was indeed correspondence from his dead brother. He sat for a moment, pondering all this, before typing another message.

> *It is you, Reggie. I didn't know. I'm sorry for all this. Where are you right now? How is this possible?*

Paul left the message short and to the point, figuring it pretty much covered everything that needed to be covered at the moment. About a minute passed and then a new e-mail arrived in his inbox. To Paul's disappointment, it was junk mail. But then immediately after its arrival, a second e-mail popped up in his inbox. This one was from Reggie. He clicked on it.

I'm in hell, dear brother, where you will be soon enough.

Paul felt a chill run down his spine. He didn't believe in hell. But that meant nothing. After all, he didn't believe in spirits or demons or the undead or whatever, somehow able to send and receive e-mails. But his not believing it did little to stop it from occurring. Whether Paul liked it or not, he could not deny this.

But what did Reggie mean when he said Paul would be in hell soon? Was he talking about after he died? Was it a threat? What was this all about?

So Paul began to type again.

Reggie, what did you mean when you said I would be in hell soon enough?

Paul once again hit "send" and waited for a response. There was nothing for a half hour or so, making Paul wonder what the hell Reggie would be doing in hell that would preoccupy him so that it would take him so long to respond. Was he watching old episodes of *Barney Miller* down there? Probably *Married with Children*, Paul thought. That would be his idea of hell. Or maybe a soap opera or one of those reality shows about baking cakes.

Finally Paul received the notification that he had a new e-mail. It was Reggie, and Paul clicked on it, opening it.

What I meant is, you're gonna pay, dear brother. You're gonna pay big time. You and me are gonna trade places. You're gonna come to hell and spend an eternity here, and I'm going to come and live in your house and live your life, selling cars and whatnot. And no one will know because we look alike. I'll just act like an asshole and no one will know the difference. They'll just think, typical Paul, acting like an asshole again.

Count your days and enjoy them while they last, dear brother, because those days are about to end. Then you'll be here, in hell, burning for all of eternity. And there will be no one to hear your cries of anguish.

So fuck you, Paul. Really, fuck you, in the face.

Be waiting for me, because I'll see you soon.

It was a threat, but it was one he didn't believe Reggie could back up. Even if Reggie still existed in hell or whatever, he had no way of coming back and taking Paul's place. How would that even work? It was ridiculous. Paul decided he would just ignore the e-mails and stop further correspondence with Reggie. If he kept sending him messages, then Paul would just close out his account and start a new one.

But no more messages came. Not one.

Months passed, and eventually Paul went on with his life, completely forgetting about the e-mails. Sure, he would think about them every now and then, but it all felt distant now, as though it was something he had seen on a television program.

One night, six months later, there was a knock at Paul's apartment door. Paul stood up from the table where he'd been eating a meatloaf TV dinner and went to answer it. When he opened the door, he was shocked to see his brother Reggie standing there, very much alive. He looked exactly as he had before he'd died. He wasn't rotted or discolored in any way. He was just Reggie.

"Reggie," Paul managed.

His brother grinned. "Aren't you gonna let me in?"

Now the fear began to set in, and Paul began to worry about what was happening here.

"Sure," Paul said. "Come on in."

He ushered Reggie in, closing the door behind him. Reggie turned around, now face to face with him, a sick smile on his face. Reggie reached out, grabbing Paul, his hands gripping the sides of Paul's head. Before Paul could say a word, Reggie twisted his head hard, making a gruesome crunching sound, and let his dead body drop to the floor.

Several days passed with Reggie living Paul's life with only the slightest modicum of difficulty. Knowing nothing about selling used cars or that Paul had had an affair with his secretary, Reggie had stumbled a little at work, but in the end all of it had worked out. It was a Tuesday morning at the dealership, and Reggie (as Paul) was looking at his computer. He found that he had received a new e-mail. Reggie looked at it and saw that it was from Paul, now in hell himself. The subject line just said "Please, Reggie." Reggie smiled, and marked the message as spam. This way he would never have to hear from his brother Paul again.

As he closed the window on his computer, his secretary Desiree sat down in the seat in front of him. He looked up at her.

"What's up, Desiree?"

The pretty young girl grinned, sexy as always. "Something's different about you these days. I can't quite put my finger on it."

"Oh yeah?"

"Yeah," she said. "You're better looking somehow. You smell better. You just seem better in every way. It's so weird. Even your dick seems bigger now. I know that's not possible, but it seems like that." She smiled awkwardly. "Am I crazy, Paul?"

"I'm afraid so," he said, taking a sip from his coffee mug.

"You're easier to get along with these days, too," she said. "Don't take this the wrong way, but there were a lot of days I just wanted to say, 'Go to hell, Paul.'"

Reggie grinned. "Trust me, darling, I know the feeling."

WYATT EARP AND THE DEVIL INCARNATE

If this ain't the way it was, it's the way it should have been.
—John Milius, *The Life and Times of Judge Roy Bean*

One: A Night at the Oriental

It was a Saturday night like any other at the Oriental. The saloon was packed, overflowing with drifters, gunmen, gamblers, and the dregs of society. Red played a ditty on the old piano, barely audible over the din of drunken patrons. The smells of cigar smoke, sex, and body odor filled the place, giving it the same generic odor found in any saloon on a busy night.

Deputy Marshal Wyatt Earp was, as was usual on such a night, holding court over the faro table. His older brother, Virgil, the town marshal, was sitting to his right, downing his fair share of free whiskey and smoking Wyatt's cigars. To Wyatt's left sat notorious sporting man and cold-blooded killer Doc Holliday—Wyatt's only friend—smoking a cigar, downing glass after glass of high-end scotch, and making lewd remarks to anyone who might indulge him with a listen.

"It's a hell of a night tonight, Wyatt," said Doc.

"I don't like it."

Doc grinned. "You don't like anything."

"I got a bad feeling." Wyatt, being a lifelong lawman, was prone to such gut feelings, and they were seldom wrong. He almost always knew when trouble was about to jump off, seeming to somehow smell the tomfoolery in the air. And now his gut was telling him things could get ugly any minute.

He scanned the room, looking for potential problems. Doc was used to Wyatt's keen ability to sense such things, so he paid him no mind. Inebriated, he just kept on blabbing about the superiority of a Georgia gentleman over just about any other man created by god.

Watching a group of cowboys over Doc's shoulder, Wyatt engaged his friend. "If you love Georgia so much, why don't you go back there?"

Doc chuckled. "You know I can't go back there, Wyatt. I love the beautiful state of Georgia, but it turns out she does not share the same love for me."

"Problems seem to follow you everywhere you go," said Virgil.

Doc raised his glass. "That does seem to be the unfortunate truth."

Wyatt continued his inspection of the room, but saw nothing out of the ordinary.

This time—once in a million—he didn't spot the trouble because it was directly behind him. But Doc saw it clearly. A little whiny troglodyte of a brute named Ike Clanton was putting his arms around Doc's traveling mate and companion, Kate Elder, and she wasn't enjoying it one bit. Ike's hand slid up to grab a handful of Kate's sizeable bosom. She slapped him away, but still Ike persisted.

Doc stood, staring at Ike. He poured himself another drink, downed it, and said, "If you'll excuse me fellas, I have pressing business to attend to." And Doc started walking towards Ike.

Virgil now saw what Doc had seen. "Aw, hell," he said.

Wyatt spun around in his chair to get a look, now seeing Ike putting his hands on Kate.

Doc approached Ike, but the damned fool didn't see him coming as he was too busy fondling Kate. When Ike saw Kate looking at Doc, he turned around and found himself face to face with Doc's nickel-plated .41 caliber Colt Thunderer.

Ike's eyes got big.

"I don't believe we've had the pleasure of introduction," said Doc. "My name is John Holliday."

Ike said nothing.

"And this woman you've been putting your grubby little paws all over is named Kate."

"I didn't mean nothin'," Ike said. "I was just foolin' around, having a good time."

Doc looked at Kate. "Then why doesn't *she* appear to be having a good time?"

"I didn't do nothin' wrong."

"Where I'm from, a man doesn't grab a lady's breast without her consent," said Doc.

"But she ain't no lady. She's a whore."

Doc cocked the pistol. "That may well be the case, but she's *my* whore."

Now members of Ike Clanton's gang were moving in to surround them. One of the men, a smart-assed cattle rustler named Curly Bill Brocius, drew his Colt .45 and put it to Doc's head. Only seconds later, Wyatt held his own Schofield Smith and Wesson to Curly Bill's head.

Doc grinned his big trademark shit-eating grin. "Well, I do believe we have us a party now. *Woo-wee!*"

Curly Bill growled, "Shut up."

Doc looked over at Wyatt. "How nice of you to join us, Wyatt."

Now Virgil jumped into the fray, waving his revolver around, telling everyone to put away their weapons. "Stop all this *now!*" he demanded, but no one moved so much as an inch.

"If you don't put down your pistol, sir, I will be obliged to shoot a big hole through your little friend," said Doc, his condescending tone an invitation to test him.

"And if you shoot him, then I shoot you," said Curly Bill.

"I guess this is the part where I'm supposed to say then I'll shoot you," said Wyatt.

"Goddammit, Wyatt!" said Virgil, losing his patience.

Curly Bill smiled, looking at Doc. "I believe it's your turn now."

"Aren't you a clever devil?" said Doc.

Tired of the bullshit, Wyatt smashed Curly Bill over the head with his revolver, knocking him to the floor unconscious.

Ike's eyes got big again. "You can't do that!"

"I believe he already did," said Doc.

Wyatt holstered his pistol. "Why don't you and your boys clear on out of here before there's *real* trouble…the kind you won't walk away from."

"What kind of talk is that for a lawman?" asked Ike. "That ain't right!"

"Let the man go," said Virgil.

As usual, no one listened to Virgil. Doc kept his gun pressed against Ike's temple.

"Come on," said Wyatt. "Put away the gun."

Doc holstered his weapon. "If you aren't the very voice of reason, Wyatt Earp."

"You boys ain't gonna get away with this," said Ike. "We'll be back."

Wyatt said, "Can't you see I'm trying to let you leave here alive? Are you really so stupid you can't see when it's the proper time to shut your damn fool mouth?"

Ike backed away, threatening, "You ain't heard the last of us, lawman."

But Doc just waved him away nonchalantly. "You may leave now, sir. I believe our business here has reached its conclusion."

Ike elbowed one of his men, motioning for him to leave with him.

Virgil pointed at Curly Bill. "And take this no good son of a bitch with you."

Virgil was pissed. Wyatt was a natural-born lawman, and Virgil was, to his chagrin, somewhat lacking as a peacemaker. Virgil didn't get the respect he felt he deserved, and what little respect he did receive came from his being the brother of the famed Wyatt Earp, legendary lawman out of Kansas. Both Virgil and Wyatt knew the score. They both knew Virgil wasn't cut out to be the marshal, but neither of them had ever said a word about this before.

"How the hell am I supposed to maintain order here with you and Doc gallivanting around here as you please, acting like a couple of damned outlaws?" asked Virgil.

Doc said, "Hold your tongue, Virgil. I am still a proud card-carrying member of the outlaw club, and I have absolutely no desire to be a lawman of any kind."

"Well," said Virgil, "you've got an excuse. But you, Wyatt, you should know better."

"And what?" asked Wyatt. "Let them get the drop on Doc? Let them run wild and shoot up the place? Let them rape Kate?"

"I appreciate the sentiment, Wyatt, but I could have taken them both," said Doc.

"Not when you're drunk you couldn't have," said Wyatt.

Doc smiled. "My being drunk is the only reason I claimed possibility to shooting only the two of them and not their whole damned inbred band of misfits and miscreants."

Wyatt and Virgil ignored this, and Virgil went on saying his piece. "We're the law here, Wyatt. We—"

"There ain't no law here!" said Wyatt. "This isn't Wichita, where you can just play happy lawman and finesse your way out. This is

Tombstone. It's a whole different game here. You have to stand up to them. You have to think on their level. You have to act on their level. If you don't, then they've already won the damn battle. So if you want to act like you're their friend, then you go ahead and do it and I'll just keep coming along behind you and cleaning up the mess."

Virgil was visibly hurt. "That's not fair."

"Fair?" asked Wyatt. "Fair's got nothing to do with it. If you're looking for a fair fight, you need to go somewhere else, Virg."

Virgil started to stutter, but Wyatt cut him off.

"When Curly Bill and Clanton threw down, you just stood there like a stump," said Wyatt. "You don't have the instinct, and they can sense that. Do you think they can't? Hell, a blind man could see it a mile away."

Doc was the first to sit down. "Let's all have a drink or two and relax a little bit before feelings get injured and whatnot."

Wyatt and Virgil weren't ready to end their conversation, but Doc, who suffered from tuberculosis, started hacking up blood. Both of them saw this and decided to table the conversation for the time being. They looked at each other, exchanging a glance which said there would be a momentary truce. They sat down on both sides of Doc.

Kate approached the table. "You ready for bed yet?"

"Ooh," purred Doc. "I do think I might get lucky tonight."

"Maybe," she said. "But only if you don't stay here too long."

"Honey, you read my mind," said Doc. "I do think I'll stay and have a couple more drinks with the boys here. Then I'll be home shortly thereafter."

Kate rolled her eyes, but accepted it. "I'll keep the bed warm for you."

"That's not the only thing I want you to keep warm for me, Kate, my dear lady," said Doc.

Kate left and Doc returned his attention to the Earp brothers.

"I propose a toast," said Doc, raising his glass.

Virgil looked at him like he was crazy. "To what?"

"To new friends," said Doc. "Let us toast our new pals, Ike and Curly Bill."

Wyatt looked at Virgil, half-smiling. "Haven't you learned yet? Doc doesn't need a reason to drink. Living's excuse enough for him."

"Regrettably this is a fact," admitted Doc. "I do fear that I am becoming somewhat of an alcoholic. I do hope it doesn't affect my girlish figure."

Virgil and Wyatt both laughed.

"If you were any skinnier, you'd be invisible," said Virgil.

"You think I'm skinny?" asked Doc, grinning. "At least that's one good thing I can say for this damnable consumption I have—I don't get fat."

Now Virgil got serious, looking his brother straight in the eyes. "I've got to ask you something, Wyatt."

Wyatt said, "Anything, Virg."

"You've been spending a lot of time with that Jewish girl. The dancer."

"Josie."

"Right. Are you two an item?"

Wyatt's cheeks went red with embarrassment. "What do you mean?"

Doc spoke up. "What he wants to know is whether or not you're having sexual intercourse with that pretty young lady."

"I'm a married man," said Wyatt. "I don't engage in that kind of activity. Not anymore."

"If you say so," said Virgil.

Doc spoke up. "If Wyatt says he's not having relations with that girl, then that's it. That's the way it is. He's a damned fool if he's not, but then nobody ever said he was the smartest fella around."

A smile touched Wyatt's lips. "You're right, nobody ever said that."

"Then let us drink," said Doc. "To willful ignorance."

Virgil said, "There he goes with another toast."

Doc was about to say something smart, but old Henry Neville came running up to the table, shaken and out of breath.

"What the hell's the matter, Henry?" asked Virgil.

Henry looked past Virgil to Wyatt. "I found a dead woman outside!"

Wyatt started to stand. "A dead woman?"

"I tripped over the body in the alleyway. I reached down and tried to wake her, but she was covered in blood!"

"Who was it?" asked Virgil.

"I couldn't see who it was. It was too dark."

"Show us, Henry," said Wyatt. "Show us the body."

135

Two: The Grisly Fate of Arlene Gates

The body Henry Neville found was that of Arlene Gates, a prostitute who worked at the Crystal Palace. Arlene had come from Nebraska with her late husband, Durwood Gates, in the hopes of striking a claim and getting rich. But Arlene never got rich. All she got was dead.

In all his years as a lawman, Wyatt had never seen such a murder as this. Hell, he'd never even *heard* of a murder like this. The killer had sliced Arlene's throat from one side to the other. Then he'd disemboweled her. And she was missing an ear.

"What the hell do you make of this?" asked Virgil, sitting behind his desk, fiddling with a pencil.

"I'll be damned if I know," said Wyatt. "It's the craziest thing I've ever seen."

Their little brother Morgan, also a Tombstone deputy marshal, asked, "Why do you suppose the killer took her ear?"

Doc said, "Perhaps the man just has a fetish for ears."

"A fetish for ears?" asked Virgil.

Doc smiled. "I have been known to nibble on a female's ear on one or two occasions."

"So what do we know about the killer?" asked Morgan.

"I think it's safe to say we're dealing with one sick son of a bitch," said Doc.

Wyatt said, "I think we can all agree that that's a fair assessment."

"Doc Goodfellow said the killer was shorter than Arlene," said Virgil.

"How could he tell?" asked Morgan

"They can tell from the angle of the cuts," explained Doc. "Those cuts'll tell you a whole story if you know what to look for."

Wyatt said, "The coroner said the incisions were extremely skillful, like those a doctor would make."

"You figure the killer's done this before?" asked Morgan.

"Could be," said Wyatt, nodding his head. "Could be."

"You figure he's somebody with medical training?"

"I dunno. At this point it could be anybody killed Arlene."

"If it's a doctor, he shouldn't be too hard to track down," said Doc.

"What about you, Doc?" asked Morgan, grinning.

Doc laughed. "While it is true that I was once a man of medicine, I myself was a dentist."

"What does that mean?"

"It means there wasn't a lot of call for me to disembowel anybody in my line of work," said Doc. "Besides, how do we know we can trust Doc Goodfellow? Maybe it was him that killed Arlene."

"Coroner by day, killer by night?" asked Virgil.

Doc said, "No killer is a killer all the time."

"Yeah," said Virgil. "Just look at you."

Doc gave him a go-to-hell look, but said nothing.

"What do we know about the blade that cut her—anything?" asked Wyatt.

Virgil said, "The coroner figured the killer would have had to use either a scalpel or a sharp razor to make incisions like those."

"Maybe the killer is a barber," suggested Morgan. "A barber would have a sharp razor."

"Anything is possible," Wyatt said.

"So we now have the search for the killer narrowed down to barbers, doctors, and coroners," said Doc. "We should have the killer in custody in no time."

"We've never seen anything like this in Tombstone before," said Virgil. "So if the killer has done this before, he may be new to town. Have you guys seen anyone new that stood out?"

"Fifty new people come to Tombstone every day," said Wyatt. "It's a boom town. Could be anybody."

Morgan said, "I did notice one person we might need to speak with."

"Who?" asked Wyatt.

"An Englishman named Eldrich Davies came in on the stagecoach the other day. He looked kind of shifty."

"What else?"

"He's a doctor," said Morgan.

"Well then, he just moved to the top of our list of suspects," said Virgil.

"A doctor," said Wyatt, mulling it over.

"And a no good Brit on top of that," said Doc, snooping through a stack of wanted posters. "He *must* be our man."

"Who else might we be looking for?" asked Morgan.

"Maybe he's a butcher," said Virgil.

Doc smirked. "Obviously."

"I mean a real butcher—as in someone who cuts meat for a living."

"I hate to shoot down your theory, Virgil," said Doc. "But a butcher hacks away at his work and uses a very big knife—not a scalpel. He wouldn't likely be able to make such a smooth incision such as those on our dearly departed Arlene."

"Did you know Arlene?" asked Morgan.

"I have only carnal knowledge of the woman."

"What does that mean?"

Doc smiled. "It means I worked with her on more than a few occasions."

"You sampled her wares?" asked Wyatt.

"Exactly, Wyatt. I sampled her wares."

"What do you remember about her?"

Doc gazed past them. "Boy, she had a mouth that could—"

"Will you guys get serious here?" said Virgil. "We need to figure out who might have done this."

"Obviously we know who we're looking for now," said Doc.

"How do you figure?"

"We just have to find a short barber with a medical degree who's new to town."

Morgan smiled. He couldn't help it—Doc always made him laugh. The man had a way with words that was unlike anything the young deputy marshal had ever heard before. "I think Doc has figured out this whole case," said Morgan.

Virgil did not smile.

"You figure the Clantons might have done this?" asked Morgan. "Maybe on their way out of town, to get back at Wyatt?"

"No, the coroner said the body had been there for at least two hours," said Virgil. "Besides, I don't figure the Clantons for it."

"Why?"

"The Clantons like to shoot their enemies in the back," said Doc. "They don't cut them up. Besides, they were all too drunk to make such perfect incisions."

"Maybe we ought to ask old Evelyn over at the Crystal Palace about Arlene's recent customers," said Virgil. "That might tell us something. Maybe she'll know if Arlene has had any trouble lately."

"That is an excellent idea to be sure," said Doc. "A fine idea indeed."

And off they went to the Crystal Palace.

The Crystal Palace was almost as dead as Arlene Gates, but this was a Sunday afternoon, so it was to be expected. Today only the bartender and the whores were there, and the place stunk of cheap French perfume.

"Business is kind of dead today," observed Wyatt.

Zed, the bartender, said, "You can say that again. We ain't had but a few customers all day. I figured for sure things woulda picked up after church got out, but not today. How are things down at the Oriental?"

Wyatt lit his cigar. "About the same. Couple of drifters at the bar, that's about it."

"What can I do for you boys?" asked Zed.

"I take it you heard about what happened to Arlene Gates?" asked Virgil.

Zed nodded. "I did indeed. Damned shame."

"Do you know if Arlene had any trouble with anyone?"

"No," Zed said, shaking his head. "Everyone loved Arlene."

"You can say that again," said Doc.

"She have any rough customers lately?"

"Not that I know of," said Zed, wiping a glass clean. "But then you'd have to ask Evelyn about that one. I wouldn't really know."

"She around?" asked Wyatt.

"Sure. Let me get her for you." Zed turned and looked upstairs, yelling out, *"Hey, Evelyn! You got visitors!"*

Evelyn, the Crystal Palace madam, appeared at the top of the stairs, smiling big. "Why hello, boys." Making her way down the stairs, she turned to Doc, saying, "Hello, Doc. I ain't seen you in a day or two."

Doc tipped the brim of his hat to her.

"Damn Doc," said Wyatt. "How much are you in here?"

"Hell," said Evelyn. "If old Doc was here any more, we'd have to give him a job. I swear he's here more than I am, and I live here."

Doc said, "You know I think you may be right, Evelyn."

Evelyn looked at Wyatt. "So I guess you boys are here to ask me about Arlene."

"Unfortunately yes," said Virgil.

"Well, I don't know what to tell you fellas. She was a great girl. Everyone loved her. She was one of our biggest earners. She'll be missed. She didn't necessarily want to be a whore, turned to it after her husband died and left her broke... But the girl did her homework for the job, and she was a real fast learner."

Wyatt asked, "What kind of homework might one do to become a whore?"

"Well, she studied the hell out of that *Kama Sutra*," said Evelyn.

"And I can assure you she put every one of those moves to good use," Doc said. "The author would have been proud."

Virgil rolled his eyes.

Morgan chuckled.

"This ain't no laughing matter," said Virgil. "A woman is dead here."

"Chopped all to hell is what I heard," said Evelyn. "That true?"

"I'm afraid so."

"I heard they cut off all her fingers, all her toes, both of her tits, both ears, and poked out her eyes."

Virgil paused before saying, "That's somewhat of an exaggeration."

"That's good to hear," said Evelyn. "That poor girl never did nothin' to no one. She was the most innocent whore I've ever known."

"Innocent whore," said Doc. "Kind of an oxymoron, don't you think?"

"She have any rough customers lately?" asked Wyatt.

Evelyn thought for a moment, shaking her head. "Not that I can recall. Again, everybody loved her."

"Apparently someone didn't," said Doc, lighting his cigar.

"I hate to ask this, but did she sleep with any of those cowboys that ride with Ike Clanton and his boys?" asked Virgil.

"Ike Clanton?" she asked. "I'm not sure I know him."

"Real hairy little fella," said Wyatt. "Dumber than a box of hammers. Full of hot air. Rides with a horse's ass named Curly Bill."

"Oh, *him*," said Evelyn. "Sure, I know that loudmouth. He's a grubby little thing, that one."

Virgil asked, "You know if he slept with Arlene?"

"I don't think so. I don't recall any of those cowboys paying for whores when they were in here. They get them up there at the Oriental?"

"Damned if I know," said Wyatt.

Doc smiled. "I just assumed every man paid for whores."

"You assume wrong," said Wyatt. "Not *every* man."

Doc rolled his eyes. "I forgot, the reverend Wyatt Earp doesn't pay for sex. Why, he's a married man."

Evelyn smiled big. "Maybe he just ain't met the right whore."

"What are you implying?" asked Wyatt.

"Maybe I could be the one to change your mind."

Wyatt grinned. "I appreciate the offer. I truly do. But no thank you."

"Can you remember any of Arlene's recent customers?" asked Morgan.

"Just one."

"And who might that be?" asked Wyatt.

"Some fancy-pants Englishman. I think he said he was a doctor."

Wyatt and Virgil looked at one another.

"You remember his name?" asked Virgil.

"It was a weird Brit name as I recall…"

Wyatt asked, "Was it Eldrich Davies?"

Evelyn's face lit up with recognition. *"That's it,"* she said. "That's him. Eldrich Davies! He was the last paying customer to sleep with Arlene before she was murdered."

"It looks like we're going to see Dr. Eldrich Davies," said Wyatt.

Three: Meeting the Good Doctor

Wyatt sent Morgan and Doc back to the jail house to hold down the fort. Then he and Virgil asked around about Dr. Eldrich Davies and learned he was staying in the Grand Hotel. Largely because most everyone had a general disdain for Englishmen, no one had anything good to say. "He looks shifty" and "there's something strange about him" were the two most frequent claims they heard from the people of Tombstone.

When they arrived at the Grand, Wyatt and Virgil questioned the hotel manager about Davies, but learned little beyond the fact that he was a good tipper and that the manager didn't much trust him either.

They also found that the good doctor was out.

"I think he went to get a shave and a haircut," said the manager.

"Any idea where?"

"Old John Hays cuts hair right around the corner. You might try him."

The two men left and walked around the corner to John Hays' barber shop. There they found a peculiar-looking, bespectacled little man sitting in the barber's chair, getting a shave. The moment Wyatt laid eyes on him, he knew what everyone else meant—there was *something* off about him, but Wyatt couldn't quite put his finger on what it was.

But the damn guy gave him the creeps. He knew that much.

Wyatt's gut told him this was their killer.

"You Eldrich Davies?" asked Wyatt.

The doctor didn't look at all surprised or worried to see two men with badges standing before him. If anything, he looked annoyed.

"Yes? Something I can do for you?"

"We'd like to talk to you," said Wyatt.

"About?"

Virgil said, "About the death of Arlene Gates."

"I have no idea to whom you're referring," said Davies. "I have no idea who this Arlene Gates person is."

"That's not what we hear," said Wyatt.

"I just got in to town three days ago. I don't know anyone here."

"Evelyn over at the Crystal Palace says otherwise."

Davies said, "Well then I'm afraid she's mistaken."

"You calling Evelyn a liar?" asked Virgil, defensive now.

Davies looked more perturbed than flustered. "I'm afraid I don't know this Evelyn person either."

"Then I guess you're gonna have to come down to the jail house with us," said Wyatt, grabbing Davies' arm brusquely. When Wyatt grabbed the doctor's arm, John Hays jumped, inadvertently cutting Davies' cheek.

Wyatt now had Davies up and out of the chair, his face still half-covered with shaving cream. Davies reached up to where he'd been cut and looked down at the dark blood on his hand.

"I'm bleeding," he said.

"What about me?" asked Hays. "This man hasn't paid me yet."

Wyatt nodded at Davies. "Pay the man his money."

"But he hasn't finished shaving me," Davies said.

Wyatt tugged on his arm. "Pay the man."

Davies unhappily reached into his pants pocket, producing a handful of change. He paid Hays five cents.

"The price is ten cents," said Hays.

"What are you talking about?" asked Davies, pointing at the wall. "The sign right there says five cents for a shave."

"But you bled all over my apron," explained Hays. "Now I'm gonna have to buy a new one."

"But you were the one who cut me!"

Virgil looked at Davies. "Kind of a feisty one, aren't you?"

"Pay the man his five cents," ordered Wyatt.

"This is most absurd," said Davies.

Nevertheless he handed over the five cents to John Hays.

"My good man," Davies said to Wyatt. "Could you unhand me momentarily so that I might remove this apron?"

Wyatt released his grip on the doctor's arm and Davies took off the apron, tossing it into the barber's chair.

"This is ridiculous," Davies said, noticeably perturbed.

They started walking towards the door. Davies grabbed his bowler hat from a peg on the wall. Wyatt looked back at Hays and said, "Give my regards to the missus."

"And you say hello to Mattie for me."

"I'll do that," said Wyatt.

The three men stepped out of the barber shop into the sunlight. There was a slight breeze, but it was still fairly warm for mid-October.

Wyatt took off his hat and fanned himself with it as they walked.

"Can I get a cigar?" asked Virgil.

Wyatt made a face as he reached into his jacket pocket. "You make more money than me, Virgil. Why don't you ever buy your own damn cigars?"

"Cause Allie won't let me."

"But she'll let you bum them off me?" asked Wyatt.

"She says money's too tight right now for unneeded expenditures."

"Excuse me, but who is this Arlene person, and what does she have to do with me?" asked Davies.

Virgil put the cigar to his lips and chewed the tip off. He then lit the cigar.

"She's the dance hall girl got killed last night in an alleyway near the Crystal Palace," said Wyatt.

"And I'm supposed to know her?"

"That's the story," said Virgil.

Davies at least tried to look like he was wracking his brain to remember. "Oh," he said. "The whore."

"Yeah," said Wyatt. "One in the same."

"I didn't even know her name."

"Just keep walking," said Virgil. "We'll discuss this down at the jail house."

And on they walked.

When they reached the jail house, Wyatt shoved Davies down into a chair.

"This is quite irregular," said Davies. "I haven't done anything wrong."

"You're our number one suspect right now," Virgil informed him.

"But even a suspect has rights."

Wyatt reminded him, "We're the law here. We decide what rights you do and don't have in this town. So shut your goddamn mouth and just answer the questions unless you want more blood on your face than there already is."

The ever-proper Englishman showed an expression of disapproval. "Very well then."

Morgan walked out from the back room and looked Davies up and down, sizing him up.

"Where's Doc?" Wyatt asked.

"He went down to play cards at the Occidental."

Wyatt nodded with understanding.

"You think this is our guy?" Morgan asked Wyatt.

"I'm not sure yet."

"This all seems very improper," said Davies. "I don't think—"

That was when Wyatt slugged him in the jaw, knocking Davies' head to the side. Davies reached up and touched his lip, finding more blood, just as Wyatt had threatened.

"Now, will you shut your damn mouth?" asked Wyatt.

"This girl, the whore," said Davies. "How was she killed?"

"Someone—some very sick cocksucker—sliced her up pretty good," said Wyatt.

"And you believe I know something about it?"

Virgil spoke up. "It was almost surgical, like it was done with a scalpel."

Davies grinned big now.

"I'd wipe that smirk off your face unless you want me to hit you a few more times," said Wyatt. "It's disrespectful to the—"

"Whore?" asked Davies.

Wyatt slugged him again, almost knocking Davies' chair over. This time Davies did not wipe away the blood. He just grinned, blood in the crevices of his teeth.

"You have nothing on me," said Davies.

"What makes you say that?" asked Wyatt.

"Because I, sir, did not commit this heinous crime."

Virgil asked, "So you admit you were with Arlene the day she died?"

"I admit that I paid her for her services," said Davies. "No crime in that, is there?"

"No, there's not," said Wyatt.

"I was lonely," said Davies. "We didn't even have sex."

"Then what did you do?"

"We talked. Like civilized people."

Virgil asked, "What did you talk about?"

"Life. The normal things a man and woman talk about."

"You expect us to believe that?" asked Morgan.

"What?"

"That you paid Arlene to...*talk?*"

"Look," said Davies. "You can't prove anything, so would you please let me go?"

All three lawmen disliked Davies' choice of words. He didn't say he didn't do it—he just said they had no proof.

"I don't like you," said Wyatt.

"Frankly, sir, I don't care much for you either."

"Do you own a scalpel?" asked Virgil.

Davies smiled. "What in the hell is this?"

"Do you own a scalpel?" repeated Wyatt.

"Of course I own a scalpel. I'm a doctor."

"Did you murder Arlene Gates?"

"This is preposterous."

"Did you kill her?"

"No, I certainly did not."

"Where were you last night between, say, ten and one?"

"I was out."

"Doing what?" asked Virgil.

"I went for a walk, and I caught the burlesque show at the theatre," Davies said. "Ask around, I was there."

"At what time?" asked Wyatt.

"Ten."

Virgil asked, "You stayed for the whole show?"

"No, I left in the middle."

"Why?"

"Because I was bored, just as I am now."

"I'm sorry," said Wyatt. "Are we boring you?"

"Yes, I'm afraid you are," said Davies, obviously trying to anger them now.

Wyatt backhanded Davies across the mouth.

This time Davies didn't flinch. He just sat there and took it, stonefaced. The condescending smile never left his face.

"You're starting to piss me off," said Wyatt.

"Well, this should be fun."

"If you didn't kill Arlene," said Morgan, "then why are you grinning like a damn madman?"

"Because you amuse me."

"How so?" asked Wyatt.

"All Americans amuse me," said Davies. "You're all so arrogant and self-righteous, all the while having no idea what complete and utter dolts you are."

"Are you calling me and my brothers dolts?" asked Wyatt, getting angrier by the second.

"I'm calling your entire country a nation of dolts."

And the man just kept grinning.

"You think it's funny that a woman died here?" asked Virgil.

"Of course I don't. Life is a very sacred thing."

"Are you a religious man?"

Davies laughed. "Not in the slightest."

"Do you believe in god?" asked Wyatt.

"No, of course not. Only an idiot would believe such superstition."

"What kind of man doesn't believe in god?"

"A man of medicine," said Davies. "Do you know how many men I've saved and how many men have died in my hands? If they lived, they lived because of modern medicine and my own skill as a physician.

If they died it was because I couldn't save them. No god had anything to do with any of it. It was all me."

"Are you comparing yourself to god?" asked Virgil.

"Every surgeon is a god in his way," said Davies. "We control life and death. We hold it all in our hands. And I assure you, gentlemen, that's the only true god you're ever going to find in this world."

"You mentioned having people die in your hands," said Wyatt.

"I didn't kill that woman."

"How do we know that?"

Davies smiled again. "I guess you'll just have to take my word for it."

After hours of questioning intermingled with the occasional punch or slap from Wyatt, they got nowhere with Davies. He would not admit to having murdered Arlene Gates. He only smiled that creepy smile and taunted them, ever insinuating that there was more to his story than he was telling them.

Finally they let him go on Virgil's orders, but he was told not to leave the city limits anytime soon.

"What the hell did you do that for?" asked Wyatt.

"What?" asked Virgil.

"Let him go. You know damned well he committed that murder."

"But we can't prove it. Until we turn up some sort of evidence, we've got nothing."

"You don't have what it takes to be a lawman," said Wyatt.

"Here we go again."

"What do you think I would have done had I been the marshal here today?"

"Probably beat the hell out of the man worse than you already did," said Virgil. "And you know what? You still wouldn't have gotten anywhere."

"We could have forced him to sign a confession," said Wyatt.

"And that's justice in your eyes?"

"Frontier justice," said Wyatt. "It's the only kind there is."

Before Virgil could respond, there was a knock on the door.

Morgan opened it, and there stood Fred Schoemehl, the editor of the *Epitaph*, the city newspaper.

"Hey Morgan," he said, still standing in the doorway. "I wondered if I could talk to you fellas about last night's murder."

"Come on in," said Virgil.

Wyatt smiled big. He had an idea.

"We got the whole story for you," he said.

"You do?" asked Fred.

"We sure do."

"Why are you helping me?" asked Fred, suspicious. "You boys are never this helpful."

"Get out your pad and your pencil," said Wyatt.

"Alright." Fred opened his bag and pulled out a pad and set to take notes.

Wyatt said, "You ready?"

"Yes, sir."

"Okay, write this name down: Dr. Eldrich Davies."

Fred looked up. "How do you spell that?"

Four: Wyatt and Josephine

Wyatt Earp had never believed in things like love at first sight. Such things were beliefs held by women and poets, and he had previously believed himself incapable of such things. So when he invited Josephine Marcus—a woman that, if truth be told, caused his heart to flutter a bit—to a picnic in the woods, he did so with the utmost belief that this could be done in the name of platonic friendship. After all, Wyatt was a strong man who had shown tremendous ability in just about everything else, so surely he could hold his urges at bay.

Or so he thought.

But here they were now, sitting on a blanket, eating sandwiches, and staring at one another, and Wyatt knew for the first time that he wanted this woman very badly. Josephine Marcus was a woman who could make a man reconsider his beliefs.

He didn't want to flirt with her, but he could feel himself doing so. Even when they weren't speaking, he was seducing her with his eyes. And she didn't mind. She was doing the same thing back.

"I've never met a woman like you before," he said.

She smiled. "There are no other women like me, Wyatt Earp."

"You're so free and full of life. That's refreshing."

"What do I care what others think of me? I have no time for such foolishness. I enjoy the company of men, and I like to have a good time. I say what I mean and I mean what I say. Life is too short for anything less."

"What will your fiancé Johnny say about us sitting here together like this?" asked Wyatt.

"Johnny Behan has nothing to say about what I do any longer," she said.

"Why is that?"

"For starters, he's no longer my fiancé."

"Really?" he asked.

"Really. And second, Johnny Behan is a horse's ass."

"There's something we both agree on," said Wyatt, smiling.

"You don't like Johnnny?"

"No, I don't. He's arrogant," Wyatt said. "But not in a self-confident way, but the exact opposite. He's a man who seems insecure about himself, so he acts like he has confidence. He's cocky. And we don't see eye to eye on anything at all."

"Nor do we," she said. "Besides that, he's a no-good liar and a cheater."

Wyatt said, "He doesn't strike me as a man who would be a good lover. He seems too effeminate for that."

"I assure you that he's no great lover."

"Then how'd he get a pretty thing like you?" asked Wyatt.

"We were traveling across the desert in a stagecoach. It was Apache territory. He and a man named Al accompanied us on the trip to keep watch and keep us safe from the Indians. That...*interested* me. Besides, he was just about the only man present, so he seemed like a catch at the time."

Wyatt laughed. "Maybe under those circumstances, but that'd be about it."

She now turned her gaze to Wyatt. "I'll bet you're a magnificent lover. Are you a good lover, Wyatt Earp?"

Wyatt blushed. "What kind of question is that?"

"It's an honest one. I really want to know."

"Well, I've never had any complaints," he managed.

"What about that woman you travel with, that Mattie? Does she have any complaints?"

"I don't really want to talk about her," Wyatt said.

"Is she your wife?"

"She carries my name and we've been together for a while, but she's not my wife."

"Hmmm," said Josephine. "That's a good thing."

"Why?"

"Because I'm now interested in *you*, Wyatt Earp."

"Please call me Wyatt, not Wyatt Earp."

"Okay, Wyatt," she said. "Tell me something about you that I don't know."

Wyatt could feel himself dropping his guard with her. There was something special about this woman; he wanted to know her, and he wanted her to know him, which was something new for Wyatt.

"I used to be a bouncer at a brothel up in Peoria," he said.

"When was that?"

"This was a long time ago. Me and my brother Morgan worked there together."

"Did you enjoy that line of work?"

"It was the time of my life. I didn't have to deal with all the trouble and worry that comes with being a lawman."

Josephine asked, "Did you have sex with the prostitutes?"

"I'll just say this: it was not a job without its merits."

She smiled. "I like you very much," she said.

"I like you, too. Tell me about yourself."

"I like to tell people I'm the daughter of a wealthy German merchant, but it isn't true," she said. "I'm not even German. I'm Prussian."

"You speak Prussian?"

She laughed. "No, Prussian isn't a language. They speak Yiddish and German there."

"Which do you speak?"

"Both," she said.

Wyatt was impressed. He'd never met a woman with such sophistication and intelligence before. She was unlike anything else Tombstone had to offer.

"How did you become a dancer?" he asked.

"By luck. My best friend Dora was a dancer, and she convinced me to join her. Now we're performing 'H.M.S. Pinafore' at the Bird Cage Theatre. You should come see the show sometime."

"I definitely will," said Wyatt. "I hear you're quite good in it."

"Where did you hear that?"

"People talk."

"So how did you become a lawman, Wyatt?"

"The job was open and I took it. That's about all there is to say."

"How long have you been a lawman?"

"A long time now," he said. "I used to be the marshal in Wichita and later in Dodge City."

"I know," she said. "As you said, people talk. Besides, you're practically a legend."

"Well, like most legends, a lot of what people say about me isn't true," said Wyatt. "I like to hear the stories myself, and they are entertaining, but they build me up so that it's difficult for me to live up to people's expectations."

"I doubt that," she said. "Tell me more about yourself."

"My brother Virgil arrested me last year, if you can believe that," he said, laughing.

"Truly?"

"I'm afraid so."

"On what charges?"

"Being a drunken ass," Wyatt said. "I got drunk and started a fight over a card game. Virgil took me to jail until I sobered up, and then he slapped me with a $25 fine on top of it."

She laughed.

"I like your eyes," she said. "They're pretty. They change colors... Sometimes they're blue, and sometimes they look gray."

"I like your eyes, too," said Wyatt. The truth was he liked everything about this beautiful, curvaceous young woman.

"What else have you done for a living, Wyatt?"

"I used to be a professional gambler."

She made a face. "Gamblers are generally dishonest people. Are you a dishonest man?"

He grinned. "Define dishonest."

"You do make me laugh," she said.

"So where did you live before you came to Tombstone?"

She looked off through the trees. "My family lived in Manhattan. In New York. It was an area known as the Five Points. We were very poor. That's why I tell people that story about being from a wealthy family."

"So why aren't you telling *me* that story?"

She smiled and gazed into his eyes, making his heart feel funny again.

"There's something different about you, Wyatt," she said. "I feel comfortable with you. I feel like I can be myself, and I don't feel that way about anyone else. Certainly not any men."

Wyatt knew what she meant. He felt the exact same way about her.

"I believe I'm going to fall in love with you," said Josephine.

Wyatt didn't know what to say, so he said nothing.

"I'd like you to call me Sadie," she said.

"Why?"

"My middle name is Sarah, and everyone back home calls me Sadie." She paused, staring into his eyes. "Can I be your Sadie, Wyatt Earp?"

Without giving thought to what he was doing, he took her in his arms and he kissed her, their tongues exploring one another's. It was a powerful kiss, and Wyatt never wanted it to end. But finally it did.

She tried to regain her composure, wiping her lips.

"You're a fine kisser," she said.

"I told you, no complaints."

They kissed again. This time it was her who made the move. Wyatt did not try to stop her. He went with it, eventually pulling his mouth away to kiss her neck. His hand moved up the outside of her dress to her bosom. She lifted her head to the skies, and he kissed every part of her body his mouth came into contact with, his hand still rubbing at her bosom.

And they made love, right there on top of the picnic blanket, rolling over half-eaten sandwiches as they did.

And it was wonderful.

When they were finished, they lay naked on the picnic blanket, staring at the clouds passing by.

"Does your job ever cause you to be afraid?" she asked.

"Not really," he said. "But this new killing… This Arlene Gates murder. It's something different. I've never seen anything like it. And that man, Eldrich Davies, makes me nervous. I've seen a lot of faces in my time, and none of them made me feel uneasy the way his does. There's just something about him. I fear he's…" Wyatt couldn't find the words.

"The devil incarnate," Josephine said.

Wyatt stared at the skies. She was correct. The killer seemed to be the devil incarnate. It was as though this woman had searched inside his brain. She somehow already knew him well enough to finish his sentences. She was a remarkable woman, to be sure.

"Wyatt?" she asked. "Why do you think people do things like that?"

"I don't know. I've known a lot of men who were just plain mean— just meaner than all hell—and there was no good reason for it. Some men are just born bad, I guess."

"How about your friend Doc? Was he born bad?"

Wyatt smiled. "I wouldn't exactly call Doc 'bad.' He's more...misguided. That's the word I would use for him."

"Why are you friends with a man like Doc?"

"He's my only friend."

"I'm your friend, Wyatt."

"Thank you for that. I meant he's the only true male friend I have. He doesn't judge me, and I don't judge him."

"Is he a bad influence on you?" Josephine asked. "Or is it the other way around?"

"Depends on who you ask, I guess. Most people think he's a bad influence on me, but Big Nosed Kate thinks I'm the bad influence on Doc."

"Big Nosed Kate?" she asked.

"Kate Elder," said Wyatt. "She's Doc's woman."

Josephine was about to speak when they were interrupted by Morgan, riding up through the trees on horseback. Wyatt sat up, trying to cover himself. "What is it, Morgan?" he asked.

"Virgil needs you back in town," said Morgan.

"What's going on?"

"There's a mob out front of the jail house. They want to string up Eldrich Davies."

"Goddammit," Wyatt said.

His plan to involve the *Epitaph* didn't seem so clever at the moment. He wanted nothing more than to stay here in Josephine's arms and make love to her again.

But duty called.

Wyatt turned to Morgan. "You go on ahead. I'll be along directly."

He turned to Josephine, now covering herself with part of the blanket.

"I have to go," he told her. "Or else they're gonna kill that damned doctor."

"But isn't that a good thing?"

"Maybe," he said. Wyatt stood and put his clothes back on, tucking his shirt into his trousers. He put his holsters on, walked to his horse, and climbed on.

"I'll see you soon."

"Be careful," she said.

He turned back to her and said, "And yes, you can be my Sadie."

And he rode away.

Five: Mob Mentality

In the latest issue of the *Epitaph*, the good folks of Tombstone got to read all about how local law enforcement officers believed Dr. Eldrich Davies to be responsible for the grisly murder of dancehall girl Arlene Gates. The newspaper sensationally referred to Eldrich as "Doctor Death," further branding him as a murderer in the minds of the city's populace.

About an hour after the newspaper had been released, a drunken mob began organizing at the Occidental Saloon. It then carried down the street to the jail house, where Davies had already checked himself in for fear of death at the hands of vigilantes. Virgil was holding the doctor behind bars in protective custody. After the mob had arrived in front of the jail house demanding he hand Davies over to them, Virgil had gone outside, sawed-off 12-gauge Greener in hand, to try and quell them.

But talking had done no good thus far, and until Morgan and Wyatt got back, it was just he and Doc Holliday.

Virgil stood on the steps of the jail house, holding up the shotgun where everyone could see it. Doc was behind him, leaning casually against the wall. As usual, Doc looked completely at ease in the situation aside from the occasional coughing fit. He was holding his own sawed-off 10-gauge Meteor.

It was big E.B. Thompson out in front of the mob, whipping them into a frenzy.

"E.B., why don't you take these people back where you came from," said Virgil. "No one's gonna take Eldrich Davies away from here today."

"Is it true he killed that whore?" asked E.B.

"I can only say that he's our number one suspect at the moment. It has yet to be determined whether Dr. Davies raised a hand against Arlene Gates."

"He gonna hang for what he done?" asked someone in the crowd.

Someone else yelled out, *"Bring out Doctor Death!"*

And soon the crowd was just as raucous as it had been in the beginning. Lucky for Virgil and Doc, Wyatt and Morgan were approaching.

E.B. Thompson looked over at them. "Wyatt ain't gonna stop us. Hell, it was him that said Davies was the damn murderer in the first place. I read it in the newspaper!"

Wyatt fired his pistol into the air, causing everyone to stop what they were doing.

"All of you had better disperse now," said Wyatt.

"And if we don't?" asked E.B.

"Then you can hang up there at that gallows with Davies," said Morgan.

This only made the crowd louder. Most of the members of the mob were already drunk at four in the afternoon, and by god they wanted Eldrich Davies dead.

"Bring out Doctor Death!" yelled someone, and it soon became a steady chant.

"I've said what I have to say," said Virgil. "We're going back inside now. If any of you sons of bitches tries to attack the jail house, you're gonna get a one-way ticket up to Boot Hill. I'm not in the mood for anymore of this bullshit!"

But still the crowd persisted chanting and screaming out threats.

"We're gonna get you Earps!" someone yelled.

Wyatt, now off his horse, waded through the crowd in search of the voice. "Who the hell said that?" he asked. But no one offered up the offender. Finally, Wyatt walked up the steps and followed Doc and his brothers inside the jail house.

They had been inside the jail house for several hours when someone threw a large stone through the window. There was a note attached to it, threatening that Davies would be burned out of the building if the Earps didn't hand him over to them.

Wyatt walked over to the window and yelled out, "You stupid sons of bitches! Do you have any idea how much one of these windows costs?" He paused, considered what he was saying, and added, "If anyone else comes up these steps, he dies. End of story."

Wyatt walked back to the jail where Davies was standing behind bars.

"The crowd's getting wild out there," Wyatt said.

"Why did you do this to me?" asked Davies. "This never would have happened if you hadn't planted that story in the newspaper."

"I wanted to draw you out."

Davies asked, "And?"

"Here you are," said Wyatt solemnly. "You know, you could make this all a whole lot easier if you'd just confess to what you did to that dancehall girl."

"I did nothing to anyone. Besides, what would confessing do? Speed up my death? Thanks to you I'm liable to die now no matter what happens."

"Then confess."

"You are, as they say, barking up the wrong tree," said Davies, still as calm and collected as ever. "I did not do a thing to that woman. As I said, we only had polite conversation."

"What if I was to go over to your hotel room and take a look at your scalpels? What would I find?"

"You are certainly welcome to do so," Davies said. "They are completely cleaned and sanitized. You will not find so much as a trace of blood on them."

"So you admit that you did it?" asked Wyatt.

"I said nothing of the sort."

Davies' arms were folded around the bars. Wyatt grabbed them and yanked them forward, pulling Davies' face into the bars. *"You confess to what you did, goddamn you!"*

"I shall do no such thing."

Wyatt turned and looked at the broken window, seeing faces in the street outside. "What if I was to let you go?" Wyatt asked. "What would you think of that, Mr. Fancy Pants? What if I was to release you to that crowd and let them do what they wanted to you? Do you think your treatment would be better or worse out there?"

"My guess is about the same," replied Davies. "You and the members of that mob share the same mentality, Mr. Earp. You need to look at yourself in the mirror and ask yourself if you're a vigilante or a constable—are you good or are you bad?"

Wyatt spit in Davies' face, but the doctor remained unflustered. The spit dangled from Davies' moustache for a moment before the doctor wiped his face with the sleeve of his jacket.

The mob had dwindled a bit by sundown, and those remaining soon began carrying torches. E.B. Thompson had given up and gone home for supper, leaving the unruly mob without a central instigator. Just after dark, the crowd began screaming epithets and threats at the jail house again.

Soon a knock came at the door, and all the Earps drew their revolvers and raised them. The door opened, and all of them were prepared to shoot down whoever walked through it. Much to their surprise, it was Fred Schoemehl from the newspaper.

"Get inside and close that door," ordered Wyatt.

Fred did as he was told.

"You kind of got us at a bad time," said Morgan. "Can't you see we're busy here?"

"Well, I wondered if I could get the doctor's story in his own words," said Fred. "You know, before they break in here and kill him."

"Now why would I allow you to tell my story?" asked Davies through the bars. "You're part of the reason I'm in this predicament. You called me Doctor Death, for god's sake!"

Virgil spoke up. "Don't you take my god's name in vain. You don't believe in god, remember?"

"I'll bet he's changed his tune on that one," said Wyatt, chuckling.

"And why would you presume such a thing?" asked Davies, haughty as ever.

"Most people in your situation would be crying and begging to the Lord by now. You mean to tell me you still don't believe in god?"

Davies sneered. "You tell me—where is your god today? Is he here with me, protecting me?"

"That's our job," said Morgan.

Davies laughed. "Exactly my point. I'm in just as much danger in here as I am out there."

"Between you and I," said Doc, "I don't much believe in god either. But then I'm just a scurrilous no-good scoundrel and a heathen, so nobody much cares about what I believe in."

It was just after nine when someone tossed a lit torch through the window, catching the wooden jail house floor on fire.

"Goddammit!" screamed Wyatt. "You boys go in the back and get some buckets of water and attend to this. I'll take care of these limp dick sons of bitches right here and now."

"Well," said Doc. "I do believe I'll join you. I do always love to watch Wyatt at work."

Davies reached out through the bars, screaming. *"What about me? I'll burn in here!"*

But everyone ignored him, leaving him locked inside the cell.

Wyatt and Doc stepped outside and a hush fell over the crowd.

Wyatt was now carrying Virgil's rifle. He held it up and fired it into the sky.

"All this bullshit stops now!" he cried out. "I'm gonna count to five, and any chicken shit still standing here when I get to five is gonna get a bullet through his heart!"

"One," he said.

Everyone in the crowd looked around nervously, trying to decide what to do.

"Two."

A few members of the mob broke away and left the crowd.

"Three."

Now the crowd parted and Curly Bill Brocious stepped out, his hand on his fancy two-gun rig. "Four," he said, catching Wyatt off-guard.

"What are you doing here?" asked Wyatt angrily.

"I hear you've got a murderer in there," said Curly Bill.

"Well," said Doc, "I'm sure you'd know all about that."

Curly Bill grinned, his hand now tickling the handle of his pistol.

"Let's have it out here, me and you, Holliday," said Curly Bill.

"I hardly think this is the appropriate time or place," said Doc.

"What are you, yellow?"

Doc was grinning now. "As much as I would so very much like to shoot you down dead in the street tonight, this is not an appropriate time or place."

"We've got business here," said Wyatt.

"I've got my own business," said Curly Bill.

"Oh, alright," said Doc. "If you really want to die tonight, I guess I could accommodate you." Now he had his handle on his own ivory-handled revolver, his eyes locked on Curly Bill's.

The moment was tense.

No one said a word.

Both men had their hands on their pistols.

Finally, just a moment before one of them would have drawn and killed the other, Wyatt reached out and smashed Curly Bill over the head with the butt of his rifle, once again rendering him unconscious.

"I do believe you've gotten quite good at that," said Doc.

"Now everybody go home or you'll end up in jail here with Curly Bill!"

The remaining members of the crowd looked about one another, confused, and slowly started to dissipate. Soon there was no one left of the mob to threaten the Earps or to make demands. The street was completely empty.

Six: The Burden of Proof

The Earp brothers slept overnight in the jail house to insure Davies' safety. Doc left to go play cards and "do some fornicating."

Bright and early the next morning, Ike Clanton and a few of his cowboys came riding in for Curly Bill. As was generally the case, Ike was in a foul-tempered mood. Having already knocked and been allowed into the jail house, he inquired about Curly Bill's situation.

Wyatt answered, "Curly Bill was arrested for inciting violence and threatening a lawman."

"I don't suppose you threatened him first," said Curly Bill.

"No, I don't reckon I did."

Ike tilted his head sideways and squinted at Wyatt, trying his damnedest to look tough. It didn't work. "What's the fine for that?" he asked.

"Thirty dollars," said Virgil.

"Well, I ain't payin' no damn $30 to get Curly Bill out of jail!" Ike proclaimed.

"Then it looks like he'll be staying with us," said Wyatt.

Ike looked over at Curly Bill, standing there behind bars in the cell next to Davies'. "Ain't you got some money?" Ike asked him.

"Nah, I ain't got no money," said Curly Bill. "Wyatt saw to that."

This irritated Ike, looking back at Wyatt now. "You took that man's money?"

"I unburdened him of it," said Wyatt. "Extra fines and whatnot."

Ike turned to Curly Bill. "How much did this sumbitch take off ya, Bill?"

"I had a roll," Curly Bill said. "Must have been two hundred if there was a dollar."

Ike looked back at Wyatt, who was grinning.

"What the hell kind of lawman are you?" asked Ike.

"The kind with $200," said Wyatt. "Now are you gonna pay the $30 to have Curly Bill here released or what?"

Ike mulled it over in his head, searching for something smart to say. When he couldn't come up with anything, he looked over at Davies, also standing there behind bars. "That there, that the man killed the whore?" asked Ike. "You're Doctor Death?"

Wyatt allowed Davies to answer for himself.

"You know how things tend to get blown out of proportion in this town," said Davies.

Ike nodded, looking back at Curly Bill. "Don't I know it."

Wyatt looked over at Davies now. "You and old Ike here would get along swell, Davies. I think you'd find that you share a lot of the same interests."

Ike glared at Wyatt. "What the hell is that supposed to mean?"

"It means you both enjoy killing people," Virgil said. "He cuts 'em all to hell, and you shoot 'em in the back."

"Maybe you should talk some more of your shit," Wyatt advised Ike. "Then you could stay here with Davies and you two could have a gay old time talking about all the criminal tomfoolery you've both been up to."

Ike was pissed. He took off his hat and shook it at Wyatt. "I don't appreciate your talkin' to me like that."

"Too close to the truth for comfort?" asked Morgan, lighting a cigar.

"Now are you gonna pay to take this miserable bastard Bill with you or not?" asked Wyatt.

Seeing there was nothing else to do, Ike reached into his pocket for his money. He counted out $30 and handed it to Wyatt. "I'd like a receipt," he said.

"Well, you ain't gettin' one," said Wyatt. "Besides, you and I both know you couldn't read it if I did give it to you. Now take this sorry son of a whore and get the hell out of my jail house."

Virgil unlocked Curly Bill's cell and let the man go free.

"We'll talk again," promised Curly Bill.

"One of these days you and I are gonna have one too many of these talks," said Wyatt.

"Meaning?"

"Meaning if Doc don't shoot you down then I might have to," said Wyatt. "Now both of you take your men and go home. I'm sure you got some cattle to steal or some square head to bushwhack somewhere."

Curly Bill just smiled, hat in hand, and headed for the door.

"We'll be back," said Ike. "Oh yeah, you goddamn Earps. We'll be back."

"Don't let the door hit you in the ass on your way out," said Morgan.

Curly Bill and Ike sauntered out through the doorway, trying to look tough.

"Good riddance," said Virgil, closing the door.

And that was that.

Wyatt sat there on Virgil's desk, staring at Davies. And Davies sat there in his cell looking at Wyatt. Each man studied his adversary, wondering just what it was that made him tick.

"When did you become a doctor?" asked Wyatt.

"Fifteen years ago," said Davies.

"What kind of medicine you practice?"

"I'm a general practitioner and a surgeon."

"What brings you to Tombstone?"

"Same as anyone else, I suppose," said Davies. "I came searching for prosperity. Besides, I heard they were short on doctors out in these parts. I thought maybe I could help."

"Yeah, you helped alright," said Wyatt dryly.

Davies stared at him. "Why do you take such delight in my misery, Mr. Earp?"

"Because I think you murdered that girl, and I'm not gonna be happy until I see you hang for it."

"Believe what you will, sir," said Davies.

"I will and I do," said Wyatt. "So answer me this—when did you kill your first victim?"

"1864."

"You admit to killing someone in 1864?"

Davies grinned. "I killed a few people that year."

"How did you do it?" asked Wyatt.

"With a rifle, just like everyone else involved in the war."

Wyatt straightened. "You fought in the Civil War?"

"I did."

"But you're a Englishman."

"I *was* an Englishman," corrected Davies. "Now I'm an American citizen, just like you."

"Which side did you fight on?"

"Why, the Union side, of course."

Wyatt nodded. His brothers had all fought for the Union side, as well.

"I respect that," said Wyatt. "But what made you turn to crime—to killin' folks and such? Did something happen to you during the war?"

Davies laughed. "Do you really expect me to answer that?"

"You should. It would help your cause."

"Were I to tell you that I killed someone, I'd be dead within twenty-four hours."

"That's true, but you could at least die with a clear conscience."

"My conscience is clear, sir."

Wyatt tried a different approach. "Are you talented with a scalpel?"

"I'm a surgeon, for god's sake."

"There you go invokin' the name of my god again," said Wyatt. "Do it again and I'll punch you in your smart limey face."

"What, *again?*" asked Davies, trying his hardest to be a smart ass.

"You just keep talking, Mr. Fancy Pants. You're gonna get yours. One way or the other, I'll see to it that you get yours."

"That much I'm sure of," said Davies.

Two days later Wyatt and Virgil were sitting in the Oriental, eating bowls of rice with chopsticks and sharing a bottle of Whiskey.

"It doesn't look like we're gonna get Eldrich Davies to confess," said Virgil. "Any ideas?"

"I've already knocked the hell out of him more times than I care to remember, and he won't say nothin'," said Wyatt. "If it were me who was marshal, I'd torture him and force him to sign that goddamn confession."

"That's not my way."

"I know," said Wyatt, leaving it there.

But Virgil wanted to speak his piece. "I didn't get into law to coerce people into signing confessions that wasn't true. I got into law to help people, and that ain't helping people, Wyatt. What if that man's innocent?"

"What if he's not?"

"That very well may be the case," said Virgil. "But right is right and wrong is wrong. There's no gray area here."

Wyatt was already turning red. "Tell me you don't think he's our man."

"I do," said Virgil. "I absolutely do. But we ain't got proof."

"But what does your gut tell you? You're a lawman, same as I am, so you know by now sometimes you just gotta trust your gut instinct."

"You already know what my gut says."

"Then make him sign that goddamn confession and send him up to Wells Spicer so he can swing for what he done," said Wyatt.

Virgil slammed his fist down on the table, angry now. "I know you think I'm weak, Wyatt, but I'm not. I'm just a better man than you are. I know what's right, and that ain't right."

"But if you let him go and let him out there on the streets, he could do this again," said Wyatt. "He could do it to another dancehall girl. He could do it to anyone... He could cut up Allie, Virgil."

"I've said all I got to say on this topic," said Virgil.

Wyatt took a drink of his whiskey and said flatly, "Virgil, you're wrong. You *are* weak. You're the weakest man I've ever known, and one of these days it's gonna get you killed. Hell, it might even get us both killed."

Virgil took offense at this. "Say that again."

Wyatt calmly poured himself another glass of whiskey and downed it. He looked up, staring his brother right in the eyes and said, "You're weak, Virgil."

Within seconds Virgil was up and shoving Wyatt back in his chair. After almost toppling backwards, Wyatt leapt to his feet and slugged his brother. Virgil delivered an uppercut to Wyatt and soon both men were rolling around on the floor, knocking over tables and set on beating the hell out of one another.

When Wyatt and Virgil walked back into the jail house, they were bloodied, black and blue just like Eldrich Davies.

"What in god's name happened to you two?" asked Morgan.

"Why don't you ask your brother Virgil," said Wyatt.

Morgan looked at Virgil. "What's he talking about?"

"We're letting Davies go," said Virgil. "We got no proof of what he did, and we can't hold him here."

Davies, who was sitting in his cell, now stood up and walked to the bars.

"What the hell are you saying, Virgil?" asked Morgan.

"He's saying he's releasing that killer back onto the streets of Tombstone," said Wyatt. "Ain't that right, Virg?"

Virgil said nothing. He just picked up the keys to the cells, and walked over to unlock Davies'.

"Thank you, marshal," said Davies.

"Don't thank me," said Virgil. "It was the law saved you. I got no proof. I can't hold you here. Hell, I can't even tell you to leave town. But if you stay, you make sure you stay out of my way, Davies. Because so help me god, I see you in front of me again, I won't be so kind next time."

Davies said, "I understand, marshal."

"One more thing," said Virgil.

"Yeah?"

"I better not find anymore sliced up whores."

And with that, Dr. Eldrich Davies walked out of the jail house a free man.

Seven: A Bad Day in Tombstone

When Wyatt walked into the Oriental the next morning, Ned the bartender was waiting to talk with him. "It's Ike Clanton," he said. "He's talking a whole lot of shit. He's saying he's gonna gun down the Earps and Doc Holliday. He's saying it's gonna happen soon."

"That's what men like Ike Clanton do," said Wyatt. "They talk."

"He's always in here shooting off his mouth about this and that, but this time it was different. This time it felt like he meant it."

"How long was he in here?"

"Couple hours," said Ned. "I think he was trying to drink up the courage to confront you boys."

Wyatt thought about it, pissed. "What else did he say?"

"He talked about having your wives murdered. He even mentioned your friend, the Jewish dancer."

"Josephine?" asked Wyatt.

"Yeah, her," said Ned.

Now Wyatt was good and angry. It was one thing to threaten his brothers and friends, and it was another thing to make threats towards their wives.

Towards Josephine.

"I'll take a bottle of whiskey," said Wyatt.

"Are you sure that's a good idea?"

"Just give me the damned bottle," Wyatt said. "I'll decide what's good and what's bad for me."

Ned didn't say another word. He just got the bottle and handed it over to Wyatt, now sitting on a barstool. Wyatt took out a cigar, bit off the tip, and went to lighting it. He sat and considered all that Ike Clanton had said, drinking and becoming angrier and angrier by the second.

Finally, when his anger could rise no further and the bottle was empty, Wyatt stood. He briefly considered going after his brothers and Doc, but then thought the better of it. This was something he could handle by himself.

"Ike didn't happen to mention where he was going next, did he?" asked Wyatt.

Ned stopped wiping glasses for a moment. "You gonna kill him, Wyatt?"

"Where'd he go?"

"He said he was heading down to the Hatch Saloon to have a few more drinks and run his mouth a little more," said Ned. "What are you gonna do, Wyatt?"

Wyatt just turned and walked away.

It took Wyatt several minutes to get to the Hatch Saloon, which was down around the corner on Allen Street. Now he was liquored up and feeling invincible. He was ready for whatever Ike Clanton and his boys had to throw at him. He walked up the steps to the Hatch and threw open the doors.

He looked around the saloon and saw Ike at once. Ike was sitting there alone at the bar, talking to the bartender. As Wyatt walked closer to him, he could now hear Ike spouting off the same horseshit he'd said back at the Oriental. "This time it's different," said Ike. "This time we're gonna gun those goddamn Earps down in the street in cold blood." The bartender looked up and saw Wyatt approaching, but said nothing. Ike just kept going. "And that damned Doc Holliday, he's the worst of 'em. Even that whore he runs around with is gonna get it."

Wyatt, now standing directly behind Ike, said, "Is that what you're gonna do, Ike? You're gonna murder my brothers and I? You're gonna shoot my friend John Holliday?" He paused for a moment before adding, *"You're gonna murder my friend Josephine Marcus?"* And he slugged Ike—*hard*. Ike fell back against the bar, bounced off and toppled to the floor.

The bartender threw up his hands. "I don't want no trouble in here."

"You should really watch who you serve in this place," said Wyatt. "You shouldn't allow patrons like this no-good pig-fucker in here. It's bad for business."

Ike was crawling around on the ground, trying to figure out what had just happened. Wyatt kicked him in the ribs.

"Say some more shit about me and my family," Wyatt said. "Go on, Ike, tell me all about your plans to murder us in cold blood."

Ike scooted his body back towards the stool.

"I didn't mean nothing," Ike was saying. "I was just talking. I didn't mean no harm."

And Wyatt knew then what he had always known—that a coward would say anything to save his ass.

But this time it wasn't enough.

He kicked Ike in the ribs again, and Ike crumpled under his boot.

"I'm sorry," Ike said, whimpering and starting to cry.

"You're right," said Wyatt. "You *are* sorry. You're a sorry sack of shit."

And Wyatt kicked him again.

And again.

And again.

Once Wyatt was finished kicking the hell out of Ike Clanton, he sat down in Ike's stool, shadowing over the man on the floor. He ordered another bottle. Then he sat there and drank glass after glass, leaving Ike lying there in his own blood, still in possession of his revolver.

"Shouldn't you take away his gun?" asked the bartender.

"Nah," said Wyatt. "The man's too much of a coward to try anything. All he's good for is talk."

And Wyatt kept right on drinking.

He'd been doing this for some time when Morgan came looking for him.

Morgan walked up behind him, smoking a cigar. Wyatt could see his brother's reflection in the mirror behind the bar.

"What is it?" asked Wyatt, not turning around. "Can't a man drink in peace?"

Morgan looked down at Ike, lying there unconscious on the floor.

"Had another run-in with Ike Clanton, did you?" asked Morgan.

"You could say that."

"We need you, Wyatt."

Wyatt turned to look at his brother. "What's the matter?"

"There's been another murder," said Morgan.

"What kind of murder?"

Morgan shook his head. "Another whore. I'm afraid it's just like the Arlene Gates murder."

"No fooling?"

"No fooling," said Morgan. "She's cut all to hell."

"Where was the body found?"

"In an alley over by Sixth Street."

"You identify the body yet?"

"All we know is she's a whore," said Morgan. "No idea who she is."

Wyatt Earp finished his glass of whiskey and stood up. He turned and stepped over Ike Clanton, and headed for the door.

This was shaping up to be one hell of a bad day.

The body belonged to one Mary Beth Shaffer, a Stover's whore out of Maricopa. Like Arlene Gates before her, Mary Beth had wound up alone in Tombstone, destitute and without family. So she did what many other women before her had done—she turned to prostitution to make her way. Little did she know it would lead to her demise.

Mary Beth's body was lying crumpled between a couple of barrels, and had gone unseen by passersby for a number of hours in the daylight before she was discovered by a drifter out of Missouri named Sutton.

"I was looking for a place in the shade to lie down and take a nap," Sutton had said. "So I lay down, and looked over, and there she was, her dead eyes staring back at me. I damn near pissed myself right there."

Now Wyatt, Virgil, and Morgan were standing there in the alleyway, the barrels moved out of the way so they could get a good look at the body. Mary Beth was fully dressed, just as Arlene Gates had been, and she'd been sliced up. Her throat had been slashed, she'd been disemboweled, and one of her ears was missing.

"Where in the hell does he keep the ears?" Virgil asked.

"I dunno," said Wyatt. "Damnedest thing I ever saw."

Morgan agreed.

"I wonder what it is he does with them," said Virgil. "What he needs with them."

"Could be anything," said Wyatt. "Crazy son of a bitch like that, who knows what he's thinking?"

A few minutes later Doc Goodfellow arrived on the scene and looked over the body. "She's definitely been dead since sometime last night," he said. "And the incisions look almost identical to those of Arlene Gates. This was definitely the work of the same person."

Wyatt and Virgil then walked to Stover's to talk with Mary Beth's boss, Gilbert Riley. Riley was a middle-aged man who'd come out of Nebraska and had made a name (and a sizeable bankroll) for himself in dry goods. Once he'd raised enough money, he then bought out Jack Stover's brothel.

"Mary Beth's dead?" Riley asked, more than a little disinterested.

"I'm afraid so," said Virgil.

"And it was just like the murder a few days back?"

"Almost identical," said Wyatt.

"The killer cut off her tits?" asked Riley. "I read in the newspaper the killer cut off the other whore's tits and cut out her eyes."

"That's nonsense," said Virgil. "He cut her up pretty bad, but she still has her tits and her eyes."

"That's good," said Riley. "She had some really nice tits."

"Have you known Mary Beth to have any problems with anybody?"

"The girl had a smart mouth on her, and a temper as quick as hell," said Riley. "It's possible she could have pissed off any one of her customers. It's completely possible. She was a real firecracker, that one."

"Do you know who any of her customers were?" asked Virgil.

"Just the regulars, so far as I know."

Wyatt asked, "You wouldn't happen to know if she'd slept with that limey cocksucker Eldrich Davies, would you?"

"No," said Riley. "We wouldn't have accepted his business anyway, on account of him being Doctor Death and all."

"Wise policy," said Wyatt.

"Mary Beth got any family around here?" asked Virgil.

"No," said Riley. "Most of the whores don't, or else they wouldn't be whores."

Wyatt nodded. "Makes sense."

"If you hear anything, you be sure and let us know," said Virgil.

Now it was Riley's turn to nod. "I sure will. And you do the same."

Wyatt and Virgil left to go have another conversation with Dr. Eldrich Davies.

Eight: Another Chat with Doctor Death

When the Earps reached the Grand Hotel, they asked the hotel manager if Davies was up in his room. He nodded, saying, "Room 22." The Earps then made their way up the stairs, guns in hands, and the hotel manager attempted to follow them up. "No, no, no," said Virgil. "This is official police business. You stay downstairs and keep everyone calm and away from us." The hotel manager looked sad and dejected, but did what he was told.

It was Wyatt who pounded on the door.

"Yes?" came the familiar voice from inside.

"Open this goddamn door, Davies."

There was a pause, and then the door was unlocked and opened. Davies looked at them, smiling a big, toothy smile.

"You better stop smiling," said Wyatt. "Or else I'm liable to knock all those pretty teeth down your goddamn throat."

Davies' smile fell away, and he looked unsure of the Earps' purpose. "I suppose you've found a new way to have me arrested," said Davies.

"There's been another murder," said Virgil, chewing on an unlit cigar.

"Another murder?" asked Davies, his face contorted.

"That's right," said Wyatt. "And we've got some questions to ask you."

"Can we come in?" asked Virgil.

Davies hesitated. "And if I were to say no?"

Wyatt said, "We'd come in anyway."

Davies swung the door wide open and walked back into the room, allowing the lawmen to follow. When they entered the hotel room, each of them scanned the place for possible clues or evidence. Wyatt walked to a table holding a chamber pot and Dr. Davies' medical bag. He reached out and grabbed the black leather bag, already unfastening its latch.

"Mind if I open this?" asked Wyatt.

"Since you're already doing it, I guess not," said Davies.

Wyatt opened the bag and dumped its contents out onto the neatly-made bed. Amidst the medical tools were two scalpels. Wyatt picked one of them up and held it to the light, turning it over in his hand.

"This what you used to kill those whores?" he asked.

"Even if I had killed them with it," said Davies, "you'd never be able to prove it. As I said, I keep my utensils clean and sanitized."

"Why's that?" asked Virgil.

"In case I have to use them. I couldn't very well operate on someone with dirty utensils. That could lead to an infection."

Wyatt sat down the scalpel, picking up the second one and turning it over in his hand. "You're a very thorough man, aren't you?" he asked.

"I try to be," said Davies.

"It's very convenient that your scalpels have been cleaned so thoroughly," said Virgil. "It makes it real hard for us to do our jobs."

"Tell me about this latest murder," said Davies.

Wyatt sneered. "As if you didn't already know."

"Humor me. Let's pretend for a moment I don't know."

"Another prostitute," said Morgan. "Killed in exactly the same way. The girl was sliced up, her abdomen cut open. And like the first girl, she was missing an ear."

Davies grinned devilishly. "What do you suppose the killer is doing with all these ears?"

Wyatt sat down the second scalpel, turned, and walked towards Davies. He got right up in the doctor's face, trying to intimidate him. While this tactic almost always worked with an adversary, Davies was completely unfazed. "Your breath is rather bad, Mr. Earp," he said, further angering Wyatt.

"Tell us about the ears, Davies," Wyatt demanded.

But Davies didn't budge. "I know nothing about any loose ears," he said.

Wyatt shoved him back against the dresser. It had to have hurt Davies, but he didn't show it. He just kept smiling that goofy grin of his, trying like hell to make them angry.

"*Tell me about the ears!*" screamed Wyatt.

"Do you figure there's a bag of ears around somewhere?" asked Davies. "Maybe the killer's made a necklace out of them, and he's wearing it around his neck. Perhaps that's the key to your investigation—simply finding a man wearing a necklace made of ears."

Wyatt reached down and touched the handle of his Schofield Smith and Wesson. "I'm gonna plug this son of a bitch right here and now." Morgan reached out and put his hand over Wyatt's, stopping him. "Let's remember what we're doing here," warned Virgil.

"I'm sorry," said Wyatt. "But this lowly bastard boils my blood."

Davies laughed heartily, as if he'd just heard the funniest joke he'd ever been told.

Wyatt backhanded him. When he did so, Davies' head didn't so much as turn. Blood came trickling down from his nostril, but Davies left it there. When the blood dripped down to his lip, he licked it, but still made no attempt to wipe it away.

"Well," said Virgil. "We're gonna have to search your room."

"For ears?" asked Davies, trying to stifle a snicker.

"Will somebody get him the hell out of here?" asked an irritated Virgil.

Wyatt turned to Morgan. "Escort him outside."

Morgan led Davies outside and closed the door behind them.

Wyatt and Virgil then began tearing the room apart. Virgil went through the dresser drawers, and found a journal. "Would you look at this?" said Virgil.

"What is it?"

"It's a goddamn journal."

Wyatt reached out and snatched the book from his brother's hand, flipping through it. There was nothing inside about Davies killing anyone. However, the entry for the night of Arlene Gates' murder was nothing more than a drawn smiley face.

"What do you make of that?" asked Virgil, looking over his shoulder.

"I don't know. Could be him mocking us."

After reading about Davies' stay in jail, Wyatt came to the entry for the previous night—the night of Mary Beth Shaffer's murder. On this page was scrawled the words "GO TO HELL, MR. EARP!" This statement was accompanied by a second smiley face.

"The bastard is taunting us," said Wyatt.

"That does appear to be the situation," said Virgil.

Wyatt looked at his brother. "You still against forcing Davies to sign that confession?"

Virgil said nothing. He just kept snooping around. He reached under Davies' pillow, his hand sliding over something. He pulled it out.

"Take a look at this," said Virgil.

Wyatt turned and looked at what Virgil had discovered—a Colt .45 revolver.

Wyatt went to the door and asked Morgan to bring the doctor back inside.

"Shut the door," he instructed Davies. Davies did.

"Well," said Davies, still grinning. "Find anything of interest?"

Virgil held up the revolver. "We found this."

Davies laughed again.

"What's so funny?" asked Wyatt.

"Since the murders were committed with a scalpel and not a pistol, that's not going to be a whole lot of help to you," said Davies.

"How do you know the murders were committed with a scalpel and not, say, a straight razor?" asked Morgan.

Davies said, "I'm just going by what you boys have told me. I'm only assuming it was a scalpel."

"What does a doctor need with a pistol?" asked Virgil.

"There a crime against that?" asked Davies. "I'm certain that dentist you go around with, Doc Holliday, has a pistol or two on him right now."

"At least that," said Wyatt.

"What do you need with a gun?" asked Virgil again.

"I need it for protection," said Davies. "After that article ran in the *Epitaph*, could be any number of people out to murder me."

"Now wouldn't that be a damned shame?" said Wyatt.

Davies looked over and saw his journal lying atop the dresser. "I see you found my journal," he said, smiling. "I do hope you had an enjoyable read, Mr. Earp."

It took everything Wyatt had not to kill the stupid bastard, but somehow he maintained his composure.

"So, are you boys gonna arrest me or not?" asked Davies.

"I'm afraid we still have nothing to charge with you," said Virgil.

Morgan looked flustered. "What the hell, Virgil?"

Wyatt was pissed, but said nothing. He just turned red and stormed out of the room.

"It looks like somebody's having a temper tantrum," said Davies.

"There were no murders while you were staying with us in the jail house," said Virgil. "I find that rather convenient. Then you get out, and all of a sudden there's another murder."

Davies kept that smile plastered across his mug. "Just lucky, I guess."

"Two things," said Virgil. "First, I'm gonna post a man downstairs in the lobby of the hotel to monitor your comings and goings. If you leave the building, he's gonna follow you wherever you go. That should keep the murders at bay."

Davies asked, "And second?"

"There's a Wells Fargo stage coming through here in a couple of days," said Virgil. "I want your ass on it. I don't care where the hell you go—you just leave Tombstone and don't ever come back."

Morgan didn't want to stay in the lobby of the Grand Hotel, watching for Davies. He doubted there would be any movement—especially since Virgil had tipped Davies off that he would be posted there. Morgan wanted to be where the action was. He wanted to hang out with his brothers and Doc, or see his wife, Louisa. And he was hungry. But here he was, stuck in this damnable hotel.

A sporting man Morgan barely knew named Manny Whitaker was sitting in the lobby, reading the story about Doctor Death's exploits in the *Epitaph*. He kept looking up at Morgan, obviously wanting to say something.

Finally he did.

"Mr. Earp," he said. "I thought you should know I was playing cards with a man named Tom McLaury this morning."

Morgan had no idea what this had to do with him. "And?"

"McLaury runs with Ike Clanton and his band of cutthroats. I believe you're familiar with them. I heard your brother Wyatt had a run-in with Ike just today."

Morgan said nothing. He just listened to what the man had to say.

"McLaury was good and drunk, and he tells me he and Ike Clanton are gonna murder you and your brothers," Whitaker said. "He told me Curly Bill Brocious was gonna gun down your friend Doc Holliday. He even said they would kill your girlfriends and wives."

Morgan thought of his Louisa and started to become angry. "He say when this was supposed to happen?" he asked.

"No. Nothing specific. He just said it would happen in the next few days. He said everyone would know his and Ike's names before the week was over."

Morgan wanted to go and tell Wyatt and Virgil this news, but he couldn't leave the Grand Hotel.

Morgan asked, "What was your feeling about what he said?"

"What do you mean?"

"Did he sound like he meant it?"

"Oh yeah," Whitaker said. "He took out his Army Colt and sat it on the table. He told me, 'This is the gun that's gonna kill Wyatt Earp.' He definitely meant what he was saying." Whitaker paused for a moment. "Now whether or not he and his cowboys actually have the skills or the *cojones* to pull off such a thing is a completely different matter altogether."

Morgan just nodded.

"I don't know McLaury," said Morgan. "What's your impression of him?"

"Of McLaury? The man's a blowhard who likes hearing his own voice. Now having said that, I still believe he was serious about what he was saying. I really think he and Ike Clanton and that other no-good sumbitch Curly Bill Brocious mean to do you and your family harm."

Nine: Danger Strikes Close to Home

Wyatt, Virgil, and Doc were sitting at a table in the Oriental, drinking whiskey and talking things out. Big Nosed Kate was off doing her thing, and the smoke-filled saloon was doing big business. Tonight there were no members of Ike Clanton's crew to stir up any trouble, and old Doctor Death was sealed up there in his room over at the Grand Hotel with Morgan sitting watch.

Tonight it felt like everything was back to normal.

Hell, even Wyatt's gut was telling him everything was alright.

"It's quiet tonight," said Doc. "You can almost hear the crickets chirping."

"Thank god," said Virgil. "I'm about ready for a night of peace and quiet around here. I don't know how long it'll last, but I'm enjoying it for the moment."

Wyatt said, "I'll drink to that." He raised his glass and Doc and Virgil raised theirs. "To peace and quiet," said Doc.

"To peace and quiet," repeated Wyatt.

"I don't think it's gonna stay this way for too long," said Virgil. "I hear there's a fella named McLaury that's been in town talking shit today."

Wyatt squinted, trying to place the name. "McLaury?"

"He's another one of Ike Clanton's gun thugs. He's been going around doing what Ike's gang does best—run his mouth. He's apparently been telling people he and Ike and some others are gonna gun us down sometime in the next few days."

"Won't that be lovely," said Doc. "I always wanted a fall funeral."

"Maybe you'll get it," said Virgil. "McLaury's telling people Curly Bill is gonna shoot you down in the street."

Doc snickered. "Curly Bill couldn't outdraw a man with no arms. He's no threat."

"But cowboys like those don't play fair," observed Wyatt. "They don't believe in a fair fight. You fight with one of 'em, you're liable to get shot in the back by any number of other cowboys from their crew. They're some real miserable sons of bitches. They like to fight when it's five on one."

"I'm pretty sure I could get five of 'em on the draw," said Doc.

"I believe you could," said Wyatt. "I've seen you do it. But just to be careful, I think we should travel in numbers for the next few days. Let's not give those limp dick bastards the chance to get the jump on us."

"What about Morgan?" asked Doc. "He's over there at the Grand all by his lonesome."

"I know," said Virgil, "but there was no other way. I needed someone sitting over there watching Davies."

"Davies is a whole other problem," said Wyatt. "When news of Mary Beth Shaffer's murder shows up in the newspaper tomorrow, there's liable to be a whole 'nother riot."

"That's the last goddamn thing we need right now," said Virgil.

"I'll drink to that," said Doc, raising his glass.

"You'd drink to your own death, Doc," said Wyatt, grinning.

Doc smiled. "And I shall drink to that, as well, Wyatt Earp."

"Let's just hope that stagecoach comes and takes Davies out of town before vigilantes go after him again or we wind up with another dead whore on our hands," said Virgil.

"He's a talented man if he manages to kill someone else while he's being tailed by Morgan," said Doc. "If that happens, I guess we'll have to assume the man was telling the truth the whole time—that he really is innocent."

"If Eldrich Davies is innocent," Wyatt said, "then I'll be a horse's ass."

Doc laughed. "I hate to be the one to tell you this, Wyatt, but you're already a horse's ass!"

Wyatt laughed. "You got me there, Doc."

Their moment of fun was briefly interrupted when a prospector named Coates and a card shark named Handsome Harry Dempkins got into a dispute over a hand of cards. Coates stood and put his hand on his pistol, threatening to pull on Harry. Harry just laughed and kept drinking his drink, but Wyatt knew Harry had his own pistol under the table.

Wyatt approached them with his hands out in front of him. "Let's just calm down, fellas," he said. "There's no reason for anyone to die here tonight. We've all had a few drinks and I'm sure words have been exchanged. Let's let cooler heads prevail here and sit down and have another drink. Tell you what: the next round is on me, Coates."

"But he cheated me," said Coates. "This bastard here cheated me. He palmed an extra ace."

"You saw him do it?" asked Wyatt.

"No, but no man in the history of this earth has ever been so lucky as this cocksucker."

"Then why keep playing?" asked Wyatt. "Why not call it a learning experience and just walk away?"

"I done lost twenty bucks to this piece of shit."

"What if I told you I'd set you up with another twenty bucks in credit?" asked Wyatt. "Would that calm your heels? Hell, I'll even throw in a piece of pussy for free."

And that was that. Coates saw the error of his ways, even if he did still believe Handsome Harry had duped him, and he went upstairs to have sex with one of the whores. After all, he said, it was a "freebie," so why not?

After Coates had made his way upstairs, Wyatt approached Handsome Harry. "Harry," he said, "at least try to make it look right. Hell, I could see you palming cards from across the room."

Harry laughed, and Wyatt returned to his table.

"Aren't you the diplomat?" observed Doc. "And you did it without bashing a man over the head. Why, I'm right proud of you, Wyatt. It looks as if you just might be maturing after all."

Wyatt and Virgil laughed at this.

"I still say we should force Eldrich Davies to sign that confession," said Wyatt. "You and I both know we'd all feel a whole lot better if that man was swinging up there on the gallows. And for a few bucks, Judge Spicer would look the other way in the name of justice."

"Your stance on the subject is duly noted," said Virgil. "I'm just ready to get Davies out of town and let him be somebody else's problem."

Wyatt wanted to argue his point further, but he saw Joe Rucker come rushing in through the front door of the saloon. Joe looked around, stopped and talked to someone, and they pointed over at Wyatt's table.

"It looks like we're about to have company," said Doc.

Wyatt nodded. "There goes our peace and quiet."

Joe Rucker made his way through the place, eventually finding his way to their table. He was out of breath and he looked anxious.

"What is it, Joe?" asked Virgil.

"You fellas are needed," said Joe.

Doc asked, "What seems to be the emergency, Joe Rucker?"

"There's been another murder," he answered, looking at Wyatt. "And the killer almost got your friend—the Jewish girl."

Wyatt was on his feet before Joe Rucker could finish his sentence.

The dead whore's name was Emma Bolinger. She was nineteen-years-old, and just like the other girls, her throat and abdomen had been slashed. This time, however, the killer had left his victim with both ears intact.

Wyatt, Virgil, and Doc interviewed the first witness, Chance Tucker, to ascertain what had transpired in that alleyway behind the Bird Cage Theatre. According to Tucker, he'd been walking past the mouth of the alley at Sixth Street when he'd heard a woman's screams.

"I yelled out and asked if they were alright," explained Tucker. "At first there was nothing at all, and then the Jewish girl from the theatre came running down the alley, screaming her head off. She said the killer had pushed her down behind the Bird Cage as he ran past."

"But you didn't see him?" asked Virgil.

"No, sir," said Tucker. "Well, I think I saw him moving down the alley behind the Jewish girl. He was really booking it. I think the Jewish girl must have scared the bejeezus out of him once she started screaming."

"But you couldn't make out who he was?" asked Wyatt.

"No, sir," said Tucker. "He was too far away, and really nothing more than a blurry movement in the shadows behind the girl. And at the time, she was running towards me and screaming. I didn't know what in Sam Hades was happening. It all went so fast, and the Jewish girl was crying and really shaken up by the whole thing."

"The Jewish girl," said Wyatt. "Do you know where she is now?"

"Yeah, one of the other dancers came outside and held her for a few minutes. Then they went back inside the Bird Cage. She said to have you go in there and talk to her when you showed up."

"Thanks, Tucker," said Virgil. "We really appreciate your help."

Wyatt, Virgil, and Doc walked over to look at the body under the light of Doc Goodfellow's lantern.

"Doc and I'll stay out here with Doc Goodfellow," said Virgil. "You go on inside and comfort Josephine and find out what she saw."

"I'm obliged to you for that," said Wyatt, and he turned to enter the theatre through the back door. When he walked inside the dark building, he made his way up a flight of stairs and found himself inside a well-lit dressing room. When one of the dancers saw him enter, she pointed him towards Josephine, who was sitting and talking with her friend Nora.

When she saw Wyatt, Josephine wiped away her tears and tried to be strong for him.

"Sadie," Wyatt said, now taking her in his arms.

She started to weep again.

"What happened?" asked Wyatt.

Josephine pulled back to look at him, tears in her eyes. "I went out to the alley to have a smoke. When I got down there, I saw a man cutting open a woman's stomach. I startled him when the door opened, lighting the alley. He must have let his hand go from her mouth, because she let out a loud scream. The man bolted towards me. He pushed me down and took off running down the alley."

"Then what?" asked Wyatt.

She started to sob harder now. "I took off running in the opposite direction towards a man asking if everything was alright. It turned out it was that man outside, that Tucker fella."

"Everything is alright now," said Wyatt, pulling her towards him. But she pulled away, looking him in his eyes again.

"Wyatt," she said. "I saw him."

"You saw his face?" asked Wyatt, his mouth agape.

"Yes," she said. "It was that man from the newspaper."

"Eldrich Davies?"

"Yeah, that's him," she said. "Doctor Death."

Wyatt asked, "Are you sure?"

"Yes, I'm quite sure. I'll see his face in my nightmares."

Wyatt pushed himself back. "Sadie, I've got to go. Virgil and I have to go and put that bastard behind bars so he can swing for he done."

And Wyatt was gone.

Wyatt, Virgil, and Doc ran towards the Grand Hotel as quickly as they could. When they finally got there, they all rushed into the front door of the establishment. They found Morgan sitting there just inside the door, watching the stairs. There was no one else in the lobby.

"There's been another murder," said Virgil.

"The son of a bitch hurt Josephine," said Wyatt. "Why did you let him go?"

There was an expression of shock on Morgan's face. "He never left here. I been here all night, and I haven't seen Davies once."

Wyatt spun around and took off up the stairs towards Davies' room. When he got there, he knocked. Getting no answer, he stepped back and ran towards the door, breaking it open.

The room was empty, and the window was open.

Davies was gone.

Ten: Davies on the Run

The Earp brothers and Doc Holliday walked out of the Grand Hotel with no idea where the hell the killer was. At first they considered each of them going his separate way in search of Davies, but then it was decided that they should split up into two groups. Virgil and Morgan went one way, and Wyatt and Doc went the other.

Wyatt and Doc walked slowly through the darkened streets of Tombstone. There wasn't much going on out here. The wind was kicking up dust, and there were a few people, mostly on foot, passing to and fro in the darkness.

Wyatt and Doc stopped around at establishments like the Alhambra and the Hafford, asking patrons if they had seen Dr. Davies. No one had. Wyatt and Doc slowly made their way towards the Cochise County Courthouse, walking up Fourth Street, and checking in every nook and cranny they came to.

They had just passed Spangenberg's Cosmopolitan Hotel when they spotted a figure walking along the building fronts, sporting a bowler hat like Davies'. They both pulled out their pistols, approaching slowly from behind. When they were about twenty feet behind the man, Wyatt yelled out, "Davies!" The man turned around, and even in the darkness they could see it was him.

Davies took off running in the direction of the courthouse.

As they ran, Wyatt kept thinking, *This son of a bitch hurt my Sadie.* This recurring thought made him angrier and angrier, spurring him to run even when he was out of breath. For a man who looked as weak as Davies did, he did an impressive job running from them without pause. Even more impressive was Doc, who suffered from consumption, running nonstop after the man they called Doctor Death.

Wyatt considered firing at Davies, but thought the better of it. He wanted the chance to beat the living hell out of him before watching him swing up on that gallows.

But Davies turned and opened fire on them. His shot struck something to Wyatt's right and careened off down the street.

Wyatt, still running, fired off a couple of volleys, but Davies just kept running. Finally Doc stopped. "I'm tired of all this goddamn running," he said, raising both arms and firing his Colt Thunderer and his Colt Lightning simultaneously. Doc only fired twice, but Davies went down hard, dropping his medical bag.

As they approached Davies, Wyatt yelled out, "Drop the gun or else we'll kill you right here and now!" Davies tossed the pistol away from him into the street. Out of breath, Davies managed, "I'm unarmed."

Wyatt walked towards him and started kicking the hell out of him.

As he did so, he said, "Eldrich Davies, you are under arrest for the murders of those three whores." And he just kept on kicking Davies until finally Doc stopped him. "Save something for the gallows, Wyatt," said Doc.

Dr. Eldrich Davies was sitting in his cell at the jail house, recovering from a wound in his right leg, three broken ribs, and a bruised and battered face. Doc Goodfellow had already been in to remove the bullet, and Wyatt had allowed Doc Goodfellow the opportunity to punch Davies in the face once.

"Damn, that felt good," the old man had said. "I think I busted my hand pretty good, but it was completely worth it."

Now Doc Goodfellow was gone, and Wyatt was standing over Davies outside the bars.

Wyatt was trembling with anger.

"You and I are gonna have us one hell of a good time tonight," said Wyatt. He unlocked the cell and ordered Morgan to pull Davies out. Morgan went into the cell and grabbed Davies, throwing him hard to the floor. He then reached down and dragged him out towards Virgil's chair.

"Sit his ass up in that chair," said Wyatt.

Morgan helped Davies stand, and then sat him back in the chair.

"You aren't gonna break my new chair are you?" asked Virgil.

Wyatt grinned. "We can always get you a new chair, Virg. Hell, I'll get you two."

Morgan shackled the injured prisoner to the chair so he could not try to escape, not that Davies could have tried even if he'd wanted to. Once Davies was attached to the chair, Wyatt took off his belt. He turned to Virgil. "Lock the door, Virg."

Wyatt swung the leather strap high in the air and brought it down hard against Davies' body, lashing him with it. He did this several times, even managing to whip the belt across Davies' face a couple times for good measure.

"That woman you pushed down in the alley?" Wyatt said. "That was my friend. That was my Sadie..." His voice trailed off before his anger reanimated him. *"That was my goddamn Sadie!"*

Davies had been beaten so long and so hard he didn't even put up a fight.

He didn't even ask what exactly he'd been arrested for.

In fact, all he did was bleed.

And hurt.

Now it was Morgan's turn. Morgan bit off the end of a nice, fat cigar, and lit it, puffing it hard as he did. Once he had a good burn going, he pressed the lit cigar against Davies' neck. The cigar made a sickening sizzling sound as it burned its way into Davies' soft flesh, sinking in like a knife in hot butter. Davies cried out in agony. Then Morgan puffed on the cigar a few more times, took it out of his mouth and blew softly on its burning embers. Davies just sat there with his head down, whimpering. Then Morgan took Davies' right hand—the one that would have cut those whores—and burned the cigar into its meat. Davies screamed out again.

Now it was Virgil's turn.

"You could have made all this much easier on yourself," said Virgil. "You could have just confessed and it would have been over. But no, you had to go and kill two more whores. You just had to do it. And you had to mock us. You know how that makes us feel, Eldrich?" He paused. "Can I call you Eldrich?"

Davies tried to look up through bloodied, slitted eyes, but said nothing.

"You made us look bad," said Virgil. "And that I cannot abide. That and killing them whores."

Virgil took out his Colt .45 and whipped Davies with it.

Then he did it again, two of Davies' teeth flying from his mouth as he did so.

Now it was Wyatt's turn again...

Eleven: Justice

Judge Wells Spicer oversaw the proceedings at the Cochise County Courthouse.

"I understand there is a signed confession," said Spicer. "Is that correct?"

"That is correct," said Wyatt.

Eldrich Davies, representing himself because no one else would take his case, attempted to speak out about the nature of his confession, but Spicer told him to shut the fuck up until he was spoken to.

Spicer read Davies' confession out loud before the court. "I, Dr. Eldrich Davies, being of sound mind and body, do hereby confess to having brutally murdered the three whores, Arlene Gates, Mary Beth Shaffer, and Emma Bolinger. I did so because I am a scurrilous son of a bitch who does not believe in god…" Judge Spicer stopped reading and looked up at the Earps, knowing full well the nature of Davies' confession, but said nothing. He then continued reading, "I, Dr. Eldrich Davies, do hereby throw myself on the mercy of the court."

Spicer then called Josephine Marcus up to the stand for good measure. He had her swear in over the good book. She then testified as to what she had seen in the alleyway that night behind the Bird Cage Theatre.

Almost the exact moment Josephine had finished her testimony, the courthouse erupted with chants of "string him up!" In what would be the shortest murder trial of Judge Wells Spicer's career, it took him a mere twelve minutes to read and listen to the testimony and ultimately pass judgment on Davies.

"Dr. Eldrich Davies," Spicer said, "I hereby sentence you to be hung by the neck until you are dead. May god have mercy on your heathen soul."

Perhaps Davies still wanted to speak and have his proverbial day in court, but no one will ever know because someone threw a large rock and struck him in the head, rendering him unconscious.

The perpetrator who threw the rock was never found.

The gallows were constructed in quick time in a lot out by the miner's cabins off Tough Nut Street. When the day of the big event came, more than six hundred people showed up to witness Davies' impending death. The large crowd consisted not only of Tombstone residents, but also those of nearby towns such as San Simon, Charleston, and Galeyville.

Vendors sold sweet confections and beverages there, and both the *Epitaph* and the *Nugget* would later report that a good time was had by all who attended. Throughout the hour leading up to the hanging, chants of "string him up" and "Doctor Death" would alternate, with entire families getting in on the act.

The Earps and their families were all in attendance. Wyatt had instructed Josephine not to attend as he said executions were no place for a woman. But really he just did this because he was bringing his common law wife Mattie with him. (Mattie had insisted on going, and there was nothing Wyatt could do to stop her.)

Virgil Earp escorted Dr. Eldrich Davies out onto the scaffold at approximately six a.m. "Dr. Eldrich Davies," he said, "Do you have any last words before you depart this world?"

"There is only one thing I would like to say," said Davies. A hush fell over the crowd momentarily as everyone waited to see what this terrible man had to say. And this is what he said: *"Fuck you all!"*

The crowd went crazy, and the roaring chants of "string him up" became deafening. A gunny sack was placed over Davies' head, the rope was tightened around his neck, and he was left to stand there awaiting his death for what must have seemed like an eternity. Now the crowd was quiet again. When Virgil finally pulled the lever, dropping the kicking man from the gallows, everyone in the crowd began to cheer again.

Everyone watched as Davies' kicking started to slow.

And finally he kicked no more.

At this, Mayor John Clum stepped up onto the scaffold and announced, "Today justice has been served!"

And the crowd went wild.

Twelve: The Aftermath

The very next morning, Wyatt came to Josephine's hotel room. His knocking awoke her from her slumber. She arose and answered the door, pleased to find her man standing before her.

"Sadie," he said, "I have important business to attend to. It's likely to be extremely dangerous. Some very bad men who want my brothers and me dead are waiting for us down at the O.K. Corral. There may be gunplay. I hope not, but we're prepared for the worst."

"Will Doc be with you?" she asked.

"Yes," said Wyatt.

"Good," she said. "Tell him I said to keep you safe."

"I have to go now. Stay here in your room and you should be safe. If anyone comes knocking, don't answer the door, no matter who it is. Do you understand?"

"Yes," she said. "Wyatt, I'm frightened."

He took her in his arms and he kissed her like there would be no tomorrow. He then pulled back and said, "I'll take care of you, Sadie."

"You promise you'll be back?"

He hesitated, unsure as to whether or not he would live through the day, but he said, "I promise, Sadie. I promise I'll be back." He kissed her hard, turned, and walked out through the door.

He turned one last time. "Be sure and lock the door," he said.

She blew a kiss to him. "Be safe, my love," she said.

And Wyatt was gone.

Josephine locked the door. She hoped and prayed her man would be safe from those ruffians who wished to hurt him.

She moved towards her dresser and pulled the drawer open. She then moved her undergarments aside. She reached in and grabbed the straight razor which had once belonged to her former beau Johnny Behan, along with the tiny satin pouch. She raised it in the hand which held the razor, and pulled at the pouch's drawstrings to open it. She looked inside at the two dried and bloodied ears it held, and vowed to get rid of them while Wyatt was handling his business at the O.K. Corral. Yes, she thought, she would feed the ears to the hogs just down the street.

Now everything would be alright, she thought.

She and Wyatt would be happy together, and all her troubles would be behind her. She hadn't felt the feeling—that sickening, overpowering urge to kill—since she'd resided in San Francisco a few years prior. There she had taken the lives of two whores, but she hadn't gotten fancy with it. She was still learning. Because there was nothing special about the two murders—their throats had been slashed, and that was it—no one had ever connected them as being the work of the same person. And she had walked away from those murders scot-free, vowing never to do such a heinous thing again.

But then she had come to Tombstone, and those old familiar urges came to her once again. She knew it was wrong, but when she took a life, she felt stronger than any woman had ever felt before. She felt immortal. She was fearless. In a funny way, she now believed the murders had been the cause of the outspoken, free-spirited demeanor she now carried with her. These were the very qualities which had caused Wyatt Earp to fall in love with her, so it couldn't be all that bad, could it?

He was her Wyatt, and she was his Sadie.

Together they would take on the world.

Together they would be happy.

Together they were one.

THE END?

THE NIGHT OL' DIRTY BASTARD
CAME TO HOBOKEN

Fair warning: The following story is a bit of an "inside baseball"-type story in that it requires some knowledge of Ol' Dirty Bastard and hip-hop music to fully appreciate it and to understand the references. It was written for an anthology of short stories based on or inspired by the Wu-Tang Clan, where it had an audience fully versed on the subject. This is not to say you won't enjoy the story without this knowledge, but the experience would certainly be enhanced if one possessed it.
I knew this story would not be for everyone, so it is presented here as a bonus story. If it's not for you, just close the book now (or skip to the story notes). You've gotten your money's worth without it.

Kevin was pretty sure his life was over. He was as miserable as a man could ever be. He couldn't bear to stare down another day of depression and failure. It had all become too much. So here he was, sitting in the middle of the night on the side of a train bridge, his feet dangling down from up high. He'd been drinking Hennessey all evening, and he was pretty sure he was going to jump off this goddamn bridge and put an end to all his suffering.

There was nothing left to live for.

That he was wanting to off himself was no surprise to himself, and probably wouldn't have been much of a surprise to anyone who knew him.

Hell, he'd already tried once.

A long time ago. When he was in high school. Kevin had driven his mother's old Station Wagon out to an isolated country road where there was no one there to see him end, or at least attempt to end, his crappy life. He started this little adventure by stretching a hose from the vehicle's exhaust pipe into the driver's side window. Then he sat there, listening to Kurt Cobain muttering to melancholy music, as the exhaust filled the car.

Finally, he started to cough and sputter, but death wasn't coming quickly enough, so Kevin tried a different approach. He got out of the car, feeling woozy as all hell, and wound up lying on the ground, sucking on the end of that hose. Now death would come with more urgency, he figured. What he didn't figure on, however, was the cop who was patrolling these back roads and had come upon him lying there, nearly unconscious, the hose dangling from his mouth like a near-spent cigar.

"What the hell you doing, boy?" asked the cop, shaking him.

Kevin was loopy and hadn't known what to say. The police officer then assisted him into the backseat of his car and took him on a little trip down to the cop shop. Kevin's father was called, and he had come down to the station to pick up his son. Kevin had been as embarrassed as he had ever been—perhaps even more embarrassed than the time his mother had walked in on his masturbating to the bras in a JC Penney catalog—and the conversation that had followed was a tough one. His father asked him why he would want to die, and Kevin had thrown the pity party for himself and informed him that he really had no friends to speak of. That he was bullied. That he hated life. This led to his father weeping in the car, and Kevin vowed to himself that he would never hurt his family this way again.

No more suicide attempts.

And yet here he was now, some twenty years after the fact, contemplating a swan dive off this bridge. Maybe, just maybe, he thought, a train would come along and save him the effort.

Kevin took another swig of the Henny, and he wept.

Kevin was not a religious man—he'd been raised the son of agnostics—but he now felt a prayer welling up from within his chest. "God," he managed. "Are you there?" Kevin looked up at the sky, but there was no response—not a plane or a bird or even a cloud.

Nothing.

And again he asked, "Are you there, God?" But God said nothing. "I need your help if you're out there," he said, warm tears now cascading down his cheeks. "I need you to show me if there's a better way."

But God remained silent.

Shit, Kevin thought. It was the same old thing—he wasn't going to receive any help or answers from the universe. And thus he concluded that there was no God. And to this, God replied, nothing.

Dammit.

So here he was, half-assedly drunk, sitting on the edge of this bridge, leaning more and more toward jumping to his death.

Again, he wept.

And then he heard a voice come from behind. A low, crazed voice, whose cadence carried a musicality unlike anything he'd ever heard.

"Kevin?"

Kevin turned and saw a black man standing there behind him. The man had crazy jingle-jangle hair sticking up from his head like rays of sunshine in a child's crayon drawing. He was clad in a hoodie, baggy jeans, and Timberland boots.

The man took a step forward, and Kevin almost fell from his perch. He steadied himself.

"Who are you?"

Now Kevin saw the Wu-Wear logo on the man's shirt and the unlikely pieces began to shift into place. Kevin knew who this man was.

"Are you Ol' Dirty Bastard?"

The man grinned, moonlight catching his gold teeth.

"You are, aren't you?"

The man nodded.

"But...you're...*dead.*"

"You believe in miracles, Kevin?"

"No."

"Can I sit down?" .

Kevin nodded towards the spot beside him and said, "Sure."

Dirty sat down, dangling his Tims over the side of the bridge. "Can I have some of that Henny?"

Kevin handed him the bottle, and Dirty took a healthy swig.

"Where are we?" asked Dirty. "Hoboken?"

"Yeah."

"I don't fuck with New Jersey."

"Why's that?"

"The women, son. The women here are crazy. I used to date a girl from Jersey. She had a big ol' fat butt. Body was slammin', but she was—"

"Crazy?"

"Right," Dirty said, nodding. "The girl was bonkers. You know, she tried to shoot my ass once. Threatened to shoot my balls off. Can you believe that?"

"Women are crazy."

"Exactly. You can't trust 'em."

Kevin agreed, thinking of his ex-wife.

"You can't get caught up in the power-u."

"Power-u?"

"The pussy, son," said Dirty. "You can't get caught up in all that. You can't even worry about that."

Kevin nodded, but said nothing.

Dirty grinned, his gold fronts glinting in the moonlight once again. "You already did, didn't you?"

"What?"

"Get caught up worryin' about pussy."

Kevin nodded. "Yeah, I guess I did."

"You know what they say about fishes in the sea..."

"No," Kevin said. "What do they say?"

"Damned if I know, but they say somethin'. I remember that much. Somethin' about the little fishies in the sea..."

Kevin just stared at him.

"So what's your problem, son?"

Kevin said, "I wanna die."

"Trust me, life is good. I miss that shit every day."

"So you're what? A ghost?"

"Yup," said Dirty. "I'm a motherfuckin' ghost, man."

Kevin was just drunk enough that this made sense to him. "So why are you here?"

"To talk some sense into you."

"How exactly does all this work?"

"What do you mean?"

"I prayed to God, but instead of God, I get the ghost of Ol' Dirty Bastard?"

Dirty grinned. "I'm a lot like God."

"How you figure?"

"Cause I'm the Big Baby Jesus, son."

Dirty took another swig.

"You know what this party needs?" asked Dirty.

Kevin said he didn't.

Dirty reached into his pocket and produced a Ziploc bag half filled with weed. "You wanna get high?"

Kevin laughed. "You serious?"

"Hell, yeah, I'm serious. I never joke about weed. We gonna smoke us a motherfuckin' blunt."

"You got one rolled?"

"Nah, but it ain't nuthin' but a thang. I'll roll us up a fat one. You just tell me what seems to be the problem, uh... What was your name?"

"Kevin."

"Right. I'm shitty with names, son."

"Now what?" asked Kevin.

"Tell me about your problems."

"Well, first my dad died this past year. That was real hard on me."

"I know," said Dirty.

Kevin's eyes narrowed. *"You do?"*

"Hell, yeah, I play cards with that motherfucker. And I'll tell you this much, he cheats."

Kevin's eyes got big. "You do? He does?"

"Hell yeah," said Dirty. "And you know what? That nigga still owe me $22!"

Kevin laughed. He didn't know what to say. Then, finally, he came up with something. "He ever mention me?"

"Sometimes."

"Oh yeah?"

"Yeah, we talk about our kids sometimes."

"What does he say?"

"Well, he's worried about your ass."

"He is?"

"Sure. Who do you think sent me here?"

Kevin nodded. "So why didn't he just come himself?"

To this, Dirty said, "Rules, man. They got rules up in Heaven. Your daddy couldn't come, so he sent me."

"My father sent Ol' Dirty Bastard to save my life?"

"Exactly." Dirty paused, paying extra attention to the spliff he was rolling. "I got cherry papers. I hope that's cool."

Kevin grinned. "Sounds good to me. This is my favorite kinda weed."

Dirty looked at him, his mouth hanging open. "What kind is that?"

"The free kind."

Dirty chuckled. "No doubt. You're right. Free weed is the best weed."

"You miss being alive?"

"Man, I miss the women on earth."

"Aren't there women in Heaven?"

"Not the kind I like."

"What kind is that?"

Dirty grinned a big, silly grin. "Hoes, mufucka. *I like hoes!*"

"Hoes don't go to Heaven?"

"They do," said Dirty, "but they change their ways. They be actin' all uppity, like they got sticks up their asses."

"Oh yeah?" asked Kevin. "Is there sex in Heaven?"

"There is, but it's boring missionary sex."

"What kinda sex do you like?"

"Man, I miss doggie style. *A lot.*"

Kevin smiled, then taking a swig.

"So what else is wrong?" asked Dirty.

"My wife left me."

Dirty nodded. "Yeah, I heard about that. She left you for some big-shot real estate agent."

"Right," Kevin said, hanging his head.

Dirty turned towards him, leaning in, getting right up in Kevin's face. "You wanna know something? That dude's gay."

"Who?"

"The guy your wife is with."

Kevin's eyes got big. "No shit?"

"No shit, son," said Dirty. "Dude's straight up gay."

"Will they stay together?"

"I don't know that, I ain't no magic eight ball. But I know he's gay."

"How gay we talkin'?"

"Liberace gay."

"That's pretty goddamn gay."

Dirty nodded.

"That actually makes me feel a lot better," said Kevin.

"I figured it would. You know what you need to do now?"

"What?"

"Get you some ass, son."

"But I thought you said pussy—"

"The *power-u*," Dirty interrupted.

"Right," said Kevin. "The power-u. I thought you said I shouldn't mess with that."

"Nah, man, you totally gotta mess with that."

"I do?"

"Yeah, but you don't wanna get tangled up in that drama. You just tap that shit and go."

"Just like that?"

Dirty nodded. "Easy-peezy Japa-fuckin'-esey."

"Huh."

"What other problems you got?"

"I'm in debt."

Dirty laughed at this.

"What?" asked Kevin.

"Everybody's in debt, nigga. That's how it works."

"I'll bet you weren't in debt."

Dirty's expression turned serious. "Then you'd bet wrong."

"But you were rich."

"You know how much child support I paid?"

"How much?"

"I got thirteen kids, man." Dirty held up the neatly-rolled blunt. "You wanna smoke this or what?"

"Hell yeah, I wanna smoke that."

"Let's do it then."

Dirty produced a Zippo lighter with a naked woman on its side. He put the blunt to his lips and lit it, inhaling deeply. Then, in a raspy voice, he said, "That shit is good, son." He passed the blunt to Kevin, who held it up and took a drag.

"So what else is troublin' you?" asked Dirty.

"I spent the last seven years working on a novel, and apparently it sucks. It's been rejected by a whole slew of publishers."

"What's it about?"

Kevin hesistated.

"What?"

"It's titled *Honkyland*."

Dirty looked at him like he was crazy. "*Honkyland?*"

"Yeah, so what?"

"Don't nobody use that word no more—*honky*. Only old men say shit like that... Them cats from the seventies who was all militant and shit. Other than them, honky is as dead as I am."

"Nobody?"

"Nope."

"Huh," said Kevin.

"So what's your novel about?" asked Dirty.

"It's about a white kid who goes to an all-black college. It's about the trials and tribulations he faces because he's different."

"Goddammit, man," growled Dirty.

"What?"

"Niggas can't have anything. We can't even have all-black universities without white kids thinking they're entitled to go there."

Kevin thought about it. "So you think it's a bad idea?"

"Hell yeah, it's a bad idea." Dirty sat there for a moment. "Is this the first book you've written?"

Kevin said it was.

"Sometimes it takes a few times to get something right. Look at RZA... He had a record deal with Tommy Boy under the name Prince Rakeem before we started the Wu. And that shit bombed. But RZA didn't quit. He went back into the lab and went to work on some new shit. The same thing with GZA. He had an album called *Words from the Genius* on Cold Chillin' Records."

"Before Wu-Tang Clan?"

"Yeah, and again, it didn't sell. But he didn't give up. He went right back to work and came up with some new shit. And look at him today..." Dirty turned and looked at Kevin. "You still wanna kill yourself?"

"Well," Kevin said. "I do feel better."

"That's the weed."

"Nah, I think it was all the stuff you said."

Dirty nodded, taking another drag. "Cool, cool."

"Tell my dad thank you."

"I'll do that shit," said Dirty.

They took turns passing the spliff back and forth, blowing thick clouds of smoke into the cool night air.

"I got a question that's totally off the subject," said Kevin.

"Yeah?"

"What contemporary rappers do you like?"

"Only the ones who were around when I was alive. Dudes like Jay-Z, Nas, Masta Ace, Sadat X, Everlast..."

"What do you think of these new cats?"

Dirty contemplated this as he took another drag from the spliff. "They all garbage, man. Every last one of 'em."

"Really?"

Dirty looked at him. "You like 'em?"

"Not really," admitted Kevin.

"They wear skinny jeans." Dirty paused and looked out at the night. "They look like girls, man. It's like that song, "Dude Looks Like a Lady." Every last one of them niggas look like girls. If I'd have ever worn those skinny jeans, I'd have whipped my own ass."

Kevin took the spliff. "Cool," he said. He took a drag. When he looked over where Dirty had been, he saw that he'd vanished.

"Dirty?"

But Dirty was gone—presumably back playing cards with Kevin's dead dad.

Kevin caught the first glimmers of the sun rising in the East.

Today was a new day.

Today would be a good day.

Kevin was going to live.

STORY NOTES

These are the notes for the stories in this collection, presented in the order in which they appear. Some people like myself really enjoy learning about the backgrounds of stories and how they came to exist, but others don't give a rat's ass about that type of thing. If you are of the "don't give a rat's ass" persuasion, do us both a favor and skip this section because you will find no joy here.

If you do choose to read these notes, however, please don't read them until after you've read the stories. There are spoilers here that will fuck up a good story, so avoid them at all costs until you've finished the original pieces.

The Dinner Guests

People ask writers where they get their ideas from, and this is the clearest example of a story that emerged from absolutely nothing. I have zero idea what inspired it. I was just sitting one day, staring at the blank screen on my laptop, and then I started typing. What eventually emerged was this silly little ditty. Even though this is one of two short stories I wrote about cannibalism in 2018, it's not a favorite topic or anything. (I personally only eat human flesh during Lent. I realize that's not how Lent is supposed to work, but I'm an atheist so I don't care. Yum, yum, yum!) It just happened that way. That's how writing works; you can't really plan it, it just happens.

She Had a Good Heart

This is, in many ways, the most personal thing I've ever written. I myself had a heart transplant on April 11, 2018. That is a day that I'll always remember. A lot of the experiences and feelings regarding the transplant that the girl in the story feels were/are my own. Other than her being a woman, our experiences are pretty much the same, save for the crazy ending. No one killed me, or, if they did, no one has bothered to tell me.

A lot of people I knew were interested in this story simply because it dealt with my transplant. After reading it, many of them would say things like "I didn't expect that kind of weird ending to an otherwise beautiful story." I wanted to say, "Have you not read any of my other stories? Do you not know what kind of shit I write?" (Hence the title of this book.)

Charles Bukowski's Command Performance

In 2015, I spent a few weeks in a coma. My wife had recently divorced me, I was facing a heart transplant, and my life was nothing but overwhelming, crippling depression. I was also battling the worst case of writer's block one can imagine. Things were pretty bad. This was the first story I wrote after after going through a lot of that. (I was still going through some of it, but I was at least able to put pen to paper, so to speak.) By nature I'm a pulp writer, and proud of it, but there are a few literary lines here and there in this story that I'm fond of. This was my attempt to be a more "serious" writer. But, as my stories always do, it found its way back into the dark places where most of my work winds up. (You will notice that death rears its head in one form or another in just about everything I write. A dime store Freud might suggest I have a fixation on death, which I won't deny, but the truth of the matter really is simply that I'm a bit of a morbid fucker at heart and that I find dark tales much more fun to write.)

As the story is about a would-be author summoning a demon to assist him with his writing, that same dime store Freud might suggest that this story was me somehow trying to conjure up some sort of muse to assist me. I think that guy would be completely full of shit, but who knows? I believe most of the time a cigar really is just a cigar, but then I did have a sled named Rosebud, so make of that what you will.

An observant reader will also note the frequency with which I write about real-life people or preexisting characters in my stories. Hell, I once wrote a comic novel about Elvis Presley as a government assassin. I enjoy imagining real people in very different situations. I had always been fascinated by Charles Bukowski the writer in much the same way I've always been fascinated with Hunter S. Thompson, but unlike Thompson, whose writing I absolutely adore, I must confess that I've never read a word of Bukowski's writing. I've had a copy of *Reach for the Sun* that I bought from a bargain bin sitting here for years, but I've never so much as cracked the covers. The truth is, I probably won't read it. Nothing against Bukowski, but his writing doesn't really interest me as much as he himself does.

Rachel in the Moonlight

I wrote this back in 2013. I read a call for submissions for an erotica anthology someone was compiling focusing on sex toys. According to the call, the stories could be about any type of sex toy and the story could go in just about any direction. Sure, I thought. I could do that. So I went about trying to decide which sex toy to write about. We all know that editor likely received several sacks worth of stories about the obvious sex toys like vibrators, butt plugs, and pocket pussies. So this had to be something different, but what? I considered this for a time, ultimately selecting a hyper-realistic sex doll. I've heard a little bit about these things, how they're becoming more and more life-like all the time, but I didn't know anything about them. Nor did I desire to. It wasn't that I was a prude, I just chose to go my own way and do what writers do, which was to just sit down at the computer and make up shit.

I knew I wanted my story to go in a different direction than the other submissions would likely go. But when I sat down to write the story, it did what most of my stories do, which was to go off into some weird, dark place. What resulted was something that was decidedly not erotica. Its sexual content is somewhat graphic, but it's not a thing that would or should arouse any halfway sane person. In the end, it became something sad and heartbreaking. Recognizing that the level of melancholy it achieves would most certainly be a boner-killer for just about everyone who read it, I decided not to submit it. Instead I stuck it away in a drawer, thinking I'd put it in a short story collection someday.

That day is today.

Sandwich Bitch

This story was the culmination of two things having to do with two separate jobs I had around the same period of my life (2000-2002). I was working at a soul-crushing, brain-numbing factory job for a brief time. I only worked there for a few months before I got fired for telling my boss to go fuck himself, but that's another story for another day. At that factory, there was a break room where employees could go and hang out and eat their pickle-pimento sandwiches or whatever. There was an old refrigerator in there filled with all kinds of food, old and new. One day I had a morbid thought: what if someone poisoned a complete stranger's food and then stuck it back in there? If the victim died, would anyone be able to pinpoint the killer, especially if the victim hadn't died until they had gone home? I obviously didn't poison anyone. Instead I just did what everyone else at that factory did, which was to drink myself into oblivion each night after work, all the while fantasizing about how preferable suicide might be to working there. But that idea stuck with me.

The second thing that inspired this story came from my working as a floor manager at a telemarketing call center. At one time I was tied with another person—one of my closest, craziest friends—as number two guy at the top of the totem pole. We were essentially running this multi-million-dollar call center. Can you imagine that? Who in their right minds would give a couple of drunken pot heads that much power? But I digress... While I was working there, another friend, Ron Riley, was also an employee. When Ron saw that one of the dumbasses we worked with had posted a hateful letter to whomever had stolen his Lunchable, Ron decided to write him back, signing the letter from "The Lunchable Bandit." The two of them traded notes for a couple of days, with Ron continuing to up the ante, writing and posting more and more ridiculous responses. Finally Ron stopped responding and the whole thing blew over.

Ron would eventually pass away in January 2018. Just after his passing, I was telling a mutual friend about the incident. Around that same time another mutual friend was suggesting I should write something about Ron to sort of ease my pain. Instead of doing that in a direct fashion, I figured out a way to combine these two separate memories into a single story. What resulted was "Sandwich Bitch," which I had a lot of fun writing.

The moral of "Sandwich Bitch" is, if you are ever someplace where there is a community refrigerator, be careful leaving your food in there unsupervised. Unless you enjoy the taste of pesticide that is. If that's the case, *bon appetite*!

Potential Spacemen

This was probably the first short story I wrote as an adult. There may have been others preceding it, but I no longer remember them. That version of the story ended up getting lost in the ether over time, and like "The Man Who Hated Pickles," which also appears here, I ended up going back years later and recreating it from scratch. The story went through several drafts and incarnations. At one point it depicted an even more bumbling redneck. That incarnation was aptly titled "Bubba Ray Versus the Spaceman." At another point the story possessed the very boring title "Crash Site." In the end, after all the rewriting and restructuring was finished, this is the story I wound up with.

I realize this story requires tremendous suspension of disbelief. I had a friend tell me once he thought it unlikely that an alien planet would be so much like Earth. To this I say horseshit. Who's to say it couldn't be? As we all know, there were *Twilight Zone* episodes and Ray Bradbury stories featuring alien planets that closely resembled Earth, so who cares? If you can believe that spacemen exist, then why is it any more difficult to believe they could have rifles and porno mags? For me, just the idea of alien lifeforms existing requires suspension of disbelief, so I don't see the difference. I don't believe in aliens any more than I believe in Jesus Christ, Santa Claus, Bigfoot, the moon landing hoax theories, or moderate Republicans.

Kind of Blue

A PR guy from Crime Wave Press (whom had just published my book *Riding Shotgun and Other American Cruelties*) contacted me and told me there was a small online crime fiction magazine out of Europe that was interested in me writing a noir story for them. The pay was something like $25. The magazine itself was interesting. It looked sort of low-rent like something some guy was printing out of his basement, but its concept was cool. So I said yeah, sure, why not? The theme of the issue was jazz music, so all the stories had to in some way involve jazz. I went to work writing the story, probably my first straight-out crime short ever. There had previously been stories like "The Hollister Job" and early versions of "The Man Who Hated Pickles" that had flirted with the genre, but all my straight-out crime stories had been longer in length.

The story's title comes from the album "Kind of Blue" by Miles Davis, which is my all-time favorite jazz record. (Yes, record, and yes, I'm dating myself.) The story's idea was basic enough—a poor schmuck trumpet player who's been fooling around with the crime boss' woman—but I particularly enjoyed the ending. I appreciated that the man won't back down, fighting until his very end.

At the time I was still sick with end-stage heart disease (before my eventual transplant) and the writing was coming along slowly, so crafting the story took longer than I'd anticipated. I wound up turning it in a few days late. As a result, the story I wrote specifically for that magazine didn't end up being published in it. But, the magazine's editor assured me he would fit it into the next issue. I thought this was weird considering the story was about jazz and probably wouldn't fit with whatever the next theme would be, but I took him at his word. Because why lie? But later, when I followed up with the guy, he informed me that he'd never really planned to publish the story after I'd missed the deadline. He'd basically just said that to placate me. So the moral of this story, kiddies, is that people are full of shit and will lie to you at every turn. But in the end, I wound up with a cool little story I would not have written otherwise, so it ended up being a win.

The story wound up appearing in a really cool magazine called *Retreats from Oblivion*, named after a novel by pulp god David Goodis. The magazine's editor, Lou Boxer, paid me one of the greatest compliments I've ever received. "'Kind of Blue' reminded me of David Goodis' writing," he wrote. "People down on their luck, whether by just bad luck or self-imposed. Either way, they literally go down fighting. Bravo to you and thank you for a magnificent piece of writing." Think about that for a moment; it's wonderful to be compared to Goodis, but even better to be compared to him by a fellow writer who was so inspired by his work that he literally named his magazine after him.

Steve McQueen and the Thanksgiving Elvis Decanter

This was a weird little story I wrote out of sheer boredom. I finished it right around the end of November 2018. Originally the gift in the story was given for the character's birthday rather than Thanksgiving, but then Clash Books' website put out a call for submissions seeking Thanksgiving stories. I made a few tweaks and *voila*, it became a Thanksgiving story. The website, *Yes Clash*, accepted the story and ran it. I considered changing it back to the original birthday theme for this collection, but I felt like the Thanksgiving element actually made it more quirky, because who gives gifts for Thanksgiving?

I worried that the twist at the end was too obvious, but it seemed to be one that a lot of people somehow didn't see coming. A lot did, but about half didn't. And either way, this story isn't about the twist as much as it is about the journey. I just thought it was a light, dopey story that was a lot of fun. And the idea of a genie coming out of an Elvis decanter made me laugh. (I'm simple like that.)

The Man Who Hated Pickles

This is an insane idea for a story I had back around 1995 or so. I was working the night shift at a group home for mentally-challenged people. I was the only employee working. I used to sit in the kitchen when everyone was asleep and read and listen to music. I was doing that on this occasion when the idea for this story came to me. I was still in the infancy of my writing at the time, but I was learning the way you're supposed to—by writing. I started writing the original version of this story by hand. I have no idea what its title was back then, but it was something different.

When I finished, I was kind of proud of it. It wasn't very good, and some would probably say this version isn't very good either, but it's certainly better. I have no idea whatever happened to that story, but it got lost somewhere between 1995 and today. In 2017 I started toying around with the story again. I don't know why, but it kind of always tickled me, for whatever reason. It's not particularly deep or meaningful, nor does it have the greatest story line known to man, but it was fun. I showed it to quite a few people and their reactions were positive. It was never meant to be anything more than a lark done simply for the sake of doing it.

And if you're wondering, I am the man who hates pickles. But I probably wouldn't murder anyone over them.

Probably.

It's Not Enough

I was reading calls for submissions and I read about an anthology someone was doing of stories based on Grimm's fairy tales. So I went to the library and grabbed a collection of the stories, searching for a fairly obscure one to re-imagine. This might have actually been the story's downfall, as it wasn't accepted. But I still think it's a solid story, even if it is about a dog and a bird. Writing about animals as protagonists is not the kind of thing I normally do, but I felt like it was something different. And I like revenge stories, even if they're about animals.

Granny Wilkins' Last Supper

This was a story I wrote back in 2013. For some reason I didn't include it in my first short story collection, *Death Rattles*. I'm not sure why. I had actually forgotten it even existed and then stumbled across it in 2018. I stumbled across a few forgotten stories, most of which deserved to be forgotten and shall remain hidden away, never to be seen again. But this one makes me chuckle every time I read it. I really like the idea of the sweet old woman poisoning her unsuspecting loved ones so they can join her in heaven for eternity.

The Sweetest Ass in the Ozarks

After my heart transplant in mid-2018, I had to make the 300-plus mile trip from where I live in Parsons, Kansas back to the hospital in St. Louis once a month for tests. These trips involve a drive through the Ozarks, which can be a pretty interesting area to visit (if a person has an interest in inbreeding and similar redneck dumbfuckery). On one such trip, on which I was accompanied by my aunt, Sherri Watson, we stopped to get gas and go to the restroom at a little middle-of-nowhere gas station. While I was in there grabbing a soda, I observed a ridiculously-attractive (and equally ridiculously-built) young woman, who looked very blonde, very snobby, and very much out of place in that hillbilly gas stop. At the same time, I also observed a guy who was likely a meth addict and definitely a scumbag. I saw him staring at her ass, as was every other male (and possibly female) in that gas station. I started to wonder what would happen if he hit on her. This line of thought led me down another path, which became the basis of this story.

Several hours later when I got home I went immediately to my laptop and started typing, working on this story. Several hours later I was finished with my first draft of "The Sweetest Ass in the Ozarks." The story seemed to resonate with people. I don't think it reinvents the wheel or anything, but it seems to be a combination of things that interests readers. On top of that, I think it's well written.

The Man Who Wouldn't Die

Back in 2014 I had a brief association with a publisher called Curiosity Quills. (At that time they were planning to publish my fantasy/action novel *M-Company in the Axis of Evil*, but I wound up publishing it elsewhere.) During my association with them, Curiosity Quills announced they were seeking short story submissions for an anthology entitled *Chronology*, which was a big deal because Piers Anthony had written a story for it. I knew the name, knew it was a big deal, but had not and still haven't ever read anything by the guy. (I think it's a guy, but don't know, don't care.) But the wheels started turning and I wrote a flurry of stories to submit for the competition. (Most of the others eventually wound up in my first short story collection, *Death Rattles*.) The story they ended up publishing was this one, which was retitled "Inmate #85298."

The editor really didn't get what I was doing. She was a nice enough lady, but she didn't care for my lean, dialogue-heavy style. (This is why we ended up parting ways and I took my work elsewhere.) But she liked this one—*mostly*. But she wanted a key change, and it was one that I hated, hated, *fucking hated*; she wanted a reason given as to why the inmate will not die. I personally thought it was more fun if we don't know why this was happening. In a lot of the old *Twilight Zone* episodes, which heavily influence my short story writing, there weren't always reasons given as to why things happened. But I did as she requested so I could get my story in the anthology so it would appear alongside old what's his name (or her name), and I made up a cockamamie reason for the inmate's immortality. (The reason, which was shit, was that the inmate had been imprisoned for killing a man, and the daughter of the man put a hex on him.) It was crap, but it didn't ruin the story too much.

But I always liked the original version far more, and I'm happy to finally present it here in its original form.

The Gypsy's Curse

I wrote this on a lark. Sometimes I like to write things for themed submission calls because they inspire me to write about things I wouldn't otherwise. This was one of those occasions. I had just been a guest on a podcast called The Deadman's Tome. I remember the night well because later, after the podcast, my girlfriend at the time, a sweet girl named Sadie Miller, who'd had a heart transplant just as I had, passed away.

A few days later, while I was still grieving, I happened to look on the Deadman's Tome Facebook page to see what the response to my appearance had been. It was then I learned that Deadman's Tome sometimes puts out short story anthologies. They had a call for submissions for one titled *Bikers vs Zombies*. I was trying to force myself to work in the midst of my sadness, so I decided to pen something for the anthology. The end result was "The Gypsy's Curse."

Whenever I submit to one of these calls, I always try to write something that will be completely different from what everyone else is likely to write. When I saw the title *Bikers vs Zombies*, I immediately knew what kinds of stories would be submitted—bikers with bikes battling shambling, flesh-eating zombies. I mean, what else would you expect? So I decided to take the story somewhere else completely. I envisioned an outlaw biker gang like the ones in *Sons of Anarchy,* who deal drugs and commit crimes. By making the story about the bikers going on a boating excursion to dump a dead body, it allowed me to place the story in a setting that none of the other stories would be set— *on water.* This also allowed me to write about a different kind of zombie—a water zombie. So the end result becomes a biker story that isn't really a biker story in which the protagonists fight zombies that aren't really zombies (at least not as we know them traditionally).

The truth is, I've come to loathe zombies. When I was a kid, I loved all the Romero movies and the Italian films by Lucio Fulci. Later on I helped make a pretty terrible STV zombie movie called *Zombiegeddon.* (I'm still proud of it, warts and all, but it's not great.) But somewhere along the line, probably because of *The Walking Dead*, I had come to hate zombie stories. They had become *passe*. So the only way I could bring myself to write such a story was to make it something different.

The Truth About Josh

I came by this story in a weird fashion. It's sort of a true story. I actually had a person tell me about a real-life encounter he'd had with a troubled friend who'd confessed that he was a werewolf. Of course he wasn't really a werewolf, at least not that I know of. Although if he reads this story and sees the similarities I might receive verification on some night when the moon is full. (Can I get some thoughts and prayers, people? Or better yet, how about a pack of silver bullets?)

Anyway, I wanted to do something different with the story. What if the guy actually turns into a werewolf? Well, that's what we expect and that would be pretty boring. Well, what if we find out he's not really a werewolf? Completely boring by itself. But what if the guy he's talking to turns out to be the real werewolf? *Ding! Ding! Ding!* Winner, winner, chicken dinner!

And that is...the truth about Josh.

Santa's Little Helper

One night my eight-year-old daughter Josslyn asked me, "Is there really an Easter Bunny?" I didn't want to let the cat out of the bag, so I told her no. But she kept pushing. She's a really smart little girl, smarter than the average bear, so she wouldn't relent. She then explained all the reasons why she felt the Easter Bunny couldn't possibly be real. She then posited a theory that parents just make up the Easter Bunny to make their kids happy. That was, of course, the truth, but I didn't want to tell her this. (Especially without her mother present, as she lives elsewhere.) For an hour straight Josslyn persisted like a little inquisitor, grilling me about the existence (or lack thereof) of the six-foot bunny.

Finally I relented and told her what she thought she wanted to hear. But it wasn't what she wanted to hear. Not really, so she cried and cried, saying she hated being so smart. (This was akin to the feelings I felt when I was thirty-five and came to conclusion that I didn't believe in God.)

A couple days later Josslyn's mother, myself, and Josslyn's stepfather (hi Adam!) all sat her down and talked to her about the Easter Bunny, the Tooth Fairy, and Santa Claus. As we sat there explaining it to her, this story formed in my head. Then, about a week later, as luck would have it, author T. Fox Dunham asked me if I wanted to write some sort of crime-themed story involving Christmas to be performed on his *What Are You Afraid of?* podcast. So I sat down and wrote this funny, dark little tale. People seem to think it's really funny and have fun with it until they realize the ramifications for the poor little boy. It's not really a very happy story at the end of the day.

Early Retirement

I'm not exactly sure what the genesis of this story was. I wrote it back in 2014. My wife at the time was a high school teacher and I think we were probably talking about teacher layoffs. But again, I'm not sure. It could also have just been a crazy idea induced by weed. (Since my transplant I can no longer smoke pot. But boy, those were the days...)

There's not much to this story, but I like it. Particularly the idea of the teacher having a break from reality and being completely unaware of the murders he's committing. In his world, it's just another day. In everyone else's world, it's a fuckin' bloodbath.

This story was written before school shootings became a popular extracurricular activity for troubled students. I'm sure someone will find offense in a story taking place in a school and involving shootings, but those things do happen and as such, stories should be permitted to depict them.

Snow White and the Seven Bastards

This was another story inspired by a call for submissions back in 2016. The call asked for updated fairy tales. They were wanting happy updates, but my mind doesn't work that way. My mind always goes straight to the darkest places. This is how I came to write a story about a white trash Snow White going on a murderous rampage against a bunch of dirty little meth-dealing dwarves. This isn't the deepest story, not particularly complex or meaningful, but it's a fun little thing. The anthology passed on the story, so I stuck it away in a drawer for several years.

Later, in 2018, I submitted it to Paul D. Brazill, a writer whose work I have the utmost respect for, and he published it on his Punk Noir website. The reader reaction was positive and it was shared on Facebook and Twitter many times. And now I'm sharing it here with you.

Enjoy.

It'll Make You Feel Better

Over the years I've known a number of people who have died. Once they were gone, I would inevitably stumble across their e-mail addresses at some point. And each time, I would sit there for a few moments, contemplating messaging them. Of course I knew they wouldn't respond. *But what if they did?* This idea occurred to me just after the passing of my friend, the aforementioned Ron Riley. The problem with this seed of an idea was that I had absolutely no idea where the story should go from there. I asked a number of writer friends if they had any ideas. Everyone seemed excited about the prospect of collaborating, but no one could ever come up with a solution. Just like me, they were stumped.

Then I met a writer named Mark Slade. Somehow we got to talking about writing, and I told him my story idea. He suggested that I check out the Harlan Ellison "Shatterday" episode of *The Twilight Zone*. He thought that might give me some ideas. Mark and I then talked some more, and together came up with some ideas that grew into other ideas. I can't necessarily say that Mark came up with the story, but I can definitely say he was a sort of muse; he led me down a path of discovery. I came up with the thing and made it work, but I couldn't have done it without his thoughts and suggestions.

Someone who read the story after it was finished asked me, "What exactly is the brother when he comes back?" I don't really have an answer for that. He's dead. But he's alive. So who knows? But I think it works. I have always liked those *Twilight Zone* and E.C. Comics-type stories like this that don't spell out everything for you. Sometimes things just happen and we as readers or viewers have to accept that. And if the story's conclusion leaves us with more questions and we have to spend time considering and thinking about the story, I think that's a positive thing.

Interestingly, the story ended up finding a home in an anthology called *Aberrant Gospels*, edited by Mark Slade. So, in the end, the loose collaboration that wasn't really a collaboration ended up being something that would benefit us both. Sometimes things just work out.

Wyatt Earp and the Devil Incarnate

In 2013 I met a guy named Troy Smith, who ran a small publishing house called Western Trailblazers. He published Western novels and novellas. When I was a kid I had read a few Louis L'Amour novels, but that was about it as far as Westerns. I liked Western movies, but the books sort of bored me. (Two of my favorite authors, Elmore Leonard and Richard Matheson, had written Western novels, and even those bored me.) But I was inspired to write something to submit to him. I basically wrote this novella just to see if I could do it, as I had never even considered writing a Western before. I actually wrote this one and another Western-themed novella *Easy-Peezy*, which later appeared in my collection *Riding Shotgun and Other American Cruelties* simultaneously, I think. If they weren't simultaneous, they were back to back. But they were close.

I loved all the movies I had seen about Wyatt Earp and Doc Holliday, but I especially loved *Tombstone*. I'm not saying it was my favorite Western ever, or even the best about those men, but I thought it was pretty badass. This set me down a path where I began to consider a story involving those same people, imagining them portrayed by those same actors as I wrote it. My mind always goes to weird, off-the-beaten-path places, so I decided to pen a story about a serial killer coming to Tombstone. I had never seen a serial killer Western, so I decided to write one. I read a bunch of books on Earp and Holliday and set about writing *Wyatt Earp and the Devil Incarnate*. I had a blast writing it and I really liked the weird ending. Is it believable? Probably not, but it's fun, so who gives a damn?

The novella was published by Western Trailblazers at the end of 2014. I had seen no proofs for the book and had not seen the cover prior to its being published. I love Troy to this day and appreciate his accepting my novella, but the cover looked atrocious. I hated it, but I kept my mouth shut, just happy it was in print. And it stayed in print for about two months before Western Trailblazers closed its doors. Then the rights reverted to me and the novella languished for a good long time. I wanted very badly to see it have a proper printing, so here it is at long last.

The Night Ol' Dirty Bastard Came to Hoboken

In 2016, Clash Books put out a call for submissions for an anthology of stories inspired by the legendary hip-hop group Wu-Tang Clan. Since everyone who has ever come into contact with me knows I'm a ridiculously huge Wu-Tang fan (I'm writing this in the morning as I wait impatiently for 10 a.m., when tickets for their twenty-fifth anniversary tour go on sale), several writer friends informed me of the call. I was incredibly excited. I kicked around several ideas for the story. I really wanted to be in that anthology more than I can possibly express.

I wanted to do something different, so I ended up writing a story about the deceased member of the Wu-Tang Clan, Ol' Dirty Bastard, coming back from the dead. In this silly scenario, ODB comes to the rescue of a man who's about to commit suicide. The man had prayed to God to help him, but instead he got ODB, who informed him he's very similar to God. It was a fun story to write and I was exceedingly happy when I received the news from editor Christoph Paul that the story made the cut. The anthology came out in 2017, and I adore it. I myself have written thirty-seven books, but this one, which wasn't even my own, may be my favorite because of my continued love and admiration of all things Wu-Tang.

I knew it wouldn't be a story for everyone, hence it is presented here as a bonus story. If you don't like it, don't hold it against the book. It was just a bonus. What more do you want?

CREDITS

"The Dinner Guests," copyright 2018. First published in *Deadman's Tome.*

"She Had a Good Heart," copyright 2019. First published in *Deadman's Tome.*

"Charles Bukowski's Command Performance," copyright 2018. First published in *The Horror Zine.*

"Kind of Blue," copyright 2018. First published in *Retreat from Oblivion.*

"Steve McQueen and the Thanksgiving Elvis Decanter," copyright 2018. First published on the Clash Books website.

"The Man Who Hated Pickles," copyright 2018. First published in *Short-Story.Me.*

"The Sweetest Ass in the Ozarks," copyright 2019. First published in *A Time for Violence: Stories with an Edge.*

"The Man Who Wouldn't Die," copyright 2019. An alternate version appeared previously in *Curiosity Quills: Chronology*, 2015, as "Inmate #85298."

"The Gypsy's Curse," copyright 2018. First published in *Bikers vs The Undead.*

"The Truth About Josh," copyright 2018. First published in *Deep Fried Horror.*

"Santa's Little Helper," copyright 2018. Performed as an audio story on the *What Are You Afraid Of* podcast.

"Snow White and the Seven Bastards," copyright 2018. First published in *Punk Noir*.

"It'll Make You Feel Better," copyright 2019. First published in *Aberrant Gospels (Fresh Fruit for Rotting Eyes and Delusions of Psychotic Profits)*.

Wyatt Earp and the Devil Incarnate, copyright 2015. First published as a standalone novella by Western Trailblazers.

"The Night Ol' Dirty Bastard Came to Hoboken," copyright 2019. A slightly different version appeared previously in *This Book Ain't Nuthin' to Fuck With: A Wu-Tang Clan Anthology*, 2017.

ABOUT THE AUTHOR

Andy Rausch is the author of more than thirty books, including the novels *Mad World*, *Riding Shotgun and Other American Cruelties*, and *Bloody Sheets*. He recently edited the short story anthology *A Time for Violence: Stories with an Edge* (with Chris Roy), featuring such noted authors as Joe R. Lansdale, Max Allan Collins, and Richard Chizmar. In addition to these things, he writes for numerous publications, is an editor at *Diabolique* magazine, and has written and appeared in numerous straight-to-video B movies. His previous short story collection was 2014's *Death Rattles*, also published by Burning Bulb Publishing.